Praise for the novels of Maggie Shayne

"A tasty, tension-packed read."
—*Publishers Weekly* on *Thicker Than Water*

"Tense...frightening...a page-turner in the best sense."
—*RT Book Reviews* on *Colder Than Ice*

"Mystery and danger abound in *Darker than Midnight*,
a fast-paced, chilling thrill read that will keep readers turning the pages
long after bedtime.... Suspense, mystery, danger and passion—
no one does them better than Maggie Shayne."
—*Romance Reviews Today* on *Darker than Midnight*
[winner of a Perfect 10 award]

"Maggie Shayne is better than chocolate.
She satisfies every wicked craving."
—*New York Times* bestselling author Suzanne Forster

"Shayne's haunting tale is intricately woven... A moving mix of
high suspense and romance, this haunting Halloween thriller
will propel readers to bolt their doors at night."
—*Publishers Weekly* on *The Gingerbread Man*

"[A] gripping story of small-town secrets. The suspense will
keep you guessing. The characters will steal your heart."
—*New York Times* bestselling author Lisa Gardner on
The Gingerbread Man

"[*Kiss of the Shadow Man* is] a crackerjack novel of romantic suspense."
—*RT Book Reviews*

"Shayne crafts a convincing world, tweaking vampire legends
just enough to draw fresh blood."
—*Publishers Weekly* on *Demon's Kiss*

"This story will have readers on the edge of their seats
and begging for more."
—*RT Book Reviews* on *Twilight Fulfilled*

MAGGIE SHAYNE

INNOCENT
PREY

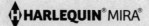
HARLEQUIN® MIRA®

Recycling programs
for this product may
not exist in your area.

ISBN-13: 978-0-7783-1658-9

INNOCENT PREY

For questions and comments about the quality of this book, please contact us at
CustomerService@Harlequin.com.

Printed in U.S.A.

INNOCENT
PREY

Prologue

Near Taos, New Mexico

Halle didn't think he knew—until he held out the test-kit wand and pointed firmly at the bucket in the corner that had been her only toilet for the past ten months.

Ten months, as near as she could figure. It must be getting close to her nineteenth birthday, and she had no reason to think she wouldn't still be here for her twentieth. She hadn't kept track of the days until after the first week or so, when she'd realized he was going to keep her alive, at least for a while. She'd never expected that she might be rescued. There was no one to come and save her, no one even to notice she was gone. The first time she woke up and was almost unable to remember what day it was, she knew she was going to have to start marking time somehow. Now she kept track of the days in the dust *way* underneath the bed. He couldn't wriggle under that far even if he wanted to, the fat fucking pig.

It was a nice bed. The nicest thing in the tiny basement dungeon. But that was only because he was so often in it. She wasn't supposed to sleep in it herself, though. She was only allowed into the bed to service him. Her bed was a dog bed. A circular one, with a single blanket, at the foot of the plush bed. In the other two corners were her bucket toilet and her shower: an ordinary cold water spigot set high in the wall, with a drain in the concrete floor underneath it.

If she slept in the bed, he would know. He always knew. And he would punish her. He would snap her ankles and wrists into the shackles attached to the wall, and he would torture her for a little while. Hot wax. A lit cigarette. Whips and paddles and clothespins. It wasn't sexy. It wasn't a turn-on. It wasn't about pleasure or surrender or any of that stuff people who consider themselves sexually adventurous fantasize about. It was horrible. It was a nightmare. It was a living hell. Pain wasn't pleasure. Pain was just pain. And this guy wasn't Christian Grey. He was a sick, perverted bastard who enjoyed hurting and humiliating women.

And now she was pregnant. And he knew. Somehow he knew.

"I—I don't have to go, sir." She always had to address him as "sir." Or "master."

"Did I give you permission to speak?"

She kept her eyes lowered, shook her head to answer and took the wand from him. Then she squatted over the disgusting bucket he only emptied when it suited him and peed on the wand, praying it would somehow lie to him. Keep her secret.

He took it from her, and she stood submissively in front of him, head down, resisting the urge to hug her short satin bathrobe around her, because that would be considered insubordination. To cover herself in his presence was a huge offense. There was no sash to the robe. She wasn't allowed to wear anything else unless he told her to, although there were clothes in a plastic bin under the bed. He bought them for her all the time and sometimes had her dress up in them. But mostly she lived in the short robe.

After a minute he sighed heavily and shoved the wand under her downturned head so she could read the results for herself. She'd already known, but somehow seeing the plus sign made it worse. She couldn't bear the thought of what he might do with a baby. What was she going to do?

"Well, you've been a good girl," he said. "You hear me? You've been a good girl. But I'm gonna have to let you go now."

She brought her head up fast, eyes widening, then quickly lowered it again.

"Why don't you pack your things while I make a phone call? Here." He pulled a plastic trash bag from his pocket. He often had one on him. He liked to smother her until she passed out sometimes. After almost dying once or twice, she'd started faking it. But he wasn't easy to fool. She had to wait until the black spots started popping into her eyes to make it convincing.

"You... You're letting me go?" she whispered, daring to meet his eyes again, briefly.

He smiled and nodded, reaching out to stroke her coarse curls. "Yes. Now pack."

Her heart jumped in her chest, but she took the bag

from him. She didn't want anything he'd given her, but she wasn't going to tell him that. It would offend him. He might change his mind. Oh, God, it was over. It was finally over.

She knelt and pulled the plastic tub out from beneath the bed, scooped everything out of it in one big armful and then rose and dropped the clothes on the bed. Quickly, she opened the bag and began shoving the clothing into it, while he stood behind her with his cell phone. She could hear the tones when he tapped the keys, and then the ringing.

She heard someone answer, and then a sound that made her heart clench tight as the cold steel of what she knew was a gun barrel pressed against the back of her head.

"I'm gonna need another girl," he said to the person on the phone.

And that was the last thing she ever heard.

Binghamton, New York

"It's time for you to face it, Stephanie. You're never going to see again."

It had been two months since she'd heard those words from the dire-voiced doctor she imagined looked like an undertaker. And they were still replaying in her mind every time she let herself drift.

Coaching sessions were one of those times.

Stevie had once believed that there was always hope, unless you were talking to a corpse. Well, Dr. Langley had talked to her just as if he were talking to a corpse that day. No hope, he'd said. No way it can happen, he'd said. It was time to begin accepting that this was her new way of life, he'd said. And it was like the light in her heart just blinked out. *No hope.*

Everything she'd ever believed about the world, about herself, about everything, blinked out with it. *No hope.* A dark curtain lowered itself across the stage of her life. She felt its weight as if she'd been standing right beneath it. It was heavy and cold and black, and she didn't think she was going to be able to keep going.

"There are a lot of blind people who live productive, fulfilling lives," Dr. Undertaker had said. "It's only one sense out of five. You have four more to fall back on."

"Look at Rachel de Luca," her mother had added.

"Fuck Rachel de Luca" had been her reply. It had shocked her to hear herself sound that dark. And it had shocked her mother, too.

That had been two months ago, and now it was May and her days were still as dark as her nights. She spent her mornings in one-on-one therapy with her shrink and group therapy with a bunch of other disabled people. Paraplegics, vets missing limbs, that sort of thing. No other blind people, though. And in the afternoons she had lessons with her coach, Loren Markovich, a mid-forties pain-in-the-ass who was constantly quoting self-help authors to her. Rachel de Luca had been one of *her* suggestions. The self-help author who'd been blind for twenty-some-odd years. Stevie's mom and her blindness coach had been shoving de Luca's self-help audio books down her throat since the accident. And she'd listened to them, eagerly sucking up the notion that she could change her reality. She'd believed it. She'd been sure she could positive-think her way out of this endless night. It had worked for the author, after all.

It made Stevie want to vomit. Anyone who would say she had created her own blindness was an ignorant fuckwit. Who the hell would *choose* to be blind?

Personally, she hated Rachel de Luca. Partly for the stupid message she'd wanted so badly to believe in, but mostly for getting the miracle Stevie wanted so much for herself. The one her gloom-and-doom doctor said she was never going to have. Rachel de Luca got her eyesight back. Stevie hated her for that.

She also hated her shrink, her therapy group and her blindness coach. Yes, there was a rational part of her mind that figured she ought to be grateful her father could afford to buy her all this help. But she didn't want it. It was all geared toward learning to live with being blind. Toward accepting it. And she would *never* do that.

She was twenty years old. Her life stretched out ahead of her like an endless black pit. She didn't want this. She just didn't want it. She figured she'd give it a year, if she could stand it that long. It had been eight months already. So four more. Maybe she would even stretch it to five, because a Halloween suicide had a nice sense of flair to it.

But dammit, she wanted to see Jake again before then. See him. That was a joke. She'd never *see* him again. But she wanted to be with him. Not that it mattered. He wouldn't even answer her calls. Not that she blamed him.

"Stephanie, are you listening at all?" Loren asked.

Stevie turned her head slightly toward her coach. It was pleasantly warm outside, early May sun pouring down and bouncing off the sidewalk. They were practicing walking with the white cane. She felt like a sideshow freak, walking along beside Otsiningo Park, waving the stupid thing and tapping it to keep track of where the sidewalk was, probably weaving like a drunk. God, she hated this.

"I'm listening."

"You need to stop drifting off into your own world," Loren said. "You have to start keeping your senses attuned to what's going on around you."

"I know. You've told me a hundred times. A thousand."

"Then why aren't you doing it?"

She shrugged. "I'm sorry. I'll try harder. What did you say?"

"I know it's not easy," Loren said.

"You don't know anything, Loren. No one can, unless they're blind, too. I don't care how many people you coach or how often you walk through the city with your eyes closed, you don't know. Stop saying you do."

Loren let her breath out in a rush; then she was quiet for a moment. "You know, eventually, you're going to have to stop feeling sorry for yourself and start living again."

"Really? 'Cause I don't think I *have to* do anything. I think I can pretty much do what I want. It's my life." Deep down inside, Stevie winced at how bitchy she was being. But she squelched the feeling. She had a right to be angry. Her life had been stolen by a drunk driver.

Loren didn't reply and Stevie figured she'd pissed her off and didn't care. But she supposed she had to cooperate if she wanted to get home and hide in her room for a while. Maybe try to call Jake again. "Just repeat your last instruction, will you? I want to get this damned session over with."

She could feel her coach's anger rise up a little bit. And then she felt it vanish again. That was weird. When she spoke, Loren's tone was calm, if a little bit cool. "Walk to the end of the block. Find the corner. Don't step off the sidewalk into the street, and *don't even think about* walking around the corner out of sight. Just locate the corner using your senses and your cane. Then turn around and come back here. Count your steps so you know how to find me. There's a bench to your right. That's where I'll be waiting."

Alone? Loren wanted her to go *alone?* Panic seeped into Stevie's veins. "I'm sorry I snapped at you." She said it even though she knew the apology was too little, too late.

"I'm not mad at you, honey," Loren said softly. "This is not a punishment. It's time for you to test your wings, just a little bit."

"I'm not ready."

"It's a hundred feet, Stephanie."

"I don't care. I don't want to do this."

Loren moved, and Stephanie heard her, knew she was sitting down on the bench she'd mentioned.

"Go," Loren said. "I'll be right here waiting. I'll watch every step you take."

"You don't even care how scared I am, do you?" Stevie accused.

"Of course I care. But that fear isn't going to go away until you face it and beat it. Stephanie, you can do this. You're strong. You're not helpless. Now go."

Stevie bit her tongue before the words *I hate you* could emerge. Yes, she was acting like a ten-year-old. She didn't care. She was furious. And terrified.

"Fine."

She tapped the sidewalk to get herself lined up, finding where it ended and the grass began on the right, and then she started walking, keeping herself in that area, so others could pass by her, if there were any others. She was so focused on staying aligned and walking straight, and so afraid of walking into something, that she barely noticed people approaching until they walked or jogged past her, and it startled her every single time. But she kept going. She kept going until she felt the sidewalk make a right angle. Then she took a few more steps forward, tapping to make sure. Yes, the sidewalk ended; she could feel the curb. She imagined stepping off that small drop by accident, figured she could easily break an ankle. It would fix Loren's ass if she did, wouldn't it? Her father would fire her for sure.

But with Stevie's luck, her replacement would probably be worse.

Carefully, she turned around, 180 degrees, tapping her way back to the inside edge, where the sidewalk turned. She lifted her head, facing the direction she'd come from, hoping like hell Loren was looking, and flipped her off, then pivoted 45 degrees and walked around the corner, out of Loren's sight.

Let her panic and come chasing after me, she thought. *Let her suffer a few seconds for pushing me so damn hard and making me do what I wasn't ready to do.* She tapped about ten steps, expecting to hear Loren come running after her. Instead she heard a vehicle stop very near her. She heard its door open, and footsteps coming toward her. A chill went up her spine, and she turned all the way around and began tapping back the way she'd come, toward the corner. But a pair of very strong arms snapped around her, and one hand covered her mouth. She fumbled for her cell phone, then dropped it as she was yanked off the sidewalk and thrown into a vehicle. A door slammed closed, and the vehicle lurched into motion as she scrambled from the floor up onto a bench seat, her hands patting the area all around her to get her bearings.

"What's happening?" she shouted. "What is this? Who are you?"

No answer. She felt her way to the side of the vehicle, running her hands over the seat, then the inside of the door in search of a handle. When she found it and started yanking on it, it wouldn't budge, but she knew by then that this was bigger than a car. It was a van. She was in the back of a van. It took a corner hard, damn near rocking up on two wheels, and she was slammed into the other side, cracking her head on metal. There didn't seem to be any glass. No windows. No one could see her.

Holding her head, she sank onto the seat and started screaming at the top of her lungs. "You fucker, you'd better fucking let me go or my father will *destroy* you! You'd don't even know—"

The driver braked to a whiplash-inducing stop, and then he was on her, all his weight on her back. He pushed her face down into the seat while she wriggled and thrashed and cried. Her hands were tied behind her with what felt like a plastic band. A zip tie. She couldn't breathe. He was smothering her.

He jerked her head up by the hair, and she sucked in a desperate breath. Then he wrapped a strip of duct tape all the way around her mouth to the back of her head. Finally he got off her and shoved her to the floor. In seconds the van was moving again.

She dragged herself up onto the seat, sobbing, trembling. She'd thought her life couldn't get any worse. It was painfully obvious that it could. And had.

God, what had she done?

1

Okay. Maybe the bullshit I wrote was a little bit true. If you wanted it, you could have it. There was more to it, of course. But that was the basis of every book I'd ever written. And it seemed like my own bullshit was determined to prove itself to me.

I'd wanted my eyesight back, I'd wanted my brother's murder solved, I'd wanted to survive the holidays— literally, *survive* the holidays. And I'd wanted Detective Mason Brown.

I pretty much had all of that now. I could still see. No complications, no rejecting of the donor tissue this time—besides on moral grounds, that is. It did come from a serial killer—my brother's killer—after all. I had survived the holidays, though it had been a damn close call. The case was solved, sort of. Tommy's killer was dead. Twice now. And *his* brother, the aforementioned Detective Dreamboat, was in my bed, if only for an hour or two at a time.

I was actually beginning to believe that the messages of my bestselling books (and calendars, coffee mugs, app and upcoming series of imprinted apparel) were valid. I was actually starting to think, as Mason did, that my unoriginal philosophies on positive thinking and deliberate creation were popular because there was some truth to them, that they were more than just regurgitated new age psycho-spiritual babble. And if I were honest with myself, it felt good to believe that. It felt damn good to think I was serving some kind of higher purpose in the world.

I choked on a sarcastic laugh from my inner bitch, and it sounded like a snort. Higher purpose. Right. Still…I was warming up to the notion that there was a kernel of truth in there somewhere. For me, that's about as close to a spiritual awakening or an "ah-ha moment" as it's ever gonna get.

So why was I still kinda miserable?

Mason rolled away from me, sat up and bent forward to pull on his jeans. I glanced at the clock on the nightstand—10:00 p.m. "This has to be some kind of a land speed record."

He stopped with his hands on his button fly and turned to look back at me. He was the sexiest man in the universe. I am not exaggerating. I didn't know why women didn't swarm him in the streets like adolescents mobbing a Jonas brother. (Yes, that's a dated reference. I'm over thirty. You're lucky I didn't say Hansen.)

Mason leaned over and kissed me nice and slow. "Sorry," he said when I let go of his lips. "But the boys will be home from the movies and—"

I held up a hand. "I know, I know. It's just…"

"Just what?" He knelt on the bed, his jeans still undone, as he buttoned up his shirt. I thought he could've been on the cover of a steamy novel. *Fifty Shades of Brown.* Mason Brown, that is.

"I really have to go," he said.

"So go, then. You remember the way, right?"

"Don't be mad."

I sighed, thinking I was acting like a sophomore pouting over her steady, which was stupid, because this was just the way I wanted it. And because I don't even like sophomores.

"Don't be dumb. I'm not mad. You're the world's greatest uncle, and you're also all they have. Besides their grandmother, the queen of cold."

"Easy, woman."

I grinned at him, pleased with myself. By insulting his mother, I'd diverted his attention from my petulant little burst of emotional ickiness. "Go on. Tell Josh and Jeremy I said hi."

He looked at me for a long time, like he was trying to decide whether to say something, or maybe waiting for me to say something more. Then he nodded, kissed me quickly and got up to finish dressing.

"I've got that meeting with the chief tomorrow," he said. "I'll call you right after, tell you what it was about."

New subject. Nice. I was uncomfortable talking about…relationship stuff. Heavy stuff. Fortunately, so was he. "I already know what it's about," I said, crawling halfway out of the bed and pulling the little plastic stairs closer. Myrtle, my bulldog, was still snoring, but now she could join me when she was ready. Moving her doggy stairs away from the bed was essential to having good sex. Otherwise she spent the whole time trying to wriggle her way in between us. It was just wrong, you know?

"Yeah? What's it about, then?" he asked, though he already knew what I thought.

"The rumors are true. Chief Subrinsky has decided to retire, and he wants you to be his replacement."

Mason shook his head, sitting down on the edge of the bed to pull on his socks. "I don't think so. This feels different."

He'd already been wined and dined with Chief Sub in the company of a congressman, everyone from the D.A.'s office, the owner of the *Press & Sun-Bulletin* and the mayor. He was clearly being groomed for the job, even while insisting he didn't want it.

I could've smacked him. It paid six figures. Low six, but still…

"'Feels different,' huh?" I asked. "You're starting to sound like me, Detective Brown."

"There are worse things." He sent me a wink and a killer smile. His damn cheek dimples were my undoing. How did I live for twenty years without once seeing a cheek dimple like that? He pulled me close and did a better job of kissing me goodbye, then dropped me on my pillows and headed for the door. "I'll call you after the lunch."

"Okay."

"Night, Rache."

"Night."

He closed the bedroom door on his way out. I rolled onto my side, curled up and pulled the covers over my shoulder, while my inner girlie-girl whined that she wished he could spend the whole night.

This is what we both want. It's perfect. Don't go thinking if a little is good, more would be better. If it ain't broke, don't fix it. Just leave it alone. Don't screw this up.

I waited until I heard his car leave, then got up, pulled on a robe and crouched beside Myrtle, who was still snoring on the carpeted floor. "I hear brownies and milk calling my name, Myrt. What do you think?"

She perked her ears but did not open her eyes. Not that it would matter if she did. She was blind as a bat.

"You hungry, Myrt? You want to eat?"

Her head came up a microsecond before she sprang to her feet and said, "Snarf!"

I scratched her between the ears. "This is good, right? Just you and me and bedtime brownies. Even if you do have to have the low-fat ones from the gourmet doggy bakery. This is the life, Myrt. This is the life."

I wasn't really convinced, but I figured if I said it often enough I could make it true.

Mason walked into The End Zone in the suit he saved for weddings. Overdressed for a sports bar, but if this turned out to be another part of the unending audition for the chief's job, then it was perfect.

Besides, he'd already worn his funeral suit to a couple of the VIP meals the chief had been dragging him to for the past few weeks.

Grooming him to take over his office when he retired, or so Rachel kept telling him. He hoped to God that wasn't the case. He didn't want the headaches of that much responsibility, the hassles of politics or the boredom of a desk job, no matter how demanding it might be.

And yet, he was raising two boys now. Their father was dead by his own hand—as were a lot of others, though no one else knew that besides Rachel—and their mother was in a locked psych unit, after trying to reclaim a bunch of her husband's donated organs. Including the corneas Rachel was currently using.

Yeah, his family was a mess. And yet Rache still hadn't run screaming. Well, she had. A couple of times. Just not from him.

The chief-of-police position would bring a massive pay raise and much longer life expectancy. Didn't he owe it to the kids to take it if he could?

But he couldn't, could he? He'd lied. He'd covered up his brother's crimes and destroyed evidence to protect his surviving family members. He didn't deserve to still be a cop at all, much less chief of police.

He spotted the chief's boxy flat-top silhouette at a table all the way in the back of the bar, swathed in shadows because the big-screen TV closest to it had been turned off. The only tables near it were empty.

Another man, taller and almost painfully thin, sat across from the chief with his body angled toward the wall and his head down. He was trying hard not to be noticed, Mason thought, and wondered why.

The chief caught his eye and waved him over, so

Mason made his way to the table, giving the place a once-over on the way. There were only a handful of other customers, and no one seemed to be paying him any undue attention. But the chief's companion was nervous, and that made Mason nervous.

Chief Sub rose and shook Mason's hand, squeezing too hard and pumping too much. It was his standard greeting. The other man looked him up and down but didn't stand, didn't shake.

Mason knew his haggard face, had always thought the man looked twenty years older than he probably was. "Judge Mattheson," he said. "Good to see you again."

"Wish it was under different circumstances," the man replied.

He honestly looked like a stiff wind would carry him a couple of blocks. And old, older than Mason recalled. The guy had to be pushing sixty, but he looked eighty-five.

"What circumstances are we talking about?" Mason walked around the table to take the chair that faced outward, toward the rest of the bar. This was not about any promotion the chief might be thinking about for him. This was something else. Something private, and something dark. He knew all that before he even sat down.

Chief Sub leaned over the table. "Howard's daughter—"

"This has to be discreet, Brown." The judge smacked the table to punctuate his interruption and make it seem just a little bit ruder. "You reading me? Discreet, until and unless we have reason not to be."

Howard Mattheson's face was age-spotted to hell and gone up close like this. No, wait, those were the remnants of freckles. He must have been a ginger as a younger man. Little remained of his hair. It was thin and had faded to a colorless shade that couldn't even be called gray. Tough to tell if it had ever been red. "What is it I'm being discreet about?"

A waitress came by to ask Mason what he wanted. He glanced at the drinks in front of the other two. Chief Sub had a Coke, straight up. He wouldn't add anything on the job. Judge Mattheson had what looked and smelled like bourbon, neat. "I don't suppose you have coffee."

"I just brewed a fresh pot."

"You're an angel."

She winked at him and left them alone.

Silence stretched like a rubber band until the chief stopped it from snapping. "Howard?"

"Yeah. All right. It's my daughter, Stephanie— Stevie, as she insists on calling herself. She's disappeared."

Mason sat up a little straighter. "How old?"

"Twenty."

"And you're not filing a missing persons report because…?"

"Because I'm not convinced this is anything other than a temper tantrum. Look, she was in a car accident last September. Drunk driver. It took her eyesight."

A month after Rachel got hers back. Mason swore silently but didn't interrupt.

"We kept it quiet. We're a private family, Brown. We

like our space. I've always tried to keep my job separate from my personal life."

"I respect that, Judge." He slanted a look at the chief. He needed to know what exactly was going on here, and he needed to know now. If there was a twenty-year-old blind girl out there on her own somewhere, they ought to be finding her and hauling her right back home.

Rachel would probably kick his ass for that reaction. He could hear her in his head right then, voice dripping sarcasm like honey. *Since when is* blind *a synonym for* helpless? *Dumb-ass.*

He almost grinned, then bit his lip just in time and pulled out his smartphone to start taking notes. "Give me everything you know, then."

The judge cleared his throat. "She was told two months ago that there was no hope of getting her eyesight back. She didn't take it well. She's furious with the world and everything in it. Moody and morose. She hasn't accepted her blindness, won't even try, and resents the help we've been trying to get for her."

"Help?" Mason asked.

The judge took a sip of his bourbon, set the glass down again and stared into the liquid at the bottom. "Therapy, a personal coach to help her learn how to live with it." He slugged back the last of the bourbon, then held the glass over his head to signal his desire for a refill. "She gives that poor woman so much trouble I'm surprised she hasn't quit."

"That woman have a name?"

"Loren Markovich." Judge Mattheson set his empty

glass down, fished a business card from his pocket and put it on the table.

Mason took it and gave it a look. It was one of the judge's own cards, but it had Markovich's name and phone number written on the back. He dropped it into his shirt pocket. The waitress came back with his coffee and another bourbon for the judge, then left without a word.

"Loren took Stevie out near Otsiningo Park the day before yesterday. Told her to walk to the end of the block and back, using her cane."

"Alone?" Mason knew he sounded more shocked by that than he should.

"It's not that big a deal, Mason," Chief Sub told him. "Your friend Rachel could tell you that."

"Well, Rachel could'a done cartwheels to the corner and back, but that's Rachel."

"Who the hell is Rachel?" the judge snapped.

"She's my— She helps me with cases from time to time."

"No one else comes in on this, Brown," Mattheson said. *"No one."*

"We know, Howard." Chief Sub nodded at him to go on.

With a stern look at Mason, the judge went on. "Loren says Stephanie was good and pissed. She didn't want to do it, but Loren pushed her, and she did it. Did just fine, too. Then at the end of the block she flipped Loren off, then kept on going, around the corner and out of sight. Just to be difficult. Just to teach Loren a lesson for pushing her so hard." He took a big gulp of his bourbon, replaced the glass harder than necessary. "Loren ran to catch up, and Stephanie just wasn't there. She just…wasn't there."

Mason nodded. "She couldn't have gone far. Not on her own."

"Yeah, well, that's just it," the judge said. "I think she had help. I think she set this up somehow. She's been acting out ever since she went blind." He lowered his head, turning the bourbon glass slowly in his hand. "I know it's horrible. I know it is. Wouldn't wish it on my worst enemy, but at some point you just have to figure out how to deal with it and go on, you know? It's terrible what happened to her, but it's not our fault."

"Did they get the guy, Judge?" Mason asked.

"You better believe it. And I made sure he got the max. Trial judge was a friend of mine."

The judge's free hand flattened itself to the table, and it was shaking. "I just… I want her found. Discreetly and quietly. I want her found."

"All right." Mason nodded slowly. "But what if this wasn't some kind of tantrum? What if she was taken?"

The judge shook his head. "I've thought of that. But there's been no demand, no phone call or ransom note."

"But you're a judge. You must have enemies."

"I'm a family court judge, son. I don't deal with criminals. Criminally bad parents, sometimes, but not criminals like you're thinking of."

"All right. All right. What if she did have help, then? Who would be the most likely accomplice?"

The judge met Mason's eyes for the first time and nodded. "She had a boyfriend all through high school.

She ran off with him once, senior year. But she hasn't seen him since shortly after that."

"Name?"

"Jacob Kravitz. Goes by Jake."

"You know where he is?"

"No. As far as I know she hasn't seen or heard from him since she graduated. She's seeing a decent guy now. A law clerk in the D.A.'s office. Mitchell Kirk. He's a good kid."

"Anyone else? Friends from college or work?"

"She quit college after the accident. Her friends called and came around for a while, and then they just… stopped." He shrugged. "My wife's a wreck."

"I told Howard I'd put my best detective on this," Chief Sub said. "And I assured him, Mason, of your absolute discretion."

"You've got it, Chief."

The judge got up. Mason did, too, and this time the older man extended a hand. Mason shook, then watched Judge Mattheson turn and thread his way around the empty tables and out of the bar.

Mason turned to look at the chief, who was still sitting. "I want to bring Rachel in on this."

"Sit down. I ordered a pair of burgers, and since Howard left, you might as well eat his."

Mason sat. As if on cue, the waitress returned with more coffee, and two plates piled high with burgers and fries. She had a much easier look on her face than before. Yeah, it had been tense. It was like a dark cloud left the bar when the judge walked out the door.

"Tell me how you think Rachel can help," Chief Sub said as he pounded the bottom of the ketchup bottle.

"Well, to start with, she was blind for twenty years. She can give us some perspective on where this girl's head is at, one we're not gonna get from anyone else."

"Mmm." The chief got the ketchup flowing and made several neat round dots of it along the edge of his plate. "Can she keep this quiet? She *is* a writer, after all."

"It's not like she's a freakin' reporter."

"I know that. The question is, do you trust her?"

"I trust her." If the chief knew the enormity of the secrets Rachel had kept for him, Mason thought, he wouldn't ask. "Actually, I can honestly say I trust her more than anyone I know."

"Is that so?" Chief Sub dipped a fry in ketchup, then ate it whole. "You and she, uh…been seeing a lot of each other, haven't you." It wasn't really a question.

"Some. Not…a lot. Really."

"Why not?"

Mason looked up, surprised by the question. "She's only had her eyesight back since last August, Chief. It's a whole new world for her."

"For you, too, I imagine, with raising those two boys."

"Exactly."

The chief shrugged. "I trust your judgment, Mason. If you think she can help you and you trust her, use her. I want Stephanie Mattheson found. Hell, I'm her god-father. Since this is off-the-books work, de Luca's an off-the-books consultant. Just don't let Howard find out you told her. You got that?"

"Yeah." Mason picked up the gargantuan burger, took a huge bite and knew he would regret it later. After he chewed and swallowed, he said, "If I don't turn anything up right away, you're gonna have to convince him to make it official. You know that."

"You let me worry about Howard."

"All right, Chief."

"There's a party at my house Friday night. My fiftieth wedding anniversary. You'll be there."

Once again, it wasn't really a question.

"I will," Mason said.

"Good. Get a sitter for those boys of yours and bring de Luca."

I had Myrtle on a leash, which was a joke, really. She was short and fat and slow, and about as likely to bolt away from me as I was from a glazed sour cream doughnut. We were doing our midday walk along the four-mile-long dirt track that passed for a road. It ran along the back side of the Whitney Point Reservoir, which really was more like a lake. There were a couple of houses at the other end of the road, near the village, but mine was the only one way out this way, just before the dead end. I loved the privacy. The quiet. And now that I had eyes, I loved the beauty of it, too. Trees and woods, all sporting their newborn pale green leaves now that spring had sprung in the Point, and the way the sun would sometimes shimmer on the water, making every ripple wink like bling on a rapper. Damn, I loved where I lived.

I had my cell phone with me in case Mason called.

But he didn't. He interrupted our walk in person, instead, breaking into our solitude with the too loud motor in his "classic"—aka old—black Monte Carlo. He pulled it over, shut it off, locked it up and got out while we stood there. Myrtle was wiggling her backside in delight, knowing it was him and overjoyed about it. (She'd have wagged her tail, but bulldogs don't really have tails. So they wag their entire asses, which I think is a much more accurate depiction of extreme enthusiasm. Myrtle agrees.)

Mason approached her first, crouching down low to rub her head on either side of her face, and she closed her sightless eyes and basked in his attention. I do the same thing when he touches me like that.

Then he stood up again, but instead of kissing me hello—which would've been hopelessly goofy anyway, so I don't even know why I was hoping for it—he said, "I need your help."

I sighed my disappointment away. "Hi, Mason. I've been having a great day. Thanks for asking. Yes, I slept just fine after you left. Myrtle is a blanket hog, but not as bad as you are. And yes, as a matter of fact, we *are* enjoying our walk."

He lowered his head, raised it again, grabbed my shoulders and pulled me in for a long, slow kiss. I let go of Myrt's leash and got all mushy inside, sliding my arms around his shoulders and really getting into it.

Then he let me go, and when I straightened my knees tried to go jellyfish on me, but I snapped them straight again.

"I missed you," he said.

I rolled my eyes. "Oh, for crying out loud, don't be so emo."

But inside I was grinning like a kid.

"So what was the lunch meeting about? Or should I ask what you need my help with first?" I picked up Myrtle's leash, and we went off the road and down toward the shore. This was one of Myrt's favorite things. The water was still cold, but she loved to put her paws in, and drink and sniff around.

Mason came and stood beside me. "It's the same answer to both questions. A judge's twenty-year-old daughter is missing. He thinks she's just throwing a tantrum and wants me to find her discreetly. Off the books. I want you to help me."

I nodded slowly. We'd had this whole "police consultant" conversation before. He thought I should work with the Binghamton PD officially. But I wasn't about to put "uncanny sense of what other people are thinking and feeling" on the application. And I would rather be drawn and quartered than labeled some kind of psychic. Besides, I already had a career. A nice lucrative one, thank you very much.

"It doesn't sound like anything you can't handle on your own."

"You can handle it better."

"Why?" I wanted to take it back as soon as I said it, because I knew that was exactly what he wanted. And now I'd opened the door. Shit.

"Because she's blind, Rache."

"Oh, for the love of—"

"Drunk driver hit her car last fall. September. Doctors just told her in March that there was no hope of ever getting her sight back. She's not dealing with it very well."

"*No one* deals with it very well."

"I just want you to come with me to where she was last seen. Walk through the moments before she vanished with me. How bad is that?"

I heaved a sigh. "Myrtle needs her walk, you know. That evil lying vet of hers still insists she's overweight."

"He has a death wish. I'm sure of it," Mason said, and then he shrugged. "Actually, walking is exactly what we'll be doing. We can bring her along. You've already got her leash."

"You know perfectly well she does not ride in a car without her designer goggles and matching scarf."

He jogged up to the road to his car, opened the door and leaned in. When he came to the edge of the road again, he held up his gift. "Doggy goggles."

They were hot pink with black peace signs all over them. I almost loved them. "Did you get those on the way over?" It took some doing, but I convinced Myrt to come back up the slope away from the water. Mason handed the goggles to me. Even the lenses were tinted pink. "And if so, where? 'Cause *damn*."

"Great, aren't they? Josh bought them for her on eBay. Used his own money, too. He put 'em in my car yesterday, but I forgot to give them to you."

"They're great." I looked at him, at the goggles, at the car. I didn't want to get involved in any sort of police work or investigation. And my reason was simple. So far, every time I had, I'd had brutally horrifying dreams about whatever was going on. Vivid, awful nightmares that were mostly true. Now, granted, I'd had weird connections to the killer and/or the victims the other times, due to our common organ donor. There was no reason to think that would continue with a case that had nothing to do with me or my corneas.

Except that I'd had some kind of freaky knowledge happening last Thanksgiving when my right-hand Goth, Amy, had been kidnapped. No nightmares. Just that...

Extra sense.

Not that. It's not that. I'm not fucking psychic.

"Come on. All I want to do is take you two for a short walk near Otsiningo Park. How bad can that be?"

We both knew how bad it could be, so I wasn't going to bother answering that one. I crouched down in front of my bulldog. "Myrt. You wanna go for a ride in the car?"

She cocked her head to one side, ears perking up, lower teeth coming out above her upper lip as she stared up at me, waiting for me to repeat her favorite words ever spoken, to confirm she had heard me correctly.

"Ride? In the car?" I said again.

"Snarf!" And the butt-wiggle dance began.

I looked up at Mason and shrugged. "There's your answer. I guess we're going." I adjusted the goggle straps and put them on my dog, told her how gorgeous she was, and promised to find her a matching scarf soon. She followed me to Mason's car. I got in the front seat and slid to the middle, where newer cars would have a console instead of a supersized bench seat. I was lucky the old—sorry, *classic*—car even had seat belts. Mason lifted Myrtle to set her on the passenger side, so she could stick her head out the window. He knew the deal.

He came around and got behind the wheel, then looked at me for a second. "Need to go lock up?"

"Amy's there. I'll give her a call."

He nodded but didn't put the car into motion, and he was still looking at me. So I braved the question. "What? What's wrong?"

"I, uh… You were a little pissed at me last night. Are we good?"

I blinked. He was checking in on the thing we both hated discussing most. Mucky, murky emotional vomit. The kind of stuff that ruined great relationships. "*I'm* good," I said. "You?"

"Mostly, yeah. Pretty good."

Which meant he could be better. Which was what I'd have said if I'd been honest. But because I was a big fat chicken, I said, "Good, then. We're good."

"We're good. Okay."

And then he turned the car around, and we were off and running. And I thought to myself that it wouldn't be so bad to help him out with another case. It really wouldn't. At least I'd get to spend some time with him in the upright and unlocked position.

This could be fun.

Right. Fun. Like, you know, jury duty. Or a small-pox outbreak. Or seeing murders in your sleep. Fun.

2

By 2:00 p.m. Mason and Myrtle and I were walking
the sidewalk Stevie Mattheson had walked just before
she'd vanished, which, I'd learned, had happened the
day before yesterday. Apparently her devoted daddy had
waited a day and a half before going to his pal the chief
to *not* report her missing. Guy was a jerk.

I know, snap judgment. That's how I roll. *Tough
times turn people's masks into windows. Believe what
they show you.* Yeah, it's one of mine.

"Nice leash, by the way," Mason said.

Hot pink, with black skulls and crossbones all over
it. "And coincidentally it even matches the new goggles
you bought her."

"Except I went with peace signs instead of the Jolly
Roger."

"Yeah, I noticed," I said.

"Hope she doesn't get confused about her own identity."

"What's to be confused about? She's a pacifist pi-
rate."

He laughed. That was what I was going for, eliciting that laugh. I could tell more from Mason's laugh than from anything he said or any vibe he emitted. He was too much a cop, played things too close to the vest, to let me read him the way I did other people. But I could still read him. It was just tougher. And his laugh was the easiest way I'd found so far.

This one rang forced and tight.

"You're worried about this."

He nodded. "Something's off about the whole thing."

"Spidey sense tingling?"

"I wish to hell you'd been a fly on the wall at lunch so you could tell me if you sensed it, too."

"Is there some reason you're doubting your eerily accurate cop instincts, Mason?"

He looked at me, then at the sidewalk. "Yeah. A couple of them." He didn't elaborate, so I didn't push it, figuring it was either something deep and emotional or something about us, and those topics were things we'd sort of agreed to avoid without really ever saying so out loud. He was no more into gooey emotional gunk than I was, thank goodness.

It was beautiful outside. Warm in that springlike way that would seem chilly a month from now, but sunny and fresh. I'd always loved that about spring, that freshly washed newborn feeling it had to it. But I loved seeing it even more. The trees were taking on a pale green cast as their buds started to become leaves. Birds were flitting around singing like extras in a Disney flick. Tulips and daffodils everywhere you looked.

And the apple blossoms were busting out all over. Out in the Point they were barely peeking out of their buds.

Myrtle hurried from one spot to the next, sniffing everything thoroughly, excited by a new place and not even keeping her side pressed to my leg. She really was getting more confident. I loved that.

"So she walked from this bench to that corner," Mason said. "Bitching all the way, according to her coach."

"Her *blindness coach*. The person her father hired to teach her how to be blind."

"Yeah." He chose to ignore the sarcasm in my tone.

"But the coach is sighted, right?"

"Uh-huh." He said it like he knew what was coming next. Hell, he probably did.

"And that makes sense because no one knows what it's like to be blind better than a sighted person does, right?"

"Of course not."

"So explain it to me, then, 'cause I'm not getting it."

He stopped. We'd walked about five steps. (Myrtle, twenty.) "I didn't say I thought it was a great idea, I'm just telling you how it went down."

"I know." I said it like it should've been obvious. "I'm just *saying*."

"Can we focus here? And stop looking at the damn birds, Rachel, we need to look at the ground."

I'd been watching a red-winged blackbird in a nearby tree. He was perched on the topmost branch, and he kept chirping this loud, long note and hunching up his shoulders at the same time, so the little red patches were more prominent. Showing off for the ladies, I bet. "*You* look for clues with your eyes. *I* look with my other senses, remember?"

"So is that bird giving you anything to go on?"

I shrugged. "It's spring. Horniness thrives. I say we question the boyfriend. She does have a boyfriend, doesn't she?"

"Two that her father felt worth mentioning," he said. "One former, one current."

"Let's talk to them both. And the blindness coach."

He nodded. "Already on my list."

"I'll be more helpful when we're doing that." I glanced ahead and saw a fat robin skipping along the sidewalk pecking at something too small for me to see. Myrtle sensed it or felt it or something, because she was focused in that direction, too, leaning forward like she was getting ready to lunge at the bird, even though she couldn't see it. "If we do it indoors," I added.

He didn't reply, so I lifted my head again, met his eyes. He was grinning at me, flashing the Dimple of Doom. My doom, at least. I made a face and started walking, scanning the sidewalk as I went, at least when I could take my eyes off my bulldog and her absolute enjoyment of the walk. Myrt really had living in the moment down, that was for sure. *Can't see? Oh well. I smell a squirrel!* was her philosophy. Frankly, I thought it was a pretty good one.

I used to have to coax and cajole and tug to get her to walk any distance at all. But today she was rushing me. She was definitely getting more fit. Mason caught me watching her, sent me a look that asked for my focus.

I know, I know, but it was my first sighted spring-time since age ten. So shoot me. "Come on, get with the program, Detective," I said. Best defense is a good offense, right? "Daylight's burning."

We completed our inspection of the sidewalk where Stevie had obeyed her coach's orders, tapping her way from the bench to the corner, and didn't find anything. Well, *we* didn't, but Myrtle did. She'd peed on a clump of weeds, chomped the blossom off a stray daffodil and picked up a discarded Pepsi can, which she was still carrying like a prized treasure.

Whatever had happened to Stephanie had happened after she'd gone around the corner. But we'd already known that. So we turned right, just like she had. And then I really slowed down. Mason walked near the inside edge, where sidewalk met park, so I took the curb, where sidewalk met road.

And there in a drain was a cell phone. It had fallen onto the grate, and wedged itself most of the way through. I'd been hanging around cops—well, one cop—long enough to know not to touch it, so I pointed it out, then crouched low, pulled my long sweater over one hand and picked it up with the sleeve while Myrt dropped her soda can and tried to grab it before I could. "Got'cha!"

I won and turned toward Mason, holding up the phone. And then I flashed back to Thanksgiving, when my personal assistant and best-Goth, Amy, had been snatched off the highway by two jerks in a white pickup truck. We'd found *her* phone at the scene, too.

Weird.

Mason came over with a plastic bag and I dropped the phone in. "Nice find," he said.

"Wish I still had that damn stylus in my purse so we could tap this thing without leaving a print. I lost it, need to buy another one." I'd had one at the scene of Amy's brief abduction. Ms. Smarty-pants had snapped a photo of the pickup, knowing it was trouble, and left it behind to lead us to her. "Mason, do you think this could be related to what happened to Amy?"

"Because of the phone?"

I nodded.

"I don't think so. Amy threw her phone underneath her car deliberately. She knew she was in danger. Even if Stevie did the same, it would only mean that they think alike."

"Right. And we have *so many* women being snatched off the streets of Binghamton that there's no way it's connected." I was being sarcastic.

He gave me a look. "Okay, I'll give you that one." He nodded, thinking on it. "Amy's twenty-five, Stephanie's twenty. That's close enough, I guess."

I thought back to the photo he'd shown me of the missing girl. "Amy's got dyed black hair and multiple piercings. Stephanie's a blonde Barbie doll. It can't be the resemblance. Still," I said, "the phones."

"Coincidence. Besides, we don't even know it's her phone."

I made a face while I tried to figure out how to say what I was thinking without sounding like a complete flake. "I'm not saying that us finding the victim's phone at both scenes is evidence that the two things are connected. I'm just wondering if it's a more…a more *woo-woo* clue."

"A woo-woo clue?" he asked, arching one eyebrow. I loved when he did that. "Is that a technical term?"

"Yes. Absolutely."

"You mean, like maybe the phone being here is the universe dropping us a reminder of Amy's abduction, just to get us thinking along those lines?"

I shrugged and averted my eyes. "If you believe in that sort of thing."

"You mean the sort of thing you put in your books and then tell me is bullshit, Rachel?"

I shrugged. "You're the one who keeps trying to convince me it might not be."

"So you've decided to believe me, then?"

Tipping my head to one side, I said, "I was just trying it out. You're right. It's bullshit." Then I took a big breath. "But if that *is* Stephanie Mattheson's phone, then it's probably safe to say she didn't run away just to ditch her coach and worry her parents."

"You're right about that."

"There's a drugstore around the corner, and I'll bet we can find a ten-pack of those styluses." I frowned. "Styli?"

He was looking at the road near the grate, though, all but ignoring me. So I looked, too. There was a parking meter there. Probably had been a few dozen vehicles in and out since the night before last, when this had gone down.

Or maybe not.

He pulled out his own phone and took a few close-up shots of the area, while I looked up and down the sidewalks and road, wondering how this chick could've been snatched against her will without someone seeing something. I mean, it wasn't a busy place, but it wasn't deserted, either.

And then I thought of Amy again. Stupid, I know, but there was something bugging me, itching at my brain. I kept feeling just like I'd felt last Thanksgiving morning, when Amy's mother had called to tell me she'd never made it home, and I had known—*just known*—that something awful had happened.

We'd tracked Amy down before it had gone from awful to fatal. One of her abductors was still with her when Mason and I caught up. Now he was with the angels. (I know, but I don't believe in hell, even for jerks like him.) We'd never tracked down the other one.

Mason nudged me with an elbow. "You seeing what I'm seeing?"

I wasn't, so I looked where he was looking, down the block to the next corner. "There's a camera on that traffic light at the intersection. Snaps automatically when someone runs the light."

"Fuckin' cops. You're like Big Brother, you know that?"

"Not the point."

I nodded. "I know it's not. What *is* the point is what difference does it make? What are the chances the kidnapper ran the light?"

"If he was going that way? Pretty good, actually. People get all hopped up during the commission of a crime. Adrenaline's surging, they're nervous, jumpy, in full-blown fight-or-flight mode."

"Walking textbook," I accused.

"What? It's as good as you wanting to check the phone for photos."

"I do *not* want to check the phone for photos. I want to see who she's been talking to. Blind women do not snap a lot of pictures, Einstein."

"I knew that." He picked up the pace as we hustled to the end of the block, and Myrtle jogged along happily for most of the way, then started snuffing at me as if to say, *Enough with the running, already. Do I look like a sprinter to you?* "I was teasing about that Einstein thing," I said, slowing my pace to accommodate my bulldog.

"I know you were."

"Could you get the traffic-light photos without making the case official? I know Judge Howie wants to keep it under the radar."

"Yeah, except it won't do any good. Look at the camera."

"What?" I looked. It had what looked like a bullet hole in its lens. "Shit."

Mason turned in a slow frustrated circle. "I feel like I'm missing something."

"Like what?"

"I don't know. The judge. Something was off about him."

I frowned at him. *That again,* I thought. "So? Elaborate already. In what way was something off?"

"I don't know. I wasn't ready. He's an old friend of

Chief Sub's, and I was expecting another power lunch, not an off-the-books case. I didn't have my game face on, you know? But there was something." He sighed. "I wish you'd been there."

Wow. That he'd said it to me twice now told me he meant it in spades. And that made my insides get mushy. My inner idiot acting up, I guess. "Maybe it's that he wants it off the books at all? 'Cause, *damn,* Mason, that has my antennae all aquiver."

"No, I can see him wanting it handled discreetly. They kept her accident and blindness quiet."

"How did they manage that? I thought it was a drunk driver. Wasn't there an arrest? A trial?"

"Must've been. The judge said he got the max. Still, the judge is in the public eye. It makes sense to keep this out of the press if Stephanie is just throwing a tantrum."

"I don't know. If my twenty-year-old kid went missing—hell, if my *dog* went missing—I'd have the National Guard on it before morning. He waited two freaking nights. And how can you say you get that? What if it was Jeremy? How long would you wait to report him missing?"

"I don't know. Ten minutes?"

"There. See?"

He nodded. "Yes. I see." Then he stopped looking at the sidewalk and turned to me. "Maybe you'll get the chance to talk to him yourself, see if you...pick up anything."

I lifted one eyebrow the way he so often did. I had practiced doing it in the mirror and thought I was pretty good at it. I loved mirrors. Looking into them, trying different expressions out on myself. It's not vanity. I hadn't had a clue what I looked like for twenty years, you know? "I'm picking up something now. From you. What do you know that I don't?"

He sighed. "You're too good at this game."

"No such thing. So what haven't you told me?"

"Chief Sub's fiftieth wedding anniversary party is Friday night at his place. The judge will be there. We're invited."

"And by invited, you mean...?"

"He told me to be there."

We'd been standing still so long that Myrtle decided to lie down. Head on her paws, she closed her eyes and was snoring with her next breath.

"And by we, you mean...?"

"He said I should bring you along."

I couldn't have been more surprised if lobsters had crawled out of his ears. "So now he's auditioning *me?* Doesn't he realize that we're not...serious?"

He got a little red in the face as he turned away. "I couldn't exactly blurt out that we were just each other's most reliable booty call, could I?"

My radar went completely haywire. I didn't know if he was being sarcastic or serious, if he was a little hurt that I'd said we weren't serious or making a joke so I'd know he agreed.

Jesus, why didn't my supercharged intuition come with an instruction manual and a twenty-four-hour tech-support hotline?

I said, "I don't like that 'most reliable' line, pal. You're my only booty call."

He looked almost relieved. "Me, too. So then, we're...exclusive."

"I guess we are." It was, I realized, the single largest declaration either of us had made in regard to our relationship, and it was more than enough for one day. For both of us.

"You don't have to come to the party if you don't want to," he said.

"No, I want to." Shit, it was getting gooey again.

He looked at me. "Yeah?"

"Yeah," I said, and quickly shifted focus back to business. "I want to see this Judge Howie and try to get a feel for what's going on. Presuming we haven't found Stephanie by then."

"Good. Good." He looked relieved to be back on topic, too. "Just...don't call him Judge Howie."

I smiled at him. "I want you to get the chief's job, remember? You're the one dreading the offer."

"I'm not dreading it. I'm undecided."

Nodding, I said, "How about we wrap things up here? Myrtle's getting hungry, and so am I."

"Myrtle's entering a coma. But okay. Back on track. You're the expert on being blind. Tell me this, just in case this turns out not to be her phone. Once she got around this corner, how far do you think Stephanie could have walked in the time it took her coach to run from the park bench to here?"

I mulled on that for a second, then got a brilliant idea. "Let's find out. I'll go back to the park bench where they started. You wait at the corner. Then, as soon as I sit on the bench, you close your eyes and start walking. I'll come running and we'll see how far you manage to get."

I could tell he didn't like the suggestion by his thoughtful scowl. "Why don't I be the coach, and you be the blind girl?"

"Uh, 'cause I *was* the blind girl for twenty years and I could walk without my eyes faster than you walk with yours. Stevie was new at this. Like you." I bent down to pat Myrtle's head. "Come on, Myrt, we're back on duty."

"I hate when you make perfect sense," Mason said.

Myrt opened her eyes and sighed heavily, then got upright again, stretched and farted at the same time.

I handed Mason Myrtle's leash and jogged back around the corner, then back down the sidewalk to the bench. I sat down and waved at him, where he stood on the corner with Myrt. "Okay, close your eyes and go!" I called.

So he scrunched his eyes tight and started walking. I got up and jogged to the corner, rounding it just in time to see him bean himself on a telephone pole, take a step back, trip over Myrtle and land on his ass. He'd made it about twenty feet.

"Jeez, don't kill yourself, for crying out loud." I made it to him, helped him up and almost choked trying not to laugh at him.

He handed me the leash and rubbed his forehead. "It's harder than I thought."

"It's harder than most people think."

He nodded, looking at me oddly. Like he was feeling sorry for me. I pointed a forefinger at him. "Don't do that, Mace. Don't put on that 'poor, poor pitiful Rachel' face. I was fine blind. Got rich and famous blind. Did better than most sighted people do."

"I know you did."

"Let's get a stylus, check that phone to see if it was hers, and if so, who she was talking to right before she vanished."

"Lunch for you and Myrtle first. Call and invite Amy to join us, okay?"

I lifted my brows. "So you don't think my feeling that there's some connection is completely insane, after all?"

"I've seen too much to think *any* of your feelings are insane, Rachel. So what do you say? Food?"

I was not one to argue when food was on the line. Nor was Myrtle, whose bulldog smile appeared the second he said the word.

3

Stevie had given up the screaming and swearing, crying and pleading, halfway through the first night. She'd given up shaking and tugging at the bars of her cage after what felt like twenty-four hours. Neither of these things had been a choice. She'd stopped screaming because she'd screamed her throat raw and could barely talk anymore, and she'd stopped shaking the bars because she had broken, bleeding blisters on both hands. After that she'd spent her time exploring her cell.

There were three concrete walls around her and prison bars in front, with a locked door. There were bunks attached to the walls on either side with chains. Two high, two low. Four beds total. There were a toilet and sink on the back wall. The water worked. There was a box under the bottom bunk on the right with a few supplies. Someone had used duct tape to drape a vinyl shower curtain in front of the toilet. It smelled new. Everything else about the place had a damp, musty smell to it. It was cool enough to make her grateful she'd been wearing a sweater.

Her captor had thrown her into the cage after a long drive. She'd lost her cell phone. She'd only realized it when he had searched her—thoroughly—while she'd still been tied up. Then he'd finally dragged her to the bars and stuck her hands through, holding them there while he went outside and closed the door with a frightening bang.

From there he'd cut the zip ties from her wrists. As soon as they were free she jerked away from him, yanked the tape from her mouth and started calling him names and demanding to be let go, and screaming and swearing. But a few minutes later she'd realized he was gone.

Her possessions were few. There were a plastic water pitcher and a few plastic glasses. Spoons but no forks. Washcloths. There were a roll of toilet paper, a tangle of brushes and three wrapped bars of soap in addition to the new bar that sat on the sink. There was a single blanket on each of the bunks. And that was it.

Every few hours he brought her something to eat. Protein bars, a bag of chips, a piece of fruit. Never a meal. Just snacks. At first she'd refused to eat, figuring the food might be drugged. Then when the hunger got bad, she decided she had nothing to lose. She was a prisoner. How could being a drugged prisoner be any worse?

She had no sense of time and no real idea how long she'd been there when she heard the door open and jumped off the bunk, lunging toward the sound in desperation, only to bang hard into a person and fall on the hard floor as the door clanged closed again. Scrambling to her feet, she shouted and threw herself at the bars, grabbing and shaking them, and swearing at her captor.

But there were only retreating footsteps.

And the knowledge that she wasn't alone anymore. There was someone in here with her, sitting on the floor now, making muffled but urgent sounds.

She turned toward the sounds, knew there were tears streaming down her own face, and felt horribly guilty for hoping it was another captive like her. "All right, all right. I'm coming." Holding her hands out in front of her, Stevie moved slowly closer, until her hands bumped against a head. She turned her palms inward, running them lower, down the sides of a face, and felt the blindfold around the eyes, the tape over the mouth, and then lower, as the poor thing sat perfectly still, shivering. It was a girl. Had to be a girl. Stevie got to the hands, zip-tied together behind her back. The Asshole, as she'd taken to thinking of the kidnapper, had cut the zip tie partway through. She bent it back and forth until it gave and the newcomer's hands pulled free.

The girl whipped them around fast, and Stevie stepped backward, waiting for her to remove the tape herself. "What the fuck is this?"

Stevie said, "I don't know. I've been here… I don't know, a couple of days, maybe."

"Bullshit. This is bullshit." The other girl went to the bars, and just as Stevie had done when she'd arrived, she shook and screamed and pounded and pulled. She didn't beg or cry the way Stevie had. She sounded strong, sure of herself, confident. Everything Stevie wasn't.

Eventually she stopped fighting the useless door, and paced the cell instead, back and forth.

Stevie was sitting on the bottom bunk hugging her sweater around her and waiting until it felt like time to talk. Eventually she tried. "My name's Stevie. Um, Stephanie."

The pacing stopped. She felt the girl looking at her. Eventually she said, "Lexus."

Stevie nodded. "How did you get here?"

"Fucker grabbed me right off the damn street is how I got here. Threw me in a van, tied me up and tossed me here." She shuffled a little. "You?"

"Same."

"He come in here? He do anything to you?"

"No. Nothing. He shoves food through the bars every little while. Never says a word. It's creepy. I'm not even sure if it's a man."

"Oh, he a man all right. I grabbed him by his balls before he got me bound and gagged, put a hurt on him he won't forget. Piece'a shit. I get the chance again, I'll rip 'em right off."

"I'd like to see that."

"Don't look to me like you see anything," Lexus said. "You blind, girl?"

Stevie nodded.

"*Shee-it,* you get all the luck, don't you?"

"Looks like."

Lexus came to the bunk, sat down beside Stevie. "A'right, then. We look out for each other, you and me. We got no one else. We got to get out of this shit, you follow?"

"I do. Maybe between the two of us we'll find a way."

"Ain't no maybe about it, girl. We will."

Stevie felt a rush of relief. There was no doubt in her mind that Lexus was older and wiser and stronger than she was. She'd been reassuring herself that her father had enough clout and connections to be turning the planet upside down to find her from the outside. Now she had help from the inside, as well. "I'm so glad you're here," she said, immediately clapping a hand to her mouth.

"Yeah, that makes one of us. Not how I 'spected to be spending my eighteenth, you know?"

"Your eighteenth…birthday?"

"Uh-huh."

She wasn't older, then. Maybe stronger, maybe braver, but not older. She was just a kid. Stevie's conscience gave her a needle-like jab. She should be comforting the teenager, not leaning on her. She was almost three years older.

Hell. Okay, all right, might as well show her around the place and see if she came up with any ideas. Stevie got up off the bunk and pulled the box from underneath. "This is everything we own. Pitcher, glasses, spoons, some washcloths and some hairbrushes."

She felt the other girl come around to crouch beside her, heard her pawing around in the box. "Four glasses. Four spoons. Four hairbrushes." Lexus paused, took a breath. "Four beds in here. Four blankets."

"I didn't realize… Lexus, do you think…?"

"I think he's gonna open that door at least two more times, Stevie-girl."

Stevie nodded. "Okay. Okay, then we're gonna have to figure out how to take advantage of that the next time he does."

Even though we had Myrtle with us, we didn't go to a drive-thru window for lunch. We headed instead to the Park Diner, ordered take-out and took it with us to a bench nearby with a view of the Susquehanna River. I liked that I could hear its rushing flow from where we sat, and I liked even more that I could see it. Bodies of water had fascinated me since I'd got my vision back. I live across the dirt excuse for a road from a lake—okay, a reservoir, but it looks like a lake—so I get plenty of time to study it. Rivers were an entirely different creature. The countless colors, the eddies and swirls, the constantly shifting patterns, the frothy bits and the way the sunlight reflects like diamonds when it hits just right.

I sat there, relishing my club sandwich with added hot sauce and sipping my Diet Coke, staring at the water until a paw on my leg reminded me I was not alone.

"Sorry, Myrt." I tore the other half of my oversize sandwich into Myrtle-sized bites and fed her one of them. "Good, huh?"

Myrt swallowed it whole and whacked my shin again. And I knew what she was saying with her sightless brown eyes. *How would I know if it's good? That bite wasn't big enough to tell. More, please. And by please, I mean now.*

I sighed. I hate depriving her of people food when she likes it so much.

Mason was ripping the cellophane wrapper from the pack of styluses we'd picked up at the drugstore. "You should carry dog food," he said. "Diet dog food."

"Shut up. She's not fat."

"The vet said—"

"The vet is partial to skinny dogs. Greyhounds and Chihuahuas. For crying out loud, he owns a whippet."

"Is his whippet good?"

I had broken off another bite and was handing it down to Myrtle, but I stopped in midmotion to send him a grimace. "That was terrible." I didn't tell him that I'd made the same joke in the exam room.

"I liked it."

"Snarf!" said Myrt.

Mason smiled at her. "See? She agrees with me."

"No. She wants her sandwich." I obliged my dog, then said, "That's all, Myrt. It's all gone."

She tilted her head to one side at the words *all gone*. Her least favorite words in history, besides *go to the vet*. Then she sighed heavily and collapsed, because bulldogs don't lie down, they just drop. I knew that she knew I was a liar, and she knew that I knew that she knew it.

Mason whistled softly, drawing my attention away from both my dog and my guilt trip. "What?"

He was looking at the phone, holding it with his napkin and using the stylus to touch the screen. "She's been calling Jacob Kravitz. Frequently."

"Jacob," I said, reviewing the details he'd given me on the way over here. "Oh, Jake. Wait a minute, isn't that the *ex*-boyfriend?"

"Yep."

"Huh. Doesn't sound all that ex, does it? How about the current love interest? Kirk what's-his-name?"

"Mitchell Kirk. And yes, there are two. One incoming, one outgoing."

"Sounds like trouble in paradise."

"All the calls to Jake were outgoing. Less than a minute each."

I nodded. "So she was calling him. Maybe leaving him messages. But he wasn't answering."

"Or calling back," Mason said, tapping the screen with the stylus but not saying much, until he finally seemed satisfied and dropped the phone back into its plastic bag. "Nothing much on there. Nothing that jumps out at me, anyway."

I looked at my watch, grinning because I didn't have to feel it. Yes, still, after almost nine months of being sighted. Hell, I still smiled when I opened my eyes every morning and found I could see. I'd had no idea just how much I'd been expecting the transplant to fail, my body to reject the new corneas the way it had all the others, and my world to be plunged back into darkness all over again, until I noticed just the other day that I'd stopped expecting that. There had been some kind of bowstring tension inside me. Waiting for the axe to fall, that sort of thing. And then one day I noticed its absence. Such a different feeling. Like I'd become seventy pounds lighter overnight.

"Rache?"

I realized I had been staring at the ticking second

hand. "Sorry. I was just wondering what's taking Amy so damned long."

"I'm here, I'm here!" she called from about fifteen feet away. She was scurrying toward our bench with a paper bag in her hand. She wore a black T-shirt dress with a neon green geometric design over leggings and black leather boots. She had spiked her purple-and-black bangs with more gel than usual, and her nose stud was winking in the sunlight. "Sorry I'm late. My mother called just as I was heading out the door. What's the emergency?"

Myrt lifted her head at the sound of Amy's voice. She was one of Myrt's favorite people, probably because Amy was the one who'd rescued her and brought her to me, then used skillful emotional manipulation to trick me into falling in love with the mutt. I don't know exactly how. Introducing us, I guess.

"It's all good. How's your mom?"

"Excellent, as always. Sends her love, says she'll send you that stuffing recipe from Thanksgiving. She won't, though. She never shares her secret recipes. Says I'll get them all when she's dead." Amy took a seat on the bench next to ours, opened her bag and took out a bag of chips. She ate one, gave one to Myrtle and flashed the bag at me when I scowled at her. "It's all right, see? They're baked. And it was just one."

"You know by the time each of you and everyone else in that dog's life gives her 'just one bite' it adds up to a couple of extra meals' worth of food a day," Mason said. "At least."

"Life's short. Dieting only makes it *seem* longer," I said.

"Oh, that's a good one, Rache. We need to put that one on a mug." Amy yanked her smartphone from her bag, wiped her fingers on her black spandex leggings and started tapping the screen. "'Life's short. Dieting only makes it seem longer.' Rachel de Luca."

Mason frowned at me.

"She's working on some new merchandising for me. We're adding mugs and mouse pads to the affirmation cards and perpetual calendars."

He tightened his lips and nodded. I couldn't tell what he was thinking and was afraid he thought I was greedy. Well, hell, maybe I am. If there's more money to be made, I'll go for it. But I share. A third straight off the top to Uncle Sam to pay for bombs and guns, of course. And I give bushels to my charities on top of that.

"So, Amy," he said, turning his full focus to my assistant. Hard not to. "I wanted to talk to you about last Thanksgiving."

She stuffed her cell phone back into her oversize bag. Black. Of course. "When those two pervs snatched me off the side of the road?" she asked. Then she looked up at him. "How come? Did you finally catch the second guy?"

"No. Just want to keep it fresh in my mind."

For a detective, he was terrible at deception. Amy saw right through him. "You *didn't* catch him. Then there must have been another kidnapping."

"No," Mason said at the same exact moment that I was saying, "We're not sure yet."

He shot me a quelling look. I waved a dismissive hand. "What? Like she's gonna go Tweet it to the world?" I looked at Amy sternly. "This is strictly hush-hush. Spill it and you'll nix Mason's shot at the chief's job."

"You told her that, too?"

"She's my personal assistant, Mace. I tell her everything."

"Yeah," Amy said. "Nice job in the sack, by the way."

He looked like he was gonna pass out before I said, "I don't tell her *that,* for crying out loud."

He closed his eyes and gave his head a rapid shake.

"So, Amy," I said. "Yes, a girl is missing. And the truth is, she might just have run off. But I keep getting a feeling it has something to do with what happened to you."

"And we all know better than to ignore her feelings," Mason added, probably relieved that I hadn't blurted out Stephanie's name, address and phone number while I was at it.

"I am so dying to help out on a case," Amy said.

"You're not helping out. And it's not a case."

I clapped a hand onto Mason's thigh. "You *are* helping out, and it's not a case *yet.* But it might turn into one if she didn't leave voluntarily. So if you can stand to go over it one more time…"

"I was driving to my mother's in Erie for Thanksgiving," she said, nodding. "I stopped for gas and noticed these guys in a white pickup pulling in behind me. I went in for the restroom and some snacks for the drive, and when I came out, they were still there. Not buying gas, not shopping, just sitting there."

"Right. We saw the surveillance footage," Mason said. "What do you remember about the second guy?"

"It's all in my statement," she said.

"I know, but you might have left something out that didn't seem important, or remembered something since. Maybe there's something you thought you told us but didn't. Just humor me, okay?"

"Okay." She ate another chip, handed one down to Myrtle, then took her sandwich out of her bag and unwrapped it slowly. "I didn't really look at the guys in the truck at that point. I just sort of noticed the truck was there as I left. I didn't get any bad vibes until I saw them pull out behind me. And even then, I thought I was just being a drama queen."

I nodded and said to Mason, "She *can* be a real drama queen sometimes, so that adds up."

Amy threw a chip at me. It landed on the sidewalk and Myrtle snapped it up before it settled. "Then my tire went flat. I still wasn't overly concerned, until they pulled over in front of me. That's when my alarm bells started going off. I snapped a quick pic of the truck with my phone and slid it under the car just in case."

"Remind me how smart she is if I ever even consider letting her go, Mace."

"I promise." He nodded at Amy to keep going.

"After they dragged me into the truck, the driver dropped the second guy off. Do you need me to describe them again?"

I looked at Mason to answer that one. He shook his

head. "No, the driver's dead, and we have the sketch you and the police artist did of the second guy on file. We're just trying to figure out why they took you. Did they say anything that might be a clue? Maybe something you've remembered since the incident?"

She frowned really hard, and I knew she was trying her best to recall every detail. "The jerk drove me off to that freaking no-tell motel and chained me to the bed. But he didn't touch me. Didn't even try. Then I said I had to use the bathroom. He cuffed me to the pipe in there so I wouldn't run off. I picked the lock and crawled out the window, then ran for it. He chased after me. Caught me and tied me up again out there in the woods, and then you guys showed up." She shrugged. "The only odd thing he said was when he was chasing me through the woods. He was calling me, only not by my name. He called me Venora."

Mason blinked and looked at me. "Was that in the report?"

I shrugged and looked at Amy. "Was it? Did you tell the cops that?"

"I think so."

"Either way, it bears looking into," Mason said. "Thanks a lot, Amy. Remember not to say anything about this to anyone. Not even your mother."

"Please, if I told my mother it would be on *America's Most Wanted* by tomorrow. That woman is better networked than I am."

Jacob Kravitz lived in an apartment above a tattoo place on Washington Avenue in Endicott, one of what we locals call the Triple Cities, the other two being Binghamton and Johnson City.

I've had Manhattanites tell me that all three combined don't really qualify as a single "city," but it works for us. We've got the river. We invented Spiedies, bits of chicken marinated in our own Spiedie sauce, served on sub rolls with cheese and other tasty toppings. Hell, we even have our annual blowout, the Spiedie-fest. And we're on the Best Small Cities in America list.

Washington Avenue is a funny place. It's got the highest-end salon we can lay claim to and drug deals going down on the sidewalk outside. It's got a Greek diner where customers come to get a whole meal for five bucks and park their Mercedes out back. It's got local celebs strutting up one side of the sidewalk and pants-falling-off gangbangers on the other.

We went through the front door and up a set of steep stairs to Jake's apartment door, rapped on it and waited.

"You lookin' for me?"

We both turned toward the guy who was at the bottom of the stairs, standing in the open door, a plastic grocery bag dangling from one hand and a six-pack of Genesee beer in the other. I sized him up visually, which was becoming way more automatic than I liked. I pick up more about people non-visually.

He was tall. Even from up here I could tell he was taller than Mason. Maybe six-three, six-four. He had *Frampton Comes Alive!* hair (I'd seen Amy's classic vinyl collection) and a rugged unshaven thing going on. Wore jeans and an army-green coat with about fifty pockets, despite that it was a sixty-degree afternoon.

"If you're Jake Kravitz," Mason said.

"I am." He came up the stairs, tucking the beer under one arm and then fishing a set of keys out of one of the coat's pockets. When he reached the top and inserted the key in the lock, he said, "You look like a cop." Then he looked at me. "And you don't."

"That's 'cause I'm not. But you're good. How could you tell he's a cop?"

He shrugged and opened his door, then waved an arm at us to enter ahead of him, so we did. The place was a hole. Sofa with a blanket over it to hide the worn spots and stains, assuming the rest of it matched the arms. Linoleum floors so old the pattern was worn off. A fat-ass-style TV set sitting on the middle of a wooden card table that was sagging a little under its weight. An open door revealed an unmade bed and scattered clothes on the bedroom floor. He walked into a kitchen with appliances that were almost old enough to qualify as retro, dropped the bag on the Formica table, took a can of beer out of the sixer and slung the rest into the ancient fridge.

He did not offer us one.

"So what do you want?"

"Wanted to talk to you about Stephanie Mattheson," Mason said.

"And to know how you knew he was a cop," I added, because I thought there was something there. He didn't like cops. It felt like he, big guy that he was, was shrinking into himself on the inside, where it didn't show. On the outside he wasn't revealing a thing, subconsciously making himself bigger. Like an animal in defense mode. I wondered if I could close my eyes without being obvious. My inner senses worked better when I drew the shades.

He shifted his gaze to me only for a second, then it went right back to Mason. "What about her?" he asked, ignoring my question completely.

It pissed me off a little, frankly.

"When's the last time you heard from her?"

He shrugged. "I don't know. A couple of years ago. Something like that." Then he popped the top on his beer can and took a slug.

I felt the lie, but that was cheating. I already knew the truth.

"Her cell phone says different," Mason told him.

I walked a few steps away, to the window that looked down onto Washington Avenue, parted the curtain like I was looking out and closed my eyes.

"If you think you already know, then why waste time asking me?"

"Because I want to hear it from you," Mason told him.

"She's been calling," he said after a brief pause. "I haven't been answering. I haven't called back. I haven't talked to her in a couple of years. Just like I said."

And that was the truth. But he was nervous as hell. I could feel it radiating from him. I said, "It's kind of important, Jake. She's missing." Just so I could feel his reaction to that.

And I did. I felt a pulse of something big. Shock? Surprise? Concern? Or was it fear that we were on to him?

"What do you mean, missing?"

I stayed right where I was. Mason would read his face, his body language. I was reading his emotions. And they were all over the place.

"Missing. As in, no one knows where the hell she is," Mason said. "Unless you know. Do you?"

"She's *missing?*"

"Her father thinks she's probably run off."

"She's *blind.* Where the hell is she gonna run off to?"

"How do you know she's blind, Jake?" Mason asked. "Her family kept it pretty quiet."

He walked a few steps, set his beer down. I heard all that. "We still have a few friends in common. I heard about it."

He still cares about her, I thought. I could feel it beneath the words.

"I don't know where she is. I wasn't lying. I haven't talked to her in a couple of years. And I didn't know she was missing." I had the feeling he was telling the truth, and then he got all tense again. "You're here because you think I had something to do with…with whatever happened to her, aren't you?"

"We're not sure *anything's* happened to her," Mason told him. "I saw your name on her outgoing calls and thought I oughta talk to you, since her father said you two ran off together a few years back. It's that simple."

I turned from the window, 'cause my senses had given me a big clue. "You don't like him much, do you?"

"Who?" Jake knew exactly who I meant. He picked up his beer, turning his back to me as he did.

"Stevie's father. Judge Howie."

He just shrugged. "I don't have any contact with the man."

"But you did. Two years ago when you and Stevie ran off together. Right? I'm sure he threw a fit about that."

"Threw a fit?" He frowned and turned to look at me. I totally got that he was searching for something in my face. Then he quickly schooled his expression into a mask. "I don't have anything to do with him. And I don't know where Stevie is. I hope she's okay. And I really have to get ready for work now."

I couldn't tell if that was sincere or not. The man had closed up tight, was keeping everything inside and showing us the door. Literally. He went to the door and opened it.

Mason sighed, and I knew he was disappointed. "Call me if you hear from her, okay?" He handed the guy a card.

Jake took it from him but didn't even look at it. "Sure."

I didn't believe him.

I waited until we were back on the sidewalk in the bright afternoon sunshine to say, "Something happened between him and Judge Howie. Something big enough that he thought we already knew about it. You need to find out what it was."

Mason nodded. "I think the guy has a record."

"Really? I didn't get that at all. How did you—"

"You get a feel for it after a while. People who've done time almost carry the scent of it. I'll run him through the system, see what pops up. Should've done that first, but I figured the judge would've told me if there was anything." He looked at me. "What else did you get?"

"I think he still cares about her. And he was either surprised to hear she was missing or surprised that we were there asking him about it." We got to the car, Mason's big black beast. I opened the passenger-side door and had to heft my bulldog out of the way to make room on the seat. Her loud snoring broke into aggravated bursts and she opened one eye, but other than that, she didn't break nap. "When do we get to talk to the other boyfriend? The current one? What's his name again? James Tiberius?"

Mason got behind the wheel and started her up. "Mitchell Kirk," he corrected, deadpan. My *Star Trek* reference went right over his head. He wasn't a Trekkie like me. "Tomorrow night at the chief's anniversary party."

"He knows the chief?"

"He's his nephew."

"Oh. I did not know that. The plot thickens." I relaxed in my seat and watched the city pass by as he headed for the highway. Ten minutes and we were back on 17, heading for 81.

"So what now?" I asked after riding in silence for a little bit longer.

"I take you home and head back to HQ to tell Chief Sub what we've found so far. See if he's ready to make this thing official yet."

A big sigh rushed out of me before I could prevent it, catching me by surprise. He shot me a look. "What?"

"I don't know." I frowned. "I think that was me being

disappointed that our day hanging out together is over. Weird, huh?"

Mason's grin made his dimple flash at me. It was a more potent weapon than his stupid handgun. "I enjoyed it, too. It's like old times, huh?"

"Old times meaning the last time a serial killer was after us? Pretty sad when I'm missing those sorts of good ol' days."

"Are you?" he asked.

I shrugged, because I didn't want to get too deep or stupid. "I think if I wrote a book about you, the title would be *Meets, Screws and Leaves*."

"Is that literary humor or a serious complaint?" he asked.

I rolled my eyes. "Never mind."

He eased into the left lane, then pressed the pedal down. He had a big, loud motor in the Beast, and even I got a little thrill when he made it roar. The nose end of the thing literally rose a little as the powerful engine kicked up a notch. I had discovered that the sighted Rachel was a little bit of a motor-head. I drove a convertible T-Bird that was a modern homage to the classic 1955 model, and I loved it. I had to admit, the '74 Monte Carlo was growing on me, too.

A little.

As he merged onto 81, he said, "Jeremy has a home game tonight. You should come."

I looked at him fast. "I wasn't hinting around for an invitation."

"Shit, Rachel, you don't hint around for anything."

"It's fine, we have the party tomorrow night. Don't overdo it or I'll get sick of you."

"I was going to ask you anyway. Josh has been griping that he never gets to see your potbellied pig anymore."

"Hey!" I punched him in the shoulder and hoped it hurt. "Fine, my gorgeous, sweet-smelling, damn near svelte bulldog and I will be there. What time?"

4

"Boys' varsity baseball is not nearly as much fun as girls' varsity softball," I said a few hours later from the bottom row of the bleachers at the Whitney Point High School's baseball diamond. Mason was sitting beside me, his nephew Josh beside him, and Myrtle was lying on the ground in front of Josh's feet. Possibly *on* Josh's feet. She was the president of the eleven-year-old's fan club. She was smiling with her bottom incisors sticking out over her upper lip, and every time the kid stopped petting her, she batted him with a forepaw.

"And you've come to this conclusion based on…?" Mason asked.

"Everything. The pitches are too fast, the hits are few and far between, the scores are too low—"

"Baseball scores are supposed to be low."

"He's right, Aunt Rache," Misty called. She and Christy, my sixteen-going-on-twenty-five-year-old twin nieces were sitting on the top row, as far as possible from us. They only insisted on being part of our conversation if it meant an opportunity to correct their too-long-out-of-high-school-going-on-spinster aunt.

I twisted my head around. "You're saying this? *You,* when your game last week ended because your team got so many runs ahead that they had to invoke the mercy rule?"

She shrugged, and returned to avidly watching the game, while her twin never looked up from the screen of her phone. Her thumbs were moving at the approximate speed of sound. Misty whisper-shouted, "Jeremy's up!"

So I turned to pay attention. Misty and Jeremy were an item, though neither had admitted it yet, and nothing was official, as far as I could tell. But it was on. I'd have known that even if I'd still been blind.

Thank God I wasn't, because it was one gorgeous spring evening. The sky was bluer than blue, not a cloud in sight, and Mason was beside me, a situation I liked way better than I had, up until now, admitted to myself. Admitting it to myself now gave me a sick feeling in the pit of my stomach. I liked things easy and casual between us. I didn't want to screw it up by wanting more.

Jeremy was crouching low, elbow up, bat moving in little circles behind him as he awaited the pitch. Then it came. He swung, and *crack!* It was outta there.

I shot to my feet, whooping and clapping and grinning so hard my face hurt as the ball sailed out of sight and Jeremy jogged the bases while we cheered. I glanced at Mason. He was smiling harder than I was. He met my eyes and nodded.

Yeah, I heard him. It had been a rough year for Jere. Last August he'd lost his father. In November his baby sister had been stillborn. At Christmas his mother had gone off the deep end and now she was in a locked psych unit. On top of all that, Jeremy had shot a man dead to save Mason's life, and mine along with it. That he was still upright and not curled in a corner, drooling, was a triumph, in my opinion.

"Okay, maybe I spoke too soon about boys' games not being as exciting as girls'," I said as he rounded third and headed home. We sat down again as the applause died down. "That was freaking awesome."

"And it means ice cream sundaes," Josh added. "You promised, Uncle Mace. If he hit a home run, we get sundaes."

"I guess I have to pay up, then," Mason said.

"Don't let him bullshit you, Josh. He'd have paid up either way."

Josh grinned, probably because I'd said "bullshit." Hell, I forgot again. I was lousy around impressionable youth. Yet another reason to keep things right where they were with Mason. He had kids now. I was not mommy material. I was eccentric aunt material. I had that gig *down*.

The inning ended, and during the approximate lifetime it always took for the teams to change sides, toss balls around and warm up the pitcher, I leaned closer to Mason. "So what did you find out about Jake?"

We'd gone our separate ways after we'd questioned Stephanie Mattheson's ex-boyfriend. Mason had dropped me at home, where I'd played on Facebook and Twitter instead of writing my daily ten pages, changed clothes and walked Myrtle. He'd gone back to the PD to talk to the chief and run a background check on Jacob Kravitz.

"He did eighteen months in Attica," he said.

"Shit, you were right." I clapped a hand over my mouth and glanced down at Josh, but he was oblivious. On the ground now, rubbing Myrt's belly in just the right spot to make her leg go, and laughing like a freckled hyena. "What did he do?"

"Pissed off Judge Mattheson."

I frowned.

"Turns out that when Stephanie and Jake ran off together, she wasn't quite eighteen yet. They crossed state lines. The judge made sure Jake got the maximum."

"That motherf— That *prick*."

He grimaced at me. "Not much of an improvement there, Rache."

"It's a *slight* improvement. So then Jake has good reason to hate the judge."

"Yeah. And to keep his distance from Stephanie. He's also got a pretty powerful motive for wanting revenge."

I nodded. "You think he's hiding her somewhere? That the two of them planned this?"

"I don't know."

"Or that he did something to her? For payback?"

"I don't know."

"I don't think he'd hurt her. Maybe he's gonna hold her for ransom, only maybe she's in on it, too, and they're going to run off to Tahiti together once the judge pays up."

He stared at me like I'd sprouted a unicorn horn. *"What?"*

"I'm telling you, Aunt Rache, you've got a novel in you." Misty had moved three levels down and was sitting behind us, leaning her head down between ours. "Now, what's all this about kidnapping and ransom?"

"Hello? Private conversation here."

She gave me an exaggerated pout and still managed to be gorgeous. "Then have it somewhere private."

"She's right," I said to Mason. "We shouldn't be working at a game. Baseball is way more important than work."

"Is that from one of your books, Rachel?"

"No, but it should be." I pulled out my phone, tapped the little blue birdie.

"You're Tweeting?" Mason asked, using the same tone he might use to say "You're reproducing by mitosis?"

"Amy says it'll have a positive impact on book sales." I keyed in Baseball is more important than work. If ur boss disagrees, he's a jackass. Then I turned the phone to show him. "I'm even learning the lingo."

"Everyone's on Snapchat now," Misty informed me in a superior tone. "Anyway, Jere asked us over tomorrow night to help him watch Josh while you two party. That good with you?"

I shot a look at Mason. He said, "Sure."

For a detective, the guy was way too easily conned. "It depends," I said. "Who do you mean by 'us'?"

The big blue innocent eyes got bigger and bluer and

innocenter. I knew she was up to something. "Me and Christy."

"Just you and Christy?"

She nodded very firmly and said, "And Rex. I mean, you know Rex."

Ronald Alexander, aka Rex (because being named Ronald and surviving high school could not coexist) was Christy's current boyfriend. I did not like him. He was hornier than a rutting billy goat, and he could not hide that from the insightful-but-don't-you-dare-call-her-psychic aunt. Aka me. Also, he smoked weed. I'd smelled it on him. It wasn't something I was judgmental about—unless you were dating my niece.

"I don't see why not," Mason said.

"And who else?" I asked.

"No one." Christy's voice had gone an octave higher. "I mean, unless Rex brings a few friends or something, but it's not like we're planning it."

"So, Mason, what my niece is asking you is, 'Do you care if a bunch of teenagers throw a party in your house when you're not home?'"

He nodded slowly. "I didn't know I had to stay in detective mode when talking to teenagers," he said. Then he looked up at Misty. "I'll have to meet this Rex person first, and it'll be just you three. You, Christy and him. No one else. And no booze. No partying."

Her smile was huge, her eyes sparkling. "Thanks, Mason. You're awesome."

Then she skittered back up to the top bleacher to lean in and whisper to her twin, who grinned and started texting even faster.

Shit, she was probably sending out a mass invitation to the rave at Mason's house tomorrow night.

The cell door slammed, sending Stevie's heart into her throat. She'd been sound asleep. Now she sat up, clutching the jagged bottom half of her handle-broken-to-a-sharp-point hairbrush in one hand and listening to the familiar footsteps walking away with a slightly uneven gait. "Lexi?"

"Right here," she said from the top bunk.

But Stevie sensed someone else near them. "Who is it? Who's there?" she asked, still whispering, if loudly.

"Ain't nobody here but you an—"

"Shh! Listen."

Lexus shut up.

The sound was muffled, but it was easy enough for Stevie to figure out why. She'd sounded a lot like that herself, trying to yell for help with duct tape over her mouth. "He's brought the third," Stevie whispered.

"Shit, we missed our chance!" Lexus slid down from the bunk and padded across the cell. "Where that damn light at?"

Stevie got off the bed and walked carefully toward the muffled sobs. "It's all right. Just take it easy," she told the newcomer. Then she felt the girl, even though she hadn't bumped into her yet. She felt her nearness and crouched down, reaching out and finding the girl's head. The girl jerked away.

"It's okay," Stevie said. "I'm gonna take off the tape. Okay? Just take it easy."

She touched the girl's head again, and this time she

allowed it. Picking at the edge of the tape over the girl's mouth, Stevie eventually got it loose enough to start unwrapping, and on the final time around she tried to be gentle and not pull out too much hair.

"What's going on? What is this? Who are you?"

The *rattle-snap* sound told Stevie that Lexi had finally found the pull cord and turned on the light. "Prisoners, just like you," she said. "I'm Lexus. Number Two. And that's Stevie. Number One. She blind."

The new girl was quiet for a long moment, looking around the cell, Stevie imagined. Taking stock.

"He got us, didn't he, Stevie? Brought Number Three in while we were asleep."

"We can't let that happen again," Stevie said softly.

The newcomer sniffled. "What...what are you talking about? Number Three what?"

"There's four of everything in this cell," Stevie told her. "So we figure there will be four of us. Sooner or later. The only time he opens the door is when he brings in a new one. Making that the only time we can try to get out."

"But we just missed our shot," Lexi said.

"That's okay. We'll have one more." Stevie moved behind the new girl and used her sharp hairbrush handle to saw through the partially cut zip tie on her wrists. "We're gonna have to sleep in shifts so this doesn't happen again. It might be even better, three against one. We'll need to find her a weapon."

"We gonna break another brush?" They'd broken two of them, then sharpened the ends against the metal bunk frames to use as weapons against their captor, the man Lexi, too, referred to as the Asshole. "That means only one left for all three of us. I ain't sharin' a brush with strangers."

Stevie shook her head. "Then she and I can use the broken-off heads." She got the girl's hands free. "Can't we?"

"Yeah. Sure." Number Three rubbed her wrists. Stevie heard it.

"You hurt anywhere, Number Three?" Lexus asked.

"Don't call me that."

"Tell us your name and I won't have to."

The girl didn't reply. Stevie heard her get up onto her feet. Then she seemed to be looking around the cell, turning slowly. Stevie could tell by the sound of her breathing. "What's he going to do to us?" she asked.

"So far, nothing," Stevie told her. "All he's done is bring in food. Never speaks to us, never touches us."

"Yeah, he workin' for someone, that's what. You know if he ain't touched the pretty one here, there a reason. He got orders to keep his hands off."

Stevie took the compliment without comment. She couldn't return it, because she couldn't see. So she continued, following Lexi's logic. "Why would anyone give him orders like that? You think we're being held for ransom?"

"Ransom. Right, that why he picked me. Dirt-poor and no family." She paced back to the bed and climbed up onto her bunk, and it squeaked under her as she wriggled around, getting comfortable again. "You got some rich relative gonna pay to get you back, Stevie?"

It was the first time Lexi had voiced this particular

question. Mostly, the girl stayed silent. But Stevie could feel her anger and frustration like electricity, crackling and snapping in the empty spaces.

Stevie didn't see any point in lying. "Yeah. My father's a judge. A pretty wealthy one."

Lexi's wriggling stopped. "No shit?" she said.

"No shit," Stevie replied.

"I knew you wasn't street, but I didn't think…" She let it go. "How about you, Number Three? You got wealthy relatives gonna come bail your skinny ass outta here?"

The new girl was quiet for a long time. Then Stephanie heard her sit down on the bunk on the opposite wall, the bottom one from the sounds of it. She felt sorry for the girl, over there all alone. She was scared. Stevie could tell. She wasn't sure how, exactly. Maybe the way her voice wavered a little bit, or how even her breaths were unsteady.

After she sat, the new girl spoke. "No family. No money," she said. "Foster care, till my last birthday. Then I was on my own."

"You aged out?" Lexi said. "Huh, me, too."

"That can't be coincidence, can it?" Stephanie asked.

"Gotta be," Lexi said. "You ain't no foster child. You ain't no— Jeez, girl, what are you *doin'?*"

"What? What's wrong?" Stevie asked.

"We got us a cutter."

"A what?"

"A cutter. She cuttin' herself." Lexus slid out of bed again and crossed the cell, and there was a scuffling on the other side. "What you got there, girl? Give me that."

"Leave me alone!"

"Yeah, right." One smack, and then the scuffling stopped. The new girl was sobbing in her mattress, and Lexus was walking back to their side of the cell. "Clever bitch, ain't you?"

Then she returned to the bedside and pressed something into Stevie's hand. It was a length of hard wire, maybe an eighth of an inch in diameter and about three inches long.

"She broke it off the bedspring," Lexi said.

Stevie nodded. "Good. We can use this. Maybe sink the end of it into a bar of soap, for a handle."

"Make a nice shiv. You think like a convict, girl."

"I guess I do." Stevie got out of bed and knelt, pulled the box from under the bed to take one of the two new, unwrapped bars of soap from it. Then she pushed the wire into the bar about halfway and stabbed her mattress a few times for practice. She felt the results. "Works."

"A mattress ain't a man, Stevie."

"I know." Sighing, Stevie took the shiv across the cell, held it out to the new girl. "Keep it under your mattress. Be ready to grab it and drive it into him the next time he opens that door. We're only gonna get one chance. You've got to be ready."

The girl took the soap-knife from Stevie's hand. "All right."

"No cutting yourself. Not here. We can't be hurting ourselves here, you understand? We are the only ones on our side. You want to be your own enemy, do it after we get out of here. All right?"

The girl sighed, but didn't answer.

Stevie shrugged and walked back to her own bunk, pausing when she got to the light, stopping right underneath it and reaching up to grab the string and yank it once to turn it off, so the other two could sleep.

She got back into her bunk, shoving her broken hairbrush under the mattress, then pulling the covers up over her shoulders.

"Good night, Lexus Carmichael. Good night, Number Three."

"Night, Stephanie Mattheson," Lexi said, picking up the hint easily. "Night, Number Three."

"It's Venora," she said softly. "My name's Venora."

Mason showed up at the butt crack of dawn. I mean, yeah, he'd said he'd pick me up in the morning, but it wasn't even 8:00 a.m. If he hadn't had a Dunkin' Donuts bag in one hand and a large coffee in the other, I'd have thrown him out.

No, I wouldn't.

I reached for the coffee. He moved the cup out of my range. "It's too hot yet. You'll have to let it cool. Might as well say goodbye to Myrt first."

I started to turn away, then turned right back again. "Is that some kind of judgment about the amount of time I spend saying goodbye to my dog?"

"What are you talking about? You mean to tell me that you take too much time saying goodbye to Myrtle every time you have to leave her for more than ten minutes? No! It can't be true. Surely I'd have noticed."

Oh, he wanted to play, did he? I snatched the doughnut bag from his hand, opened it. "Which one of these babies is yours?"

"Glazed. I got you the Boston cream."

I reached in, broke an inch-wide piece out of the glazed doughnut and handed the bag back to him. Then I turned around and went to where Myrtle had been lying down.

Only she wasn't where I'd left her. She was on the couch.

I blinked at Mason. "She did it! She got up on the sofa!"

"And this is a good thing?"

"She's been trying ever since she came to live here, Mace. But it was too hard on her. She gave up." Why did I feel like tearing up? "She's getting stronger."

"She's getting leaner, and those long walks you take her on are toning up her unused muscles a little bit. You're good for her."

"We're good for each other." I looked at the doughnut bit in my hand, sighed. Mason opened the bag, and I dropped the doughnut back in. Then I went over to Myrt, lying on my nice pretty sofa with her head on a throw pillow. Queen of the World. I sat beside her, scooching her over with my hip. She growled. Didn't mean anything. She always growled if you moved her while she was napping. It was just old-lady griping.

I rubbed her head and neck, and she sighed but didn't bother opening her eyes. "Amy will be here in a little while, girl. In a little while. Okay?"

Deeper sigh. I leaned down and kissed her nose.

She shot her tongue out to wipe off my germs. "See you later, boo-dog."

Then I joined Mason at the still open door and we headed out to meet with Loren Markovich, aka the Miracle Worker. I phoned Amy from the car to see if she could try to arrive for work early today, so Myrt wouldn't be lonely.

Mason rolled his eyes and said now that she could climb on the furniture, she'd be too busy trying out a nap on every single piece to get lonely. Yeah, yeah. Very funny. Also probably true.

We arrived at Loren's house, an adorable Cape Cod in a tidy suburban neighborhood that looked like everybody's idea of the perfect place to live. All the lawns were mowed. All the driveways were paved. All the mailboxes were straight.

We pulled over onto the shoulder of the road instead of up into the drive. My coffee was half-gone and just the right temp. I hated like hell to leave it behind. We got out of the car. I was in jeans and a yellow T-shirt that said, I'm Here. What Were Your Other Two Wishes? on the front. My hair was in a ponytail. Not my usual attire, but for some reason this detecting gig brought out the "don't fuck with me" part of my personality. Or maybe I'd just done this enough by now to know running shoes beat heels if you were being chased, say through a snowy pine forest. Jeans beat skirts for just about anything short of book signings and TV appearances. T-shirts were just…easy. And they had the added benefit of being mouthy if you wanted them to be. Which I did.

Besides, when I put on my aviator sunglasses, I looked badass in this getup. Lara Croft badass. You know, in my opinion.

Have I mentioned my obsession with mirrors and all things visual? Twenty years, yada yada. You know the deal by now.

So we walked up this perfect sidewalk to the front door and rang the bell. I heard barking from the other side, followed by a harsh *"Nyet!"* and dead silence. Then footsteps, and then she opened the door.

She wasn't what I expected. I don't know what I expected, actually. But she was pretty, probably around forty, with dark brown hair in the helmet style of a 1950s TV mom. She was wearing a pencil-slim gray plaid skirt and she almost had the hips to pull it off. Not quite, but almost. A white shell was tucked into the skirt, and she was pulling on a little pink sweater that had the soft, fuzzy look of cashmere.

"Detective Brown," she said as she opened the door. "And you must be Rachel de Luca. I can't tell you what an honor it is." She shook my hand. Warm and enthusiastic, that greeting.

My eyes shot to Mason with a "you told her who I was?" look. To which his eyes replied, *Nope. Wasn't me.*

Loren let us in, leading the way through a living room that looked lived in to a small eat-in kitchen. Then she waved us into chairs and poured coffee without asking. "So tell me what I can do to help you find Stephanie."

My immediate reaction was *How the hell am I supposed to hate this woman?*

I looked at Mason. Usually I left the questioning to him and just hung out to run the answers through my internal lie detector. He'd spoken to the blind coach on his own already—just briefly, he'd said—but she'd been busy and had agreed to see him again.

"I don't know," he said. "I'm hoping we can go over her disappearance again and maybe stumble on something we missed before."

She sighed, shaking her head slowly. "I can tell you one thing," she said, and she looked at me when she said it. "She did *not* leave on her own. This isn't a play for attention, as her father thinks it is. Someone took that girl."

"Did you see something that makes you believe that, Ms. Markovich?"

"No." She lowered her eyes, shaking her head slowly. "No."

"Then why are you so sure?" I asked her. Because she really had been adamant.

"She was afraid, Ms. de Luca. She was afraid to even walk to the corner by herself." A sigh rushed out of her. "I've tried to get her to find her inner strength. Her mother and I have both tried. Even your books haven't helped, and I was sure they would if anything could." She smiled a little. "They've helped me."

"Thank you," I said. So she was a fan. Huh. Go figure.

"I just don't believe she would have had the courage to run off on her own. And besides, it doesn't make sense to think she would've argued so hard against taking that walk by herself if she'd been planning to dodge around the corner and leave. What if I had given in?"

"I see what you're saying," Mason said. "Have you voiced these concerns to the judge?"

"I've tried, but he doesn't listen. And as for Mrs. Mattheson, she's falling apart as it is." Again a heavy sigh. She sipped her coffee, didn't look at her watch or the clock on the wall behind her while the silence lengthened. She wasn't in any hurry today.

I took a sip of mine. It was damn good coffee. Then I set the cup down and said, "She was giving you a pretty hard time that day, wasn't she?"

She smiled. "Stephanie gives me a hard time every day. Lucky for her I raised two brothers."

"Is one of them blind?" I asked. Just to see how she would react to that.

She closed her eyes briefly. "One of them is dead."

"I'm sorry. I am so sorry."

"I know. You lost a brother last year, too, didn't you?"

"Yeah." It would've been hard to live in the vicinity and not know about that. Tommy had been one of the victims of the only serial killer ever to hit the Triple Cities. It had been big news.

Mason cut in before I figured out a way to change the subject. "Rachel's been curious how you come by your expertise in helping the blind adjust to their new situation."

She shrugged. "I don't know if I'd call it expertise. My mother was blind. I lived with it my entire life. I heard about the judge's daughter from another employee."

"Another employee?" Mason asked.

She nodded. "I was working as a temp in his office at the time. At any rate, I went to him privately and offered to try to help. He was furious that I'd heard about it at all, but when I explained my extensive experience with my mother's blindness and told him it might have happened for a reason, he calmed right down. I told him the universe knows what we need and always provides. Maybe I was put into his path because he needed me." She smiled at me and I knew she'd gotten that "universe provides" line from one of my books. Yeah, I had one for every occasion. Hence the quote-a-day perpetual flip calendar.

"Oh. So you *don't* do this for a living," I said.

"Not at all." She shrugged. "And the way it's been going with Stephanie, it'll probably be my first and last effort. Answering phones and managing files is way easier."

"I'll bet."

"What else can I tell you?" she asked after another sip.

"Did Stephanie ever mention anything about either of her boyfriends?" Mason asked.

"Either of them?" she asked, lifting her brows. "I thought Mitchell Kirk was the only one?"

"He is, as far as we know," I said. "Mason's referring to her ex. Jake…something."

"Kravitz. Yes."

Mason shot me a quick look. "You know him?" he asked.

"I know who he is, yes."

"But you've only been working for the judge for…"

"On and off for two years now. Whenever one of his staffers is out and he needs a temp. And yes, Mr. Kravitz and Stephanie had broken up before I came to work for them. But once I started coaching Stephanie, His Honor made sure I knew who Jake was. If I saw him anywhere near her, I was to report it."

"And did you? Ever see him around Stephanie?" I asked.

She shook her head. "No. She never mentioned him to me, either, not that she'd be very likely to confide in me about her love life."

Mason nodded. He didn't take any notes. I knew he was committing everything to memory and would scribble it somewhere as soon as we were in the car. He said note-taking tended to make suspects nervous. He liked them to be relaxed when he was questioning them. Which was kind of crazy, because who can relax while being questioned by a cop?

"How about the current boyfriend, Mitchell Kirk?"

She shrugged, but the telltale way she lowered her eyes told me something. Shit, there I went, using my eyes instead of my gut again.

"I don't think he really loves her," she said softly, bringing my gaze right back to her.

"Why not?"

She shrugged. "Have you talked to him yet?" she asked me.

"Not yet."

"But you're going to."

"Yeah," I told her. Tonight, actually, at the chief's

anniversary party, but that wasn't anything she needed to know.

"You'll see, then," she said. "He just seems…fake. To me."

He wouldn't be able to get that past me, though.

Finally she seemed to notice how much of her time we were taking. She got up from the table. "Was there anything else?"

That was our cue. We got up, too.

"Nothing I can think of at the moment," Mason said. "If you think of anything, or hear from Stephanie, give me a call?"

She took his card and nodded, tucking it into her pocket, giving it a pat for good measure. Then she walked us to the front door, opened it for us. "Detective, is it true that the case isn't official? That you're looking into this privately, as a favor to the judge?"

"Who told you that?" he asked.

"I went over to pick up some things I'd left at the house. The judge and his wife were arguing about it." She shifted her eyes between the two of us. "Is it true?"

"I can only tell you we're doing everything we can to find her," he said. "Thanks for your cooperation, Ms. Markovich."

"Mrs., actually."

"Oh?"

"Widowed," she said. There was a wistfulness to her tone. "Long time now."

We stepped outside, and she closed the door. Then we walked back to the car side by side and got in. Mason started the engine, then pulled out a phone to key in his notes.

"Gimme that, for Pete's sake." I took the phone from him, opened the notepad feature and started tapping letters with my thumbs, jotting down every detail I could think of.

"What did you think?" he asked when I paused to search my brain for a word that refused to surface from the murky writerly depths.

"Of her?" He nodded, and I frowned. "I thought she was telling the truth."

"About what?"

"About everything. I didn't get a lie vibe from her once, and barely any emotions at all."

"Yeah?"

"Yeah. When she mentioned her brothers there was warmth, and sadness, too, for the one she lost. When I asked her about Stephanie giving her a hard time, I think she was a lot more irritated than she admitted to. But I'd have done the same thing in her place. You don't want to call a bitch a bitch if the bitch in question is in danger of turning up dead, right?"

"Right. Especially when you work for her father."

"Right. And then when she said she was widowed. Little bit of an 'I don't want to talk about this' vibe."

"Right. Anything else?"

"She thinks you're hot," I told him.

"Oh, for crying out—"

"Seriously, babe. She was totally feeling the Brown magic."

"That sounds like toilet humor."

"Only to an eleven-year-old."

"Josh will enjoy it, then."

"Are we done yet, boss?" I asked. "I've got books to write, followed by a date with a detective."

"I'm taking you home as we speak."

"Good." I took a deep breath, watched the trees go by for a while, then turned to him. "Something bad is happening to that girl, Mason. I think we have to convince her father to make it official."

"I think we have to make it official whether we convince the judge or not," he said.

Stevie didn't know how she knew Venora was cutting, but she did. The cell was heavy with darkness and sleep. She'd been sleeping, and Lexus was snoring a little bit on the bunk above her. But there was that sound, soft as a fingertip dragging across paper. And in her mind she saw the sharp edge of a broken cot spring slicing across Venora's skin and leaving a trail of ruby beads behind it.

"Venora, hey," she whispered.

The sound stopped. Stevie thought she smelled blood, then decided that was impossible. You couldn't smell blood. Could you?

"What?" Venora asked, almost defensive.

"Just…hey. That's all. How are you doing? You okay?"

Venora didn't reply. The silence drew out until Stevie rolled toward the wall and pulled her blanket over her shoulder, thinking the girl would never answer. And then she said, "I had a dream I was gonna die."

Stevie sat up. It wasn't entirely voluntary. "When?"

"Before the Asshole grabbed me. Before anything happened. I dreamed I was gonna die."

Stevie shook her head, denying it automatically. "You know, some people say if you believe in that shit, you can make it come true." That crock-of-shit writer de Luca that her mom and Loren kept pushing on her, for one. "So stop believing it. We're gonna be fine. We're gonna get out of here. All of us."

"I don't think so, Stevie."

Stevie got out of the bed, pulling her blanket with her. She crossed the room and sat on the edge of the other girl's cot. "Shove over."

"What the hell?"

"Put the damn shiv down and shove your ass over, Venora."

Venora moved over. Stevie lay down on the bunk beside her. She tucked her own blanket around her.

"What do you think you're doin', Stevie? You think you're my mamma now, is that what this is?"

"I think you're not gonna cut yourself anymore tonight, that's what I think. Now get some sleep."

Venora lay very still for a minute. Then she sighed and rolled onto her side, facing away from Stevie. But still touching.

5

Mason put on his wedding suit, and made a mental note to invest in a new one. This one was getting old, and he needed something for Jeremy's graduation, which was only seven weeks away now. Hard to believe.

He jumped behind the wheel of the black 1974 Monte Carlo he'd modified himself. Driving the Beast was one of life's most cherished pleasures. He would never admit it to de Luca, but driving her T-Bird was a close second. It would be even better if she would let him get under the hood and tweak it a bit, but she wanted no part of that. What? Risk getting grease on the yellow paint just for a few extra horses and a sweet growl? No way.

He drove through the open gate and up to her lakefront home. Yep, driving this car was one of his favorite things to do. Being with Rachel was another, but he couldn't really tell her that. She wanted to keep things light and easy. He did, too. Or had.

Now... Now it felt like it was time for a little bit more. Maybe. But if he said so, he might ruin what they already had, so he wasn't going to say so. Rachel wasn't exactly the shy-and-retiring type. If she wanted more, she would tell him. Until then, he'd just have to—

"Ho-lee crap."

Rachel came out the front door, and started down the steps and toward his car. She was wearing a short, clingy black number with sexy lace sleeves and a pair of open-toed stilettos, the kind he had personally heard her refer to as "fuck-me shoes."

He got out of the car and actually wobbled. When he finally finished devouring her from the feet up and met her eyes, she was smiling.

"Apparently you approve."

"You look like a million bucks."

She flashed him her trademark smile. "Yeah, I clean up okay." She nodded at his suit. "Your wedding suit?"

"Yeah. I've worn the funeral suit to too many of these already."

"Maybe it's time for a new suit? You're gonna need one for Jere's graduation."

"Stop reading my mind. And PS, I hate suits."

"Reason number five thousand, three hundred and seventy-five not to take the chief's job?"

"At least." He went around the car and opened her door.

"Gee, I put on a dress and get treated like a lady. Go figure. If we come to a puddle, are you gonna throw your jacket over it for me?"

"If that'll get me out of wearing it."

She grinned at him as he took his spot behind the wheel and got them underway.

"You know," he said, "now that you mention it, I

should probably start planning a graduation party for Jeremy."

When she didn't reply he looked across the car and saw her staring at him wide-eyed. Then he started noticing little flecks of green hiding in her blue-sky irises—or at least it looked that way in the dashboard lights—and he forgot what they'd been talking about.

"You haven't even *started* planning Jere's party yet?" I said when I'd finally managed to stop gaping like a fish out of water. He was staring into my eyes in a weird way that tripped about twenty alarms in my brain and body, including the two labeled "uncomfortably close to mushy" and "horny." I set them aside to go with "irritated at him for being such a typical male about some things."

Not many things. There wasn't a lot about Mason Brown I'd call *typical.* But in this…yeah. "I figured it was already all done," I said, feeling the biggest "damn, why didn't I bring this up?" moment ever. "You never mentioned it, so I assumed you and your mother had it covered. Jeez, Mason, you realize it's in, like, six weeks, right?"

"Seven."

"Seven weeks!"

"So? I buy some food, order a cake…"

"You need invitations. You need decorations. You need a location, for crying out loud. This is a big deal."

He glanced my way, maybe a little alarmed. "A location? I thought the backyard would…"

"Backyards only count if they have something in

them. Like a pool or a baseball diamond or a lake. Yours just has a barn. What the hell are they gonna do with a barn? Square-dance?"

"You think I still have enough time?"

"If I help. And Amy helps. And my sister, Sandra, helps. And the twins help. And we start tonight. Yeah, you have time."

"What if you help, and we start tomorrow?"

I realized I was sounding a little psycho and reined it in. Then I made a face and sucked air through my teeth in an exaggerated manner. "I don't know, man. Could be dicey."

He nodded slowly, a little relieved, I think, to see me off my freak-out wagon. "Ordinarily we'd have thrown the party up north, at the lake house, but…"

He trailed off. He didn't have to say the rest. I filled it in myself, in his voice. *But since my dead serial-killer brother used it as a dumping ground for his victims, it's kind of lost its charm.* The house had been for sale since January. Not. One. Nibble. Too soon, I figured, since the dragging of the lake for bodies. Lots and lots of bodies.

"We can have it at my place," I said. "It's huge, and we have the reservoir right there. We can rent a pontoon boat, maybe even some of those paddleboats, too, and let the kids have at it. Of course, we'll have to make sure someone's watching at all times and probably breatha-lyze them first," I said.

He frowned at me like I'd lapsed into Swahili.

"Mace, you know how graduation parties work, right? You remember?"

"I didn't really have one."

"What the fuck do you mean, you didn't have one?" I bit my lip, held up a hand. "No. We'll talk about that later. Right now I'll remind you how they go. Each parent throws a party for his or her own kid, to which all the relatives come. Each kid spends an obligatory hour at his own party and then goes to another kid's party. And then to another. And then to another. If they can cop a drink at each one, they're buzzing by nightfall. It's easy to do, because everyone has an Uncle Ken who thinks one drink on graduation day is harmless and well-deserved. After they've finished hitting all their friends' parties, they retire to an isolated spot in the state forest, around the back side of the res, where there will be a fire pit, a mountain of junk food and a tapped keg, and they drink themselves into a state of oblivion and sleep right there in the woods."

He had, I realized, stopped at a red light that had since turned green and was staring at me like my hair was on fire.

"What?" I asked him. "Weren't you ever eighteen, Mason?"

"I just… That's not how I remember it."

Having met his mother, I thought I understood. He'd probably led a sterile, pretentious "don't get dirty" sort of a childhood. Poor Mason. No grad party? No tapped keg in the woods? Even I'd had that experience, and I was freakin' blind. Man, it stunk on ice to be him.

"And that's *definitely* not how it's going down with my nephew," he added.

"Oh." I shrugged and bit back the stream of sarcasm

itching to come out. When I could safely speak again, I said, "Okay then."

"If he thinks for one minute that he's going party hopping and drinking—"

"I know. I know."

"It's zero tolerance, Rache."

"Got it. You want to drive the car now, Mace? The light's gonna turn red all over again any second now."

He looked at the light like he'd forgotten it was there and drove through as it turned from green to yellow. Then he went back to talking party. "Your house sounds good. And thanks for the offer. But no alcohol."

"Not even for the grown-ups?" I asked, pouting and wishing I could take it all back. He was sweating over it now. I hadn't meant to make him worry. But damn, the guy was living in a bubble where those boys were concerned. "Not even a secret stash, a tiny little one, for the adults?"

"I'll buy you a round during cleanup if you'll help me with this."

"Make it a double. By then we'll both need it," I said, and knew it was true. What the hell had I gotten myself into?

We were only a half hour late, which, I assured my gallant date, was actually on time. I figure you get a ninety-minute grace period at fancy-ass gatherings of three or more hours in duration. No, it's not an arbitrary number. It's one of a whole series of opinions I've developed over time. I reached this particular conclusion by timing my arrivals at fancy-ass parties a bit later and a bit later until I hit the point where I felt the pissed-off reaction of the hostess. Just past 90 minutes. Hence my rule. You can get away with an hour and a half, not one minute more.

At any rate, we were only a half hour late, which is actually on time, as I've explained. We saw the crowd of beautifully dressed people milling around on a side patio and headed that way to join in. Judge Mattheson's wife was already three sheets to the wind, which is actually drunk. It's just a more polite term for it. Or at least a more descriptive one. As a writer, I appreciate such things.

Mrs. Mattheson was leaning heavily into her husband's arm near the buffet table on the edge of the patio when Mason whispered, "That's Judge Mattheson and his wife, Marianne," and indicated them with his eyes.

"There you are!" Chief Subrinsky boomed from just inside the open French doors. He waved at us, so we meandered around the bodies spilling onto the patio and made our way into the house, which was stunning. The main room had a cathedral ceiling with a crystal chandelier bigger than any I'd ever seen. Not that I'd seen that many.

"I was starting to think you weren't going to make it," Chief Sub said, then turned to the guests standing with him. "For those who don't know him already, this is the detective I've been telling you about, Mason Brown."

The chief was surrounded by well-dressed, fat white men past their prime, who all looked our way. Talk about an old-boys network.

Mason drew me by the hand until we were a part of the circle, then had to release my hand to shake all of theirs. He clearly already knew many of them, the assistant D.A., some retired cops, a couple of lawyers. There was even a congressman. I was impressed.

"The man who brought down the Wraith," said the politician, shaking Mason's hand and clapping his shoulder. "It's a pleasure to meet you, Detective."

I couldn't help my inner scanner's quick burst of activity. It read: *Kissing ass, laying the groundwork in case he needs Mason's help later.*

It was the same kind of feeling I got from the whole bunch of them as they greeted Mason. Flattering and predatory. It made me shiver, and I was so busy getting my hackles up that I let my focus drift a little.

Then an uncomfortable silence brought me back, and I had to quickly review. Right, Chief Sub had said, "And this is Rachel de Luca, Mason's..."

He'd stopped there, looking to Mason to save him by filling in the blank.

Mason was paling before my eyes as he searched his panic-stricken brain for the right word.

I took pity and saved him. "Favorite author?"

The fat white men all laughed. Then they shook my hand, too, and most of them said they knew of my work but hadn't read it. All their handshakes were too fleshy, too warm, and some of them were damp. *Ick.*

I complimented the chief on his home, asked him to point out his wife so I could wish her a happy anniversary. He did, and I followed his finger and reacted in surprise. His wife looked like she belonged in a commercial for the innocence and natural beauty of Wyoming. "What anniversary did you say this was, Chief?" I asked.

"Forty." He was gazing at her across the room as he said it. She met his eyes, and I closed mine fast, because I wanted to feel that *thing* that passed between them. And I did. It was warm and deep and old and *real*.

Then I looked up at Mason and caught him looking back.

He leaned closer to me while the chief started talking about something else, and whispered, "I didn't bring an anniversary card."

"Yeah, I didn't figure you would." I was prepared. I pulled my just-in-case card from my handbag. "It says the gift is on its way," I whispered in his ear. "I suggest you go online and order something as soon as you get home. I signed it 'Mason and Rachel.' Is that okay?"

"Of course it's okay. You saved my ass. Thank you."

He totally missed the point of my question. He didn't get that signing the card "Mason and Rachel" meant something. It was significant. It labeled us a couple.

Dammit, maybe it was too soon.

"Rache?"

"Uh, yeah. You're welcome."

He took the card, and I told my head to get back on the job. We were here for a reason. Okay, we were here because his boss had told us to be here, but we were also here so I could wrap my senses around some of the principals.

"I'm gonna get busy," I told him.

"Okay." He leaned in for a peck on the mouth.

"Well, that was weird."

"Yeah, it was."

"What are we, Ozzie and Harriet now?"

"I know. Sorry." He was looking me in the eye, searching for what, I don't know.

"Stop looking into my eyes, Brown, my boobs are down there," I said, pointing them out with my chin.

He grinned. "Get to work, will you?"

I wandered away from him toward the chief's wife, not just because it was her party and I ought to greet her and wish her well. But because she was in deep conversation with Judge Howie's wife and looked a little bit alarmed.

I meandered, doing the nod-and-smile thing, while keeping eye contact minimal enough not to get drawn into conversation. It was a new skill and one I was still working on perfecting. Too far one way, you look rude, too far the other, everyone thinks you want to cozy up for a nice long chat.

Eventually, though, I made my way to the two women without looking like that was what I was attempting to do. And then I bumped into Mrs. Chief. "Sorry! Oh, Mrs. Subrinsky! Hi. What a wonderful party. Happy anniversary."

"Thank you."

"I'm Rachel," I said, extending a hand, but then I froze, because Marianne Mattheson had gulped a little, drawing my eye, and it was obvious she'd been crying. "I'm interrupting. I'm so sorry."

"That's all right," the chief's wife said, her right hand going momentarily to the other woman's shoulder. "I'm

Liddy, by the way. That 'Mrs. Subrinsky' stuff gets old."
She extended her hand and tipped her head to one side.
"So you're Mason's Rachel?"

She was so sweet, it was a shame I was going to
have to kill her later for that comment. Hair the color
of honey, a few crow's-feet at the corners of her amber
eyes, a few freckles across her cheeks and the bridge of
her nose. She wore a simple black dress, but I got her
as a jeans-and-cowboy-boots sort of woman. She liked
country music, and she went to church and meant it. I
liked her so fast I almost scared myself.

I said, "I'm not sure it's reached that point yet."

She let go of my hand and returned hers to the older
woman's shoulder. "Marianne," she said, "this is Rachel de Luca, the author."

Marianne blinked twice as she looked at me, then
her penciled-in eyebrows arched. "The author. Oh, my.
This is bizarre, isn't it?"

I frowned at her, not too clear on what she meant or
even whether *she* was. I'd already decided she'd been
drinking, but now I wondered if there was something
else in Marianne Mattheson's bloodstream. Her pupils
were pretty dilated.

"Why do you say that, Marianne?" Liddy asked.

"Because…because Stephanie has her books. Audio-
books, I mean. I bought them for her before she…"

Liddy aimed a quick glance at Marianne, who
stopped running off at the mouth.

"I'm really sorry," I said. "I'm clearly interrupting
something here." But maybe I'd found a way in with the
judge's wife. And who knew what I might learn from

her. "Marianne, I can see you're upset. I know about your daughter's condition. I was blind for twenty years, so I understand how she must be feeling."

"I know. I know, that's why I…" She bit her lip, lowered her head. Her hair was gray at the roots and sorely in need of a trim. I bet the look was short and sleek when she kept it up, but she'd missed an appointment, maybe more than one. Something had been stressing her out for longer than her daughter had been missing. The accident. The blindness. Her daughter's refusal to accept it. I thought about my mom. I'd only been eleven. It must have been a similar kind of hell for her to accept that her child's eyesight was gone. But she'd never let on. Not so much as a hint.

Whatever Marianne had started to say, it looked like she'd decided not to finish. So I had to end this. It was getting a little awkward. "Well, if you ever want to talk…" I flipped a card out of my clutch, trained by years of networking among the rich and famous to always have some on hand, even though this wasn't the same kind of thing at all.

On second thought, it kind of was. This was all part of Mason's audition for the role of Binghamton police chief. And me being auditioned as the girl most likely to become chiefette.

"Just call me, okay? Maybe I can help."

Marianne smiled crookedly at me and nodded, and I figured it was enough. I sent Liddy Subrinsky an apologetic smile and said, "Nice meeting you. Thanks for inviting me to your gorgeous home."

"Thank you for coming. Maybe we'll find some time to chat later on."

"I'd like that." *Can I ask her how to get what she has with Chief Sub? Can I ask her what there is to adore so much about the grouchy old paunch-bellied gray-haired coot anyway? Probably not the latter. Maybe the former, though. How do you do that? How do you do it for forty years?*

I heard Marianne whispering to Liddy, "Everything happens for a reason. That's so true, isn't it?"

That's right, lady. You met me for a reason. So you can spill what you know about your daughter and I can help Mason find her. Let's not take all night about it, either.

I spotted Mason again out by the patio bar, deep in conversation with Judge Howie. They were off in the shadows, away from other people, so clearly it wasn't a conversation I wanted to interrupt. I made my way to the inside bar instead, deciding a vodka with Diet Coke wouldn't impair my abilities, and that I'd already accomplished tons tonight without even trying.

I eased up to the bar and said, "Vodka Diet, please. Do you have Svedka?"

Smiling and nodding, the bartender reached for a glass. I relaxed and looked around. Ice chinked into the glass, followed by the glug of the Svedka bottle and the hissing of soda bubbles.

I felt the approach of a hunting horndog about three-point-five seconds before he showed up beside me and said, "Unique drink order."

"I'm a unique girl," I said, turning to look at him.

Hey, wait, I knew him. I'd seen his face on Stephanie Mattheson's phone. He was Kirk Something. Good-looking, dark curly hair, kind of a little-boy charm to him.

"I like unique," said the missing girl's boyfriend.

"You don't like *this* unique," I replied.

"Try me."

I shrugged. "Lesbian dominatrix. With herpes."

He actually backed away, the way you would back away from someone with really horrible breath, you know? Hands up, sort of grimacing in a "don't let it get on me" way.

"I'm kidding," I said, so he'd relax. "I'm Rachel de Luca. Came with Mason Brown. You're Stephanie's boyfriend, aren't you? Kirk…something."

"Mitch Kirk," he said, regaining his composure quicker than I'd expected. He was good. "You know Stephanie?" he asked.

I sipped my drink without answering that. "I was expecting to see her here tonight. Her folks being such good friends with your uncle. Where is she, anyway?"

He shrugged.

"Is she okay?" I asked him. Then I looked down at my drink and tried to shut off my visual circuits. When I really wanted to feel what was going on with some-one, it was easier if I closed my eyes. But doing that in public looked…weird, and I didn't want people to think of me as a weirdo.

Okay, a lot of people already did. From those who knew I wrote self-help books that claim you create your own reality, to those few who knew I sometimes helped out my favorite cop using senses not among the top five. Senses I'd developed over twenty years of living with only the top four.

But as I had often written, what others think of me is not my business.

"Why do you ask?" he replied.

I shrugged. "'Cause her mom is kind of having a mini-meltdown over there, and she's not here, and I can add two and two. You two break up or something?"

"Of course not." But I'd lost him. He was scanning the room now, and he stopped scanning when his eagle eyes picked out Marianne Mattheson. "Excuse me, I'd better make sure she's okay."

And he headed toward her.

I watched him go. She seemed glad to see him when he reached her, and he tucked her arm inside his and walked her out of the house and onto the patio, still scanning the crowd until he found her husband, interrupting his conversation with Mason. The little bastard.

The judge shook Mason's hand, then turned to his wife and apparent future son-in-law, and the three of them left. Not a word of goodbye to their hosts. Nothing. Just walked off the patio and onto the path that led to where all the cars were parked.

Mason was staring after them, too, but when they were out of sight, he turned and found me with his eyes. He started toward me as I started toward him. I wondered if anyone looking at us would sense the connection I'd sensed between Chief Sub and Liddy. I tried to see in his eyes what had been in the chief's. I tried to feel what I imagined Liddy felt like when she looked across the room at her husband of forty years, but I had no idea if it was even close.

Damn, this relationship stuff was hard.

We met in the middle. He said, "Saw you getting to know Mitchell Kirk. You get anything?"

"Besides hit on, you mean?"

A really pissed-off expression crossed his face. I saw it, and something inside me did a secret little happy dance while he rapidly averted his eyes. "Doesn't say much for his devotion to the judge's daughter, does it?"

"Nope. But then, she's not too devoted to him, either, if all those calls to Jake were any indication."

He nodded.

"I told the chief I had to leave early. Kids make a damned fine excuse."

"They really do. People get pissy if I say I have to get back to my dog."

"It's sheer prejudice," he said. "But I used it in advance, and we've been here an hour. That's sufficient. You ready to start the 'thanks for having us' round?"

"Beyond ready," I said. He reached around me, resting a hand on my hip and steering me through the crowd. Leaning close to him, I whispered, "Did you ask Judge Howie why he didn't tell you that he railroaded his daughter's ex?"

"I didn't put it exactly like that." He took my empty glass and dropped it on a passing waiter's tray. "He said, and I quote, 'You're a cop. I didn't think I'd have to spoon-feed you details that are on the public record.'"

"Ouch. And did you ask about the name Venora?"

"Yes, I did," he said. We were approaching the chief

and his wife, who were smiling, arm in arm, clearly happy. We stopped nearby, waiting our turn among the well-wishers. "He said he'd never heard it before."

"Oh." I frowned up at Mason, 'cause I'd picked up on something in his voice. "Then why am I feeling like you found out something major?"

"Because he was lying," he said.

Venora was cutting again.

"Girl, you got to stop that," Lexus said. It was the wee hours of the morning, according to Stevie's best guess. Lexi said it was getting lighter, said there must be windows somewhere down the hall beyond their cell, because the light made its way to them. None of them were sleeping. "You gonna kill yourself, you keep that shit up."

"Leave her alone, Lex. She's not hurting anything."

"She's hurtin' herself!"

"The opposite, really. She's self-medicating," Stevie said.

"What?" Lexi was leaning over the side of her bunk.

"She's making herself feel better." Stevie turned to face Venora, even though she couldn't see her. "That's why you do it, you know. Cutting releases the same chemicals in your brain that an antidepressant would. You probably oughta get on something when we get out of here."

"What do you know about it?"

"I know enough to tell you to try snapping yourself with a rubber band or pinching yourself instead. It'll do the same thing, with less damage and no risk of getting some nasty infection."

"Rubber band. Shit."

Stevie shrugged and tried not to take the pouty, petulant tone of the girl's reply personally. "I read a lot about it in college. Cutting. Eating disorders. Drug abuse. I was planning to go into youth counseling. Maybe even psychology. Wanted to work with teenagers. You know, before my life got derailed." She wondered briefly why she was opening herself up to the other two. It wasn't like her. Something about being with them seemed to have tweaked a long dormant part of her to life again. They were teens, really troubled teens. The kind she'd always wanted to help. That was probably it.

"How'd it happen?" Lexus asked. The bunk above squeaked as she rolled into a more comfortable position. "You goin' blind, I mean?"

"Car accident. The other driver was drunk, veered into my lane. Forced me off the road. My car rolled and flipped down a steep grade."

Lexus swore and Venora whistled softly.

"They had to cut the car apart to get me out. There was a metal rod stuck into my brain."

"Holy shit." Lexi leaned over the bed again. "You lucky to be alive."

Stevie sighed. "I've been miserable about it."

"Who the hell wouldn't?" Lexi asked.

"Lots of people. Rachel de Luca, for one."

"Rachel de-who?"

Stevie sighed. "Nobody. Never mind. It's just hitting me that I've been kind of a nasty bitch to everyone who's tried to help me. I mean, I knew I was. I just thought I'd have time to get over it and make it up to them eventually. Now maybe I never will. You don't think about that when you're throwing your hissy fits, you know?"

"Yeah," Venora said softly. "I know."

"I just hope I get the chance to tell my mother I'm sorry." Stevie choked up a little.

"You will." Venora's cutting had stopped. Stevie heard fabric rustling, like she was changing clothes.

"She cuts on her belly," Lexus whispered. "So no one gonna see."

"I can hear you, you—" Venora stopped herself when a door opened down the hall and they heard those familiar footsteps, along with shuffling, scuffling sounds. Stevie tensed and sat up on the bunk, feet on the floor, ready to spring. "Get ready," she whispered urgently. "It's now."

Lexi scrambled off the top bunk and took her position near the barred door. They'd discussed this, planned, practiced.

Stevie got her broken hairbrush from under the mattress. Venora would have her bar of soap shiv in her hand.

The steps came closer. The muffled pleas of another girl, bound and gagged, came with them. Number Four sounded terrified. Then the cell door opened.

"Now!" Lexi shouted.

Her job was to grab the cell door and yank it open wider, pulling their captor inside with it. It sounded as if she'd done it, so Stevie scrambled off the bed and lunged at where the Asshole would be if it had worked. She held the smooth handle in her palm and slammed the pointy end into what she sincerely hoped was some part of him. Lexus and Venora were doing the same.

The Asshole sent the new girl stumbling away from him as he grunted, swore and jerked away from her, taking her weapon with him, and then he punched Stevie in the face. She landed hard on the floor next to the bound and struggling newcomer. But she scrambled to her feet again and lunged forward, because the fight was still going on. She would attack with her hands, her feet, her—

A gunshot rang out.

6

Mason got the call at 7:00 a.m. It was a Saturday morning, and he'd intended to sleep. It seemed to him that planning to sleep in was the surest way to guarantee an early morning wake-up call. But that was part of being a cop, and he'd never really wanted to do anything else.

"Shit, I've got to get out of here," Rachel whispered while he groped for his cell phone on the nightstand. "The kids are gonna wake up anytime now."

"I don't think we're really fooling them," he said. "Josh, maybe, but—" He found the phone, picked it up. "Brown, what is it?"

"Mace, it's Rosie."

Mason rolled back onto his pillow, and watched Rachel pulling on a pair of jeans. And then he thought how lucky he was. 'Cause, *damn.* "Hang on one sec, Rosie," he told his partner. "Let me grab some clothes before we get ambushed in here."

"We, huh?" Rosie said in a wink-wink, nudge-nudge tone of voice.

Mason chose not to respond as he set the phone down and looked for his clothes. He'd thrown them off in something of a hurry once the kids had finally gone to sleep last night.

After the party, he and Rache had gone to her place just long enough to pick up Myrtle and a change of clothes, then they'd headed back to his house for the evening. The whole teenage crew had wanted to stay over, so they'd assigned Josh to Jeremy's room and let Rachel's nieces take Josh's. He grabbed a clean pair of jeans and quickly put them on.

They had *not* allowed Christy's boyfriend to join the slumber party. He'd asked, but he had a car and no reason not to get his ass home, as Rachel had put it. Christy wanted to go with him. Rachel said no. When Christy demanded to know why, Rachel had walked up to the guy, who towered over her by a foot, reached into his jacket pocket and yanked out a tiny plastic zipper bag with a joint in it. "That's why. Any questions?"

"How the hell…?" Rex demanded.

"Fuck you, kid. I could smell that a mile away. And here's a news flash for you. If you're dumb enough to bring pot to a cop's house, you're way too dumb to date my niece. Out. Now." She'd pointed at the door.

He'd left. Christy had rolled her eyes and stomped upstairs to mope. Jeremy had insisted he hadn't known about the weed, nor had anything been smoked in Mason's house. Mason believed him because *that* he would have smelled.

He dug in the dresser for a fresh T-shirt, while watching Rachel. She leaned toward the mirror, wrinkling her nose at her reflection, trying to force her hair into some semblance of order with her hands. It wasn't helping.

His feelings for Rachel had grown even bigger when he'd watched her boot the jock out the front door last night. He hadn't identified what those feelings were just yet, but he was starting to worry that they might be evolving into the big *L,* which scared the hell out of him, because she didn't want anything that big and serious, and neither did he.

Rachel was staring at him, having caught him staring at her. Her jeans were unbuttoned, and she was wearing nothing but a bra on top. She winked, pleased with herself, and pulled on a tank top and a denim shirt. Then she picked up her clothes from the night before and tiptoed out of his room.

"Mason? You there?" said the tinny voice from the phone. That wasn't Rosie's voice anymore. It was the chief's.

He grabbed the phone fast. "Sorry, sir, I was distracted. What's up?"

"We've found a body," Chief Sub said softly. "A girl."

Mason straightened. "Is it her?"

"Don't know. I'm on my way to the scene now. Rosie's with me, but he's limited, with his leg. I need you. Meet me there."

"I'm bringing Rachel," he said, blurting it without forethought. "I need her on this, Chief."

"She's not an official consultant."

"It's not an official case." *Yet.*

"All right. Bring de Luca. Just tell her to keep her head down and stay under the radar."

* * *

I phoned my sister from the passenger seat of Mason's Black Beast and asked her to go pick up her still sulking firstborn (by about seven minutes) daughter. Misty wanted to stay and hang out with the boys, and Myrtle would be happy and well cared for by Joshua. They'd all be fine. Jeremy was making everyone breakfast when we left, and he'd seemed okay.

He really did seem okay more and more these days. I didn't think he'd liked Christy's jock boyfriend anyway. Last night he'd seemed as glad to see him go as I had. I believed Jere about not knowing about the weed, and I told Mason so.

I could see the load that took off his shoulders. See, I thought, my *powers* came in handy every now and again. Then I rolled me eyes, 'cause the word *powers* was so ridiculous it didn't even make a good internal joke.

A half hour later Mason pulled the car to a stop in a vacant lot behind a small strip mall. A big wine-colored SUV was already there. The chief's, I presumed. I saw Rosie sitting in the passenger seat.

Mason vanished before my eyes, and his alter ego, Detective Brown, took his place. *He* was sharp, focused, undistractable, unshakeable and dead serious.

We both got out, and I followed him over to the SUV. Rosie nodded hello, then focused on Mason.

"Chief's already down there. So's Joe Kramer. Go left about a hundred yards. Ambulance drove right down."

Mason nodded. I followed him down a scraggly incline to the sidewalk-wide stretch of pavement known as the Rail Trail, where Triple Cities area health nuts walked and jogged. Where employees at the nearby businesses came to sit on benches during their lunch breaks to eat and smoke. Where locals walked their dogs, and most of them even remembered to bring little bags to clean up after them. This section of the trail ran alongside the Susquehanna River.

"Was that a crutch Rosie had next to him in the car?"

Mason nodded. "He got a bad sprain playing basketball with the boys. I told him he was too old." He met my eyes for a second, and I thought, *There you are.*

"Who's Joe Kramer?" I asked.

"Crime scene photographer." And he went right back into cop mode.

We hit the paved trail and headed in. I could see the ambulance, which had squashed the neat gravel shoulder on one side of the trail, driving over it. The chief and the medics were pointing at the river.

When we reached them I saw why. It was a beautiful spot, really. Lush young grass, still light green and naturally short. A wild apple tree, just starting to blossom in the palest pink imaginable. I thought the scent was heady, and apparently the bees bumbling from one flower to the next agreed. The river burbled and tumbled over rocks in the shallow bend at the edge of the trail. The sun streamed down, sparkling on the water. It was the kind of spot you'd choose for a picnic.

Except for the body that had apparently run aground in the shallows. Water rushed around and over the girl.

Her hair was dark because it was wet. Impossible to tell the color from here.

I stayed under the apple tree, and tried to tell my brain to think about the aroma and the petals and the bumblebees, and not that a girl was lying dead in the water right now. Or about Stephanie's already broken mother getting the news that her daughter…

Yeah, I wasn't having much luck not going there, was I?

Mason was pulling on a borrowed pair of waders from one of the first responders, a paramedic. Another man, one I presumed to be Joe Kramer because of the camera in his hand, already had a pair on.

The jogger who'd probably called this in sat in the grass near the water's edge, staring and rubbing the goose bumps off her arms, though it wasn't cold outside. She looked like a nice woman. Thirty, maybe. Wedding ring, probably had a couple of kids. Short blond hair with long sideswept bangs. I could feel her from here. Her heart was all tied up in knots over the dead girl.

Mason and Joe Kramer waded into the water and out to the body. Kramer took a few shots, then moved to another position and took a few more from the new angle. He did this until he'd taken shots from all sides of her, and then Mason took the girl by her shoulders. I knew he was being as gentle as he could when he pulled her off the snag and into the deeper water. Her body floated, and he just steered her all the way to shore. The medics met him there, with a gurney collapsed to its lowest height. They'd stretched an unzipped black body bag over it. Joe Kramer handed his camera to one of them; then he and Mason lifted the girl onto the gurney, water running from her in streams, and the medics carried it back to the trail, set it down and raised it to its normal height.

My eyes were glued to that girl, my brain pulling up pictures of Stephanie Mattheson and telling myself to look at this girl's face and compare, but nothing was computing. Probably because I kept getting stuck on the big bloody patch on the front of her blouse. I assumed that was what had killed her. Even when I forced myself not to look at that anymore, I still couldn't bring myself to look at her face. I didn't want to see the judge's daughter. Like it mattered, right? She was somebody's daughter, either way.

One slender arm dropped over the side of the gurney, and I found myself staring at her hand. It was a young hand. Small and feminine. Long but ragged nails with old pink nail polish all chipped and fading. And on her forearm, a series of scars. Recent ones. Like hash marks, five of them, each a couple of inches long.

I frowned and moved closer. "Mason, her arm…"

"I see it." He nodded at the photographer, who snapped a few close-ups.

Mason was wearing gloves. They reminded me of the kind women are supposed to wear while washing dishes. You know, because we're pure and made of sugar and will melt in dirty water.

He pushed the sleeve of her blouse up higher on her arm, then checked the other one, which was not within my range of vision, but apparently there were similar marks there, because more photos got taken.

The chief stood beside the stretcher with his head down and one hand on his forehead. "I knew Stephanie, and even I can't tell if it's her," he said.

My eyes disobeyed me then. I looked at her face. It was all puffy from being in the water, and tinted blue.

"Did Stephanie have any scars, Chief?" Mason asked. "What about that accident that blinded her, was she—"

"Yes, of course. There's a scar on her head, right about here." As he spoke, he leaned over the girl, holding out a hand and snapping his fingers rapidly.

The photog handed him a pair of gloves, and the chief pulled them on hurriedly, then squinted and leaned closer, moving the hair on the back of her head. "It's hard to see, with all this hair."

"There was another surgery," Rosie called. We all turned to see him hobbling along the trail with a crutch under one arm. "Her spleen was ruptured, wasn't it, Chief?"

I was still under that apple tree, between the body and Rosie on the trail. I turned to see the chief's response to Rosie and noticed Mason hadn't. He was looking at me. I met his eyes briefly, knew he was checking to see if I was okay. Well, I wasn't, but I was a helluva lot better off than the girl on the gurney was. I gave him a very slight nod, and he nodded in response. Then he turned back to the girl and carefully lifted her blouse. And then he got the oddest look on his face.

"Chief?"

The chief lowered the hand that was shielding his eyes from what he feared was the body of his friend's child. I couldn't help myself. I walked across the tender spring grass and, standing opposite Mason, I looked at the girl's exposed torso.

There was no surgical scar. There were names carved into the skin of her belly. *Lexus Carmichael, Stephanie Mattheson, & me, Venora LaMere*

Something happened to my head for a second. I swayed forward and automatically shot my hand out to catch myself. I touched the dead girl's hand instead, and there was this flash. I saw her lying on her back on a bunk bed, looking down at her belly and scratching her skin with a metal rod that looked like it was slightly heavier than coat hanger wire.

It was there and gone, just that fast.

What the fuck was that?

"You okay, Rache?" Mason asked.

I nodded. "Yeah. You see the names?" Venora, I was thinking. Venora, the same name Amy said her kidnapper had called her.

"I see them."

The chief was staring at the names, too. Mason said, "Venora was the name Rachel's assistant said her kidnapper called her during that episode last November."

Chief Sub frowned. "Can't be coincidence. And Stephanie's name is there, too. She was with her."

"It's all connected," I said softly.

"Good God." The chief shook his head. "So have we got one killer abducting young women one after another? Or some kind of ring?"

"I don't know," Mason said. "But there's no question

now that the judge's daughter is in trouble. We have to make this case official."

Chief Sub nodded. "Oh, it's official all right. I told him last night that was happening today no matter what." Then he looked at the dead girl again, reached out and pulled the body bag closed over her. "Get her to the morgue," he told the EMT. "Tell the ME not to touch anything. We need a forensic pathologist on this."

"Got it, Chief." The medic zipped the body bag closed.

"Mason, we need to find the connection between these girls. And include Rachel's Amy Montrose in that. There's got to be something."

"Yes, sir."

I felt the judge's approach before I heard his wheezing, and I heard his wheezing before anyone else. Judge Howie came hurrying down the path toward us. He was deathly white. Almost gray.

"Where is she?" Then he focused on the body bag on the gurney. "Is it her? Tell me it's not her!"

He was breathing like a lifelong smoker walking up a hill, looking nothing like the controlled, contained man I'd seen at the party the night before. He staggered to a stop, his hands on his knees, eyes fixed on that body bag, and Chief Sub hurried over to him and put his hands on the older man's shoulders like he was steadying him. "It's not her, Howard. It's not Stephanie."

The old man—and that was what he looked like, just then, an old, old man—kept his eyes glued to the black bag. "I have to see for myself." He moved past the chief, who gave a nod to the EMTs. One of them unzipped the bag and folded it open as the judge approached. I stepped away from them. I didn't want to risk touching her again, not yet.

I was still shaking like a leaf from whatever the hell had just hit me.

Okay, I'd had some weird shit happen before. I got donated corneas and wound up with some kind of mental link to the people who'd gotten other organs from the same donor. I'd had dreams and visions and premonitions. But it all had a physical reason that the believers of the world called cellular memory and the scientists of the world called bullshit.

It was the only answer I had, so I decided science would catch up later.

This, however, was different. I had no connection to this girl. I didn't have any of her organs in my body. So why that flash?

A little buzz in my brain told me to get out of my own head and pay attention. Judge Howie, who'd told Mason he'd never heard the name Venora before, was looking at the dead girl's face. He frowned hard, then looked closer. Something was going on. I closed my eyes so I could feel him. Mason had thought he was lying when he said he didn't know the name.

"Who is she?" he asked. Not because he wanted to know the name, I thought. Because he wanted to verify or nullify something his brain was telling him.

"We think her name is Venora LaMere," Mason said.

And a jolt went through the judge. I felt it.

"You *think?*" the judge asked. "What do you mean, you think?"

I need to know for sure, my whatchamacallit translated. (I'm working on a name for it, I swear.)

"Show him," I said, because I wanted to feel his reaction.

I felt Mason's eyes on me after I said it, and I knew the chief and the judge were staring at me, too, with "who the hell are you to even be here?" looks on their faces. I didn't need to see them to know. "What do you gain by not showing him?" I asked.

"Whatever it is, show me." The judge made it an order.

I heard the zipper move lower, so I knew they were complying. Someone must have lifted the blouse, because I heard the sharp breath the judge sucked in. "What the hell does this mean?"

"We don't know for sure yet, Howard," Chief Sub told him.

"Bullshit. You, Brown, what do you think it means?"

I sharpened my senses. I can't tell you how I do that, but it's like aiming your satellite dish in the right direction. I was completely attuned to the judge's frequency, whatever the hell that means.

Mason said, "I think it means that this girl was held somewhere with your daughter and the other girl. Lexus Carmichael. The wounds are recent."

"Jesus." And my brain whispered, *Something big is coming for him. Something bad. Freight train.*

"Judge, have you ever heard of these other girls before? Venora LaMere? Lexus Carmichael?"

"No. Never." I felt the lie right to my toes. Then he

added, "Not to my recollection, at least. Do you know how many girls like them come through my courtroom?"

"Girls like them?" I said it without breaking my concentration or changing position at all. Mason knew what I was doing. He knew and appreciated it. I felt that, too.

"How did she die?" The judge had apparently decided to ignore my question.

"She was shot—at very close range, I think," Mason said.

The freight train hit. It felt like a baseball bat to the skull. I opened my eyes, brought my head up fast.

Judge Howie was looking even grayer than before.

"You need to sit down," I said, but the chief was talking over me.

"The case is official now, Howard," he said. He put a hand on the judge's shoulder, and urged him to turn and start walking away. "Stephanie's in trouble. We need to bring every possible resource to bear on this so we can get her home safely."

The judge nodded.

"Mason, something's happening," I said. I didn't even say it quietly. The EMTs heard me. So did the chief and the judge, and even Rosie, who had finished up with a pad and a pen and the jogger, and was crutching toward us.

Mason pulled me into step behind the two older men. "If there's anything you haven't told us, Judge," he said, "now would be the time."

The two men stopped walking and turned to look at him, the chief with a kind of furious "how dare you?"

expression, and the judge with one that might as well have been a neon sign flashing the word *guilty*.

"Dammit, Mason, that's not what I meant. Something's *happening* to him." I looked at the judge. "Shit, it's a stroke. You're having a stroke."

He opened his mouth to say something, and then he just dropped. You know how it looks when they demo a building, the way it collapses straight down, dropping its rubble into its own basement? That's how he fell. Like his legs had dematerialized underneath him. And it happened the instant I was reaching for him. If I'd lived in the Dark Ages they'd have burned me as a witch.

The chief crouched beside him, hands on his shoulders, rolling him onto his back. Mason shouted, and waved at the ambulance that had just finished turning itself around behind us.

It sped over to us, and the EMTs jumped out and took over.

"It's a stroke."

"How do you know that, ma'am?"

"If she says it's a stroke, it's a stroke," Mason barked. Then he encircled my shoulder with one arm and moved us out of the way, to where Rosie stood on the trail.

The chief was pushing a hand through his hair as he walked over to join us. "Why the hell would you accuse him like that?"

Mason started to defend himself. "Chief, I—"

"Because he was lying when he said he'd never heard of Venora and Lexus."

Then one of the EMTs shouted at the other, "She's right, he's stroking out. We've gotta transport STAT."

Chief Sub's anger changed to fear. I felt it. He looked at me, then at Mason. "She *psychic* or something?"

"Or something," he said.

"I am *not* fucking *psychic*." And just like that I knew what to call my extra-sharp intuition. NFP. Not Fucking Psychic…ism. Hey, I didn't say it was perfect.

My attention shifted back to the EMTs as they moved the body bag onto the floor of the ambulance and dragged the gurney over for the judge.

Stevie sat on her bunk, reliving what had happened, trying to figure out what the hell she'd done wrong. Everything, she guessed. Who the hell was she to make escape plans and lead attacks? Who was she to lead anything or anyone? She couldn't even see!

Over and over the whole thing played out in her mind, and in her mind she could see it. Her and Venora and Lexi, jabbing and stabbing at their captor. The way he'd shoved her away, and then that punch to the face. She'd hit the floor but scrambled up again and flung herself back into the tangle of people, and the gun went off, and she thought her ears would bleed from the sharp crack of it.

She'd hit the floor and then searched her own body with her hands, sure she was shot. Until she felt the warm blood on the floor, flowing toward her, not away. Lifting her head she said, "Lexi?"

"It's Venora. Bastard shot Venora!" Lexi screamed, then she yelled again, but facing away from her this time, probably shouting through the bars. "You fucking asshole! You shot her, you bastard! You come back in here again I'm gonna eat your liver, you spineless son of a—"

"Venora." Stevie said her name softly as she crawled to where the girl lay and put her hands on her shoulders, and then tried to put her hand on her heart to feel for its beat. But she felt a small hole instead, and the steady pulsing way the blood rushed from it with every heartbeat. "It's okay, Venora. It's okay."

"Yeah," Venora whispered. "It is."

"Lexus, get the new girl untied before she hyperventilates and passes out!"

Lexus pounded on the bars one more time, but then Stevie heard her working on freeing up the new girl, who apparently got a look at Venora as soon as her blindfold came off, because she said, "Oh God oh God oh God."

Stevie got Venora's head up into her lap. She had her hand pressed to the wound, but she didn't expect it to do any good. That beating pulse. The spot where the bullet was. It had to have gone into her heart.

"I'm sorry," Stevie told her. "We shouldn't have tried that. It's my fault."

"I…was going out either way, Stevie. I told you, I knew I was. I'm glad I died fighting."

"You're not gonna die." The pulsing stopped. Just like that.

Stevie frowned and bent closer to listen for Venora's breath.

She exhaled the words "I'll save you," warm and soft on Stevie's cheek, and then…nothing.

She didn't breathe again.

The door opened down the hall. Stevie heard more than one set of footsteps outside the cell. Lexi roared, "You come on in here, you sons of bitches! You come on in he—"

There were three quick soft sounds. Something stabbed into Stevie's arm, and she heard Lexi fall to the floor and the new girl gasp, all at once. And then she passed out as a voice that was distorted and came from very far away said, "Get rid of the body and clean this mess up. Make it fast. We gotta move them. Someone might've heard the fucking shot."

7

Chief Sub tossed his keys to Rosie after we walked across the weed lot to where we'd all parked. The ambulance had trundled on ahead of us and was out of sight on the highway now, heading for Binghamton General. I felt bad for Rosie. He'd managed to keep up with us, his sense of urgency and commitment to his job bigger than his common sense, if you asked me. He was walking on that sprain and hurting like a bitch. And no, I didn't need NFP to know it.

"Take my wheels, Jones," the chief said. "Get back to headquarters and start looking for a connection between these girls. Including Rachel's assistant, Amy Montrose."

With a nod, Rosie headed for the big SUV.

"Keep your weight off that ankle," I called after him. "And when you get to your office, for crying out loud, put it up and ice it, okay?"

Mason frowned at me.

"Nieces. Varsity basketball. *Real* familiar with ankle sprains," I explained.

The chief frowned like he didn't know quite what to make of me. Yeah, I get that a lot. Then he went right back to business. "Mason, you're driving me." He started for Mason's car. Front seat. Passenger side. Aka my spot.

"Sure, Chief. Where to?"

"The hospital. I need to be there."

Nodding, Mason opened the back door for me. I'd just as soon have gone home, because I needed to think about what had just happened out here today. Okay, picking up on the judge's impending medical crisis was the kind of thing I'd normally do. But that flash when I touched Venora LaMere's hand was just…freaky.

Mason held the door for me. "You look shaky," he said when I slid past him into the car.

"I'm good," I said with more conviction than I felt. Because he had a job to do, and seeing to my needs wasn't a part of it. I could handle that myself, thanks. As soon as there was an opportunity to go home, I'd go. Until then, I wasn't going to turn into a fragile wilting flower who couldn't handle looking at a dead girl. A dead girl who was less than two years older than my nieces.

Mason's look lingered. He knew me too damn well, and his cop sense was as good as my NFP. No, that wasn't true. Not anymore. My NFP was hopped up on crack or something. But before. It was just as good before. And he knew I wasn't okay, but he also knew there was nothing he could do about it right now. And he'd better also know that I had a handle on it and didn't need his help.

Mason drove faster than he normally would have,

but that didn't bother me. We both liked to cut loose on deserted stretches of pavement every now and then. My T-Bird hadn't been souped-up like his Monte Carlo had, but I could do a pretty decent burn.

So he drove, and the chief called the judge's wife and told her to meet us at the hospital. Poor woman had barely been holding it together with the runaway daughter. Now she had to deal with a stroked-out husband and her runaway kid being upgraded to kidnap victim.

After the chief hung up with her, he and Mason went back and forth with each other about the case, and I sat there and tried to figure out what the hell I'd seen in that flash of mine. I mean, yeah, I was shocked by it, and completely confused, but I also knew what to do with it. Just like in the other visions or dreams or whatever the hell I'd had in the past, I had to revisit it. Look for details. Figure out what they meant.

But for the life of me, all I kept getting was the springs of the bunk above Venora's, and the sight of her belly, all trailed in ruby lines, and her hand dragging that piece of metal across her skin.

We were at the hospital before I knew it, parked in back and headed for the emergency-room entrance, even though that wasn't protocol. Chief Sub got his badge out and used it like Moses's staff to part the waters ahead of us as we ran through. He accosted the first nurse he saw. "Judge Howard Mattheson. He was just brought in."

"Yes, we have him. Are you family?"

"No. I'm the chief of police. I was with him when he—"

She put a hand on his shoulder, stopping his stream

of words. "Call his family." Her tone was saying a lot more than her words. Jeez, the judge might not pull through.

And how the hell was he going to tell us what he'd been holding back if he died?

Don't worry, you seem to have some kind of a line to the dead.

Fuck you, Inner Bitch.

Mason said, "Look, there's the waiting room. Let's get out of the way, Chief."

The chief nodded, a little spaced out, I thought, and I found myself taking him by his arm like he was my grandpa or something. If he'd been himself he'd probably have resented that. As it was, though, he didn't even seem to notice as I guided him into the waiting room. He found a chair and sank into it. I went to the vending machines. One for soft drinks, one for coffee and one for snacks. I leaned on the snack machine and looked through the glass at the selections inside.

Then I heard a woman's voice. "My husband," she said. "Howard Mattheson."

"Marianne!" Chief Sub sprang out of his seat and hurried out of the waiting room in her direction.

I no longer knew what I was looking at, and my head sort of lowered itself between my outstretched arms.

Mason came up behind me and put his hands on my shoulders, rubbing like a pro. "You okay?"

"Uh-huh."

"What happened back there?"

I brought my head up, shook it. "Damned if I know,

Mace. I got some kind of flash when my arm brushed across her hand."

"Flash?" His hands on my shoulders stilled, and he turned me around. "Like before?"

"Yeah, except I wasn't sleeping and I don't share an organ donor with this kid. Or maybe I do. I don't know. Maybe she got a bone graft or something from your brother?"

He was watching my face like it was going to tell him the secret of life. "We've both seen the recipient list. The name Venora LaMere wasn't on it. We'd have remembered if it had been, even if Amy hadn't heard it. It's an unusual name." He took a breath, then asked, "What did you see?"

"Her, cutting her belly with a piece of wire. The lines of blood on her skin. And a bunk above her."

"Bunk above her," he repeated.

"Yeah. She was lying on her back, on a narrow bed, and there was a bunk above her. I could see the springs, sagging down in the middle."

"So someone was in the bed above her, then?"

My brows went up. "I don't know. Maybe it was just old."

The chief came back, Marianne Mattheson tucked within the circle of his arm. She was shaking her head and crying softly. There wasn't a hell of a lot I could do, so I offered to get them all some coffee from the cafeteria, which had to be better than what the machine had to offer.

By the time I got back with it, Marianne's sister had arrived to be with her. Marianne seemed to be getting hold of herself and was urging the chief to go back to work trying to find her daughter. I didn't think he'd told her yet that it was pretty certain Stephanie had been kidnapped, or that one of her fellow abductees had been found shot to death. If he had, I figured, she'd have been on a stretcher herself.

I felt about as comfortable at the Binghamton Police Department as a Muslim going through U.S. airport security. I didn't have a damn thing to hide, but I was sure everyone there thought differently. Or anyone who recognized me, at least. A celeb—even a minor one like me—at a police station was high test fuel for the gossip machine. And when you were known as a lifestyle guru, your own life was always a juicy target for the naysayers.

Besides, I'd given the people here a pretty hard time when my brother, Tommy, had gone missing last summer. Especially the woman at the information desk, who looked almost exactly the way my mind-camera had projected her on my inner private viewing screen. She was heavy, with thick glossy ringlets in her hair and a snotty expression on her face when she looked my way. I could hear her expression loud and clear. *You again?*

I shrugged and said, "I don't like it any better than you do," as I followed Mason and the chief past her desk like a trained puppy.

The hospital had been kind of a useless detour, but I understood the chief's need to see his friend in good hands at the E.R. and talk to the worried wife before he could focus again. He seemed like he'd bounced back.

Worried, yeah, but he didn't look lost anymore. He was back to being large and in charge.

"Mason?" I needed to go home. I'd done my duty, but I was done now.

He turned to look at me just as Rosie appeared. "Glad you're back."

Rosie had a doughnut in one hand and a very badly stained *The Cleveland Show* ceramic coffee mug in the other. I had to bite my lip hard to keep from laughing, because "Cleveland" and Roosevelt Jones bore more than a slight resemblance.

He fell into step beside us, and we all wound up in the chief's office. I had no idea why I was being included in this inner-circle huddle, but there didn't seem to be a way to get out of it gracefully, so I tried to stand unobtrusively near the office door and keep my mouth shut.

The chief was sitting behind his desk, and he looked right at me and said, "Close the door, please."

"Look, guys, I don't really need to be here for this, so, um—"

"Stay put. I wanna talk to you. And close the door."

I closed it. The chief was hard to argue with.

"Rosie, where are we on finding a connection between the four girls?"

"I only found one connection, sir, but it's a big one. Venora LaMere and Lexus Carmichael were both wards of the state. Foster care."

The chief frowned. "That's too odd to be coincidental. But I don't see how Stephanie could be connected to two girls in the system."

"Maybe 'cause her father's a family court judge?" I said. "Which begs the question, why did he lie about knowing the names? I mean, who's gonna forget a name like Venora?"

Mason blinked at me like I'd just suggested that Jesus was a pagan.

"*What?* Like it's not obvious? Or do we just pretend not to notice things that look bad for the guy because he's in the hospital and a friend of the chief's?"

Rosie looked at his shoes, and Mason said, "Rachel…"

The chief held up a hand. "No, she's right." Then he looked me in the eye. "Sit down, Rachel."

The words *I don't work for you, so don't fucking tell me what to do* were on the tip of my tongue, but I bit them back. He was being bossy, but he'd been through a lot and I'd just sort of insulted his friend. So I sat. I imagined Mason was about to fall over dead and ask the chief how the hell he did that, but now wasn't the time.

"What made you think the judge was lying about not knowing those names?"

I heaved a giant sigh, and looked at Mason and then at Rosie, who sort of knew about my…quirks. Neither of the men flanking me were any help, though, so I complied. "Look, Chief, I was blind for twenty years."

"I'm aware of that."

"When you're blind, you depend on your other senses. Mine got really strong. I can tell a lot about people by hearing them talk."

"Tone of voice. Pitch. Steadiness. I get that," he said.

"Mason thought he was lying, too," I said. "His cop instinct. It's a lot like that."

"So how did you know he was about to have a stroke? You hear that in his voice, too?" He was watching me like I watch a dwindling bowl of M&M's.

I didn't know how the hell to answer him, so I went with the truth. "I felt it."

"You felt it. Like an…intuition?"

"More like a baseball feels a home run hit."

He blinked once, then shot an accusing look at Mason. "She's a fucking psychic."

I sprang out of my chair. "Don't call me that! I'm not a fucking psychic!"

"That's how she helped you nail the Wraith?" The chief went right on, undeterred by my most menacing tone. "With E-S-fucking-P?"

"I'm standing right here and can speak for myself, and it's *not* ESP."

"Then what the hell is it?" Chief Sub demanded.

"I don't know. *You* try being blind for twenty years and then you can tell me what it is, how's that sound?"

He glared at me. I glared back.

"You don't like me," I said, my tone low and even. "You don't like people who don't back down when you roar, and you especially don't like it from women. You like it even less that I think your friend the judge might be up to his elbows in some kind of kidnapping ring, and you're kind of freaked out by someone who's more perceptive than any cop on the force." I sent Mason and Rosie a quick look. "No offense, guys."

"None taken," Rosie said.

I barely paused, 'cause I was on a tear. It doesn't happen often, but, baby, when it does...

"The thing is, Chief, I don't fucking care what you think of me. I don't even want to be here right now. I have no interest in being an amateur sleuth, and if it'll make you feel better, I'll swear on a stack of chocolate chip pancakes not to get mixed up in any more of your cases. That work for you?"

He opened a drawer, rifled around until he pulled out a sheet of paper, then slapped it on top of the mess on his desk. "No, I'm afraid it doesn't. Scribble your name and social on there and sign it. I'll fill in the rest."

I looked at the paper but didn't reach for it. "What is it? A restraining order?"

"It's for the W-4 I have to file to make you an official police consultant."

"I just said I didn't want—"

"Yeah, I got that." The chief was completely calm but deadly serious. "Fact remains you're needed here. If you can help us get those girls back alive—and after what I saw today, I think maybe you can—then you've got to. You know that as well as I do, don't you, de Luca?"

I closed my eyes, not to feel anyone but to block out the big fat guilt trip being heaped on me by Chief Soulful-When-They-Wanna-Be Eyes. It didn't work. I leaned forward, picked up the paper.

"As far as anyone needs to know," Chief Sub went on, "we're using you because you can give us a unique perspective on Stephanie Mattheson's situation due to your years of blindness. No one is to use the phrase *police psychic*. Ever."

"You hired a psychic?" I asked. "'Cause you can't be talking about me after I told you—"

"Down, girl."

My eyes widened, and I looked at Mason. "Did he just 'down, girl' me?" Then Chief Sub. "Did you just 'down, girl' *me?*"

Ignoring me, Chief Sub shifted his attention to Mason. "Now, there's one more thing."

I stood there holding the form and wondering how the hell I'd just been out-argued, bossed around and dismissed. None of my usual tactics worked with this guy.

"What's that, sir?" Mason asked.

"According to Rosie's report, Venora LaMere's last known location was two miles across the state line in PA." He said PA, not Pennsylvania. No one in the Triple Cities calls PA Pennsylvania. It's too close and we say it too often to waste time. Or syllables. "It looks pretty solid that's where she was abducted. The state line was crossed."

"By two miles," Mason said.

"Doesn't matter. That makes this federal. I've spoken to the FBI already. They're sending a field agent. Be here by the end of the day. You'll be working under him. For now, get over to Social Services and start digging into those two girls' files."

"I'm gonna need a warrant for that," Mason said.

"It'll be there before you are."

Mason got up and opened the door. Rosie went through it, and I started to follow, the chief's form still in my hand.

"Scribble your Hancock on there and leave it, de Luca," the chief said.

"Chief, I don't sign things without running them past my—"

He tapped his desk with a forefinger, three insistent times. I slapped the paper down, picked up a stray pen, scribbled my Social in the appropriate spot and signed the bottom. Then I pushed the paper across the desk toward him, lifting my head to look him in the eye.

He looked right back. And then he smiled. "Your antennae are off, by the way. I actually *do* like you, de Luca."

"Only because I let you win Round One," I said. "Just don't get used to it, Chief."

"I love a challenge. Get out of my office."

8

Stevie woke up with a heavy throbbing head and a bad case of cotton mouth. She was in bed. At least it felt like a bed. She stretched her arms out to the sides. She was right. It was an actual bed, not a hard little cot. And there were pillows and sheets and everything.

Her heart jumped and beat faster. Had she been rescued? Was she safe again?

"Hello? Is anyone there?"

A soft groan was her answer, then Lexi's voice. "Damn, my head…"

"Lexi?" She scrambled to the edge of the bed, feeling her way. "Where are you?"

"In a bed, same as you." Stevie moved closer, following Lexi's voice, feeling her way. She bumped into a small table, rectangular and low, then an overstuffed chair, before she found the other girl's bed and sat on its edge.

"Where's Number Four?"

"Sissy," Stevie said, thinking hard and finding the name in the foggiest depths of her memory. "I heard the Asshole call her Sissy before I passed out altogether."

"Sissy, huh. How the hell you remember anything? Fucking drugged us like animals. Freaking darts."

"Lexus, where is she?"

"Still sleepin', by the look. Tell you what, we got us some better digs, that's for *damn* sure."

"Tell me."

"First, it's round. And there ain't no windows. I think it must be a basement or something. You know? Walls made outta stone blocks."

"Cinder blocks?"

"I guess. Except they're curved. There're four beds, sort of evenly spaced around the edge. One part of the right curve is walled off, with a door in it. Then in the middle, looks like somebody's livin' room. Got a little table, a couch, a couple chairs, a stack of board games." She sighed. "Ain't no TV, though. Damn, I miss TV."

"Me, too. And the internet. And my phone."

Sissy whimpered in her sleep. Stevie got up and started feeling her way to the other girl's bed. "Four, huh. Must be they're still gonna bring in one more girl."

"Looks like."

She made it to Sissy, sat on her bed and touched her shoulders. "Easy. You're okay."

She felt the girl come awake. It was nothing in the way she moved or anything she said. Just a shift in the feeling of her. It was odd how easily she could distinguish awake from asleep. She wondered if she'd been able to do that before.

"Where are we?" the new girl asked.

"I don't know. But it's better than where we were."

Stevie heard Lexi get up and walk around, heard a

door open. "It's a bathroom. Shower and everything." There was the sound of running water. "It works." Lexi moved back into the main room. "I don't see no door. How the hell they get us in here without a door?"

"There has to be a door somewhere," Stevie said. "Maybe there's a trapdoor in the floor or something. Under one of the beds or—"

"I see the door." Sissy's voice trembled when she said it.

Lexus took a few more steps. "Oh, *hell* no."

"What? What is it?"

"The door… It's way up in the ceiling. And there's no way up there. No steps, no ladder." Lexi released a shuddery breath. "Girl, we definitely underground."

"Oh, my God. Oh, my God, we're underground!" Sissy wrapped her arms around Stevie, buried her head against her chest and sobbed.

Stevie was stunned by that, she didn't know what to do, so she just did what her own mother would've done. She stroked the girl's hair and told her it would be okay. She was damned if she believed it, though.

"I miss my dog," I said, when we arrived at the building that housed the Office of Children and Family Services. Judge Howie's courtroom was right across the street.

"Aw, come on, Rache. You've been away from her a lot longer than this before." Mason parked the car and got out. I got out, too.

"I don't care. If I'm going to be bullied into working on this case, then I'm bringing her with me from now on."

"Yeah, because she'd rather be dragged around with us all day than home playing with Josh. And no one bullied you."

"What the fuck do you mean, no one bullied me? Your chief—"

"Don't even try that with me. If you didn't want to be here, you'd have crumpled the paper in your fist, bounced it off his head and told him where to shove it, and then you'd have been out the door. But you're here, aren't you?"

I narrowed my eyes on his stupid gorgeous face. "I hate that you know me so well."

"Yeah, well, if you really want me on the other side of the chief's desk, you're gonna have to lighten up on the old guy."

"Never."

He smiled at me. "Good."

We approached the entrance to the building. An officer in uniform waited outside, official papers in hand. Our warrant, I guessed. He handed them to Mason, who thanked him by name. I was no longer paying attention. There was too much else going on. A guy was sitting on the sidewalk a few yards away, wearing a heavy green military-looking coat, even though it was in the mid-sixties outside today. He was skinny as a rail, and his gray-flecked brown beard probably had things living in it. He was humming real soft. Too soft to attract anyone else's attention, but it had mine. He had a beautiful voice and a heart of gold and a head that was all mixed up.

"Rache?"

"Yeah?" But the guy met my eyes just before I looked away and flashed me a grin dentists must see in their nightmares.

I fished a twenty out of my wallet, walked over and handed it to him. He took it, pocketed it, broke eye contact and went back to his song.

"That's Randy," Mason said when I got back to him. He held open the door, and we went inside and started up the stairs of the sterile office building.

"Randy, huh? So you know him?"

He nodded. "Sleeps at the Y when it's cold but prefers to be outside. Keeps his stuff in a wrecked car out behind Phil's Auto Graveyard. Sleeps there sometimes, too. He's fine as long as he stays on his meds."

"And he's on them now?"

"Oh, yeah. Trust me, you'd see a different guy if he wasn't."

"Different how?"

"Shouting, swearing, violent."

"Schizophrenic?" I asked.

"I think it's technically schizoaffective disorder. It's a shame. He's a sweet guy."

"Yeah, I can tell." We were walking down a hallway. Other people came and went. There was a very clear difference between the clients and the workers. The workers were all in professional-looking suits or skirts and blazers, the women with their hair and makeup in decent shape. The clients wore jeans or sweats and T-shirts. They were mostly either overweight or severely underweight, and their hair was just the way it had grown, though sometimes in a ponytail. And at both ends of the spectrum, they were mostly women.

The social worker who met us halfway across the child welfare office was an exception to that rule. He was a super-good-looking, blue-eyed blond male who was way more interested in checking out my guy than me. "Chief Subrinsky phoned and told me you'd be coming by. You're Detective Brown?" he asked.

Mason nodded and accepted the man's handshake.

Hot Gay Guy finally got around to me. "And you're Rachel de Luca. I can't tell you how much your work has meant to me. It's truly a pleasure to meet you."

He shook my hand, too, clasping it with both of his and squeezing like he really meant it. I was getting used to that. People saying my work had helped them, changed their lives, saved their lives or their marriages or jobs or whatever, and on and on. I'd given up believing it was all complete bullshit. Mason had convinced me there had to be something to it, and I'd been coming around to thinking that way myself. But I hadn't wanted to dig too deeply into that end of things. Because, frankly, I didn't want to screw it up. The stuff came to me, I wrote it down, tweaked it with my own attitude and voice and it worked. If I started taking it as some kind of spiritual mission, I was going to fuck it up for sure.

But now there was this new twist. The NFP and its new level of weirdness. And I had to wonder if the one thing had anything to do with the other. And if so, what? And what did it mean? And what was I supposed to do about it?

"I'm Rodney Carr," the social worker said. "We can use my office. Right this way."

So we went straight through the bustling reception area—no, it was too glum to be called that, it was a waiting room, a stark, unpleasant, crowded waiting room. Going straight back without even warming a seat there earned us hate-glares from some of the women sitting in the chairs that lined its walls. They held their runny-nosed toddlers by their chubby arms to keep them from wobbling away. Waiting for their appointments, I guessed.

What was it with the runny noses, though? There seemed to be an age where a kid just had a perpetual snotty face. Thank God Mason's boys were way past that, because *ick*.

Carr's office was small but had fresh white paint on what I could see of the walls. Which wasn't much, because there were photos everywhere. Kids, all ages and races, were plastered all over the place. They stood in cheap frames on every surface, and were tacked and taped to every available piece of wall. I looked at them, then at the plaque on his desk and read it aloud. "'There's no such thing as a bad child.'"

"Only bad parents," the social worker said. "But with so many of them in here every day, I needed a plaque that left that part off."

"Probably a good idea." I sat in one of the chairs in front of the neat but completely covered desk. Carr sat in his chair behind it. Mason stood beside me, ignoring the vacant seat to my left.

"The chief was vague on the phone," Carr said. "What's going on?"

Mason looked at the photos again. "I'm sorry to have to tell you this, Mr. Carr. We found a girl's body this morning," Mason said. "We're still waiting for positive ID, but we have reason to believe it's Venora LaMere."

"Venora?" That reaction was real. The news hit him where he lived. No one could fake me out that thoroughly. "Venora's *dead?*"

"I'm sorry," Mason said again. "You knew her?"

Blinking fast, Rodney Carr got out of his chair and went to the wall, pointing at a photo of a smiling teenage girl with short, Gothic-black hair and a pierced nose, smiling at the camera. But not with her eyes. They were empty, I thought.

"This is Venora." His voice seemed thicker than before. "It was taken a year ago. Her mother's an addict who abandoned her. She was living with an uncle last we knew. What happened to her?"

"Last you knew?" I asked. "You mean, you don't keep track?"

He was looking at the photo, not at me, as he heaved a huge sigh, and I thought he might cry any minute now. "She turned eighteen last year. I don't have funding or authority to follow up on the girls once they age out of the program." I frowned at him, so he went on. "We basically set them adrift to sink or swim on their own. Happy eighteenth birthday. Good luck surviving to see your nineteenth."

Mason went to the photo, looked at it closely for a long time.

"Now that you've seen the photo—" Carr began.

"Yeah. I'm sorry, I'm more sure than I was before."

The social worker blinked three times, lowered his head. "How did she die? She didn't use drugs, at least not—"

"Looks like she was shot," I said, earning a quick look from Mason that told me I wasn't supposed to be revealing stuff like that.

"Oh, come on, how's it gonna hurt to tell him that? The jogger knew. You really think she's not gonna Tweet that she found a body on her run down the Rail Trail this morning?"

"Jeez, Rache, you want to show him the case file while you're at it?"

I shrugged. Rodney Carr wasn't paying attention to us. He was still looking at the girl in the picture. "I can come in, if you need someone to…identify the body."

"You don't have to do that," Mason said. "We do need her file, though, along with the file on Lexus Carmichael."

That got his notice. He sent Mason a sharp look. "Why? Is Lexi in trouble, too? What's going on here, Detective Brown?"

"We don't know yet," he said.

So Carr looked at me instead. Right, you want to know something, ask the blabbermouth. I shrugged one shoulder. "It's true, we really don't know," I said.

He nodded, believing me. Not Mason. Then he turned to one of the file cabinets lining the walls of his office. It was stuffed so full he could barely pull out the file he chose. He handed it to me, then moved to another and repeated the entire process. "These should've been archived by now, I'm just…way behind on filing."

Too busy trying to make a difference in the lives of kids no one else gave a shit about, I thought. I liked the guy.

"Lexus was living in an apartment downtown with an elderly great aunt. The address should still be good. She only aged out of the system two months ago."

"Wait a minute, she aged out, too?" Mason asked.

"Yeah."

"Mr. Carr, about how many girls in the system have turned eighteen so far this year?"

He tapped a few keys on his computer. "Forty-seven," he answered, and I heard what he didn't say. Every last one of them was a knife in his bleeding heart. God, how a guy like this survived in the business he was in was beyond me.

"I'm gonna need their names. I need to check on every last one of them," Mason said.

Carr picked up the warrant from his desk, scanned it, shook his head. "The warrant doesn't cover that. Just says to give you the files on Lexi and Venora. If I comply without a proper warrant, I could lose my job."

My impression of him took a nosedive. "Yeah, but you could save some girls' lives."

"I do that every day. But if I'm not here, I won't be able to do it anymore." He lowered his head, licked his lips nervously, then said, "I'll tell you what I can do, though. I can check on them myself. At least make some calls, unofficially, while you work on getting a new warrant."

Okay, I liked him again. 'Cause that was pretty much above and beyond his pay scale, I thought.

"If some of them seem to have…dropped out of sight, you'll let me know?" Mason asked.

"Of course I will."

Mason nodded, handing me the two bulky files so he could take a card from his shirt pocket and pass it across the desk. Rodney Carr took the card and walked back to Venora's photo, then closed his eyes. "Is there anything else I can do?"

"Are there any photos of the girls in these files?" Mason asked.

"Yes, of course. Photos and fingerprint cards on every child in the system. Just in case."

Nodding, Mason took the files back from me. "Thanks for your help," he said.

"Yes, thanks. You've been more help than you probably know," I added.

"Will you let me know…about Lexi?"

"Sure we will," I told him. Then I shot a look at Mason and said, "*I* will, that is."

Back in the car, I said, "Okay, I know your cop instincts are usually supersonic, but damn, Mason, how can you find fault with that guy?"

Mason sent me a look, that one where he raises one eyebrow. I wanted a picture of him sending me that look. It should be on a calendar. "I think *that guy* gets a little too close to the girls in his care."

"Yeah. 'Cause he cares more than most."

"Yeah. Which is suspicious as hell."

"Yeah. If you're a dirty-minded pessimist."

"Or a cop who's seen this kind of thing way too often."

I frowned at him. "I think your radar's off. And I'm positive your *gaydar* is. Maybe you've seen too much. Maybe you're just a little bit cynical, you ever think that?"

"Every day."

"I think he's sincere."

"Yeah. They always are." He shot me a look. "Maybe you're the one whose radar is off. You thought Jake was an okay guy, too."

"And you didn't like *him,* either. What's up with that? We're usually right on the same page."

He shrugged. "He's an ex-con."

"And that makes him bad." It wasn't a question.

"Yep."

"Every time? No exceptions?"

"Let's just say I have yet to see an exception."

"He's not your garden-variety ex-con, Mason. He shouldn't have done time to begin with. I mean, for running off with his girlfriend?"

He shrugged. "Doesn't much matter what he was in for. He was in."

I frowned at him. "So even if he was a decent guy when he was sent to prison…?"

"He comes out a criminal. Prison is like…college for crooks. You go in clueless, you come out with a master's in bad."

I didn't say anything, just gaped at him until he looked my way and caught me.

And then he said, "What?"

"I had no idea you were that jaded. Damn, Mason."

He was quiet for a second or two, his gaze jumping back and forth between the road and me. After a minute, he said, "So...?"

I shrugged. "It's the first thing I've found not to like about you." I tipped my head to one side, leaning over slowly to put some distance between us. Then I popped upright again. "Okay. I can deal with that."

He looked at me, then looked again. "Tell you what, you prove me wrong and I'll consider softening my hard-ass stance. Come back to the station with me and we'll look over Jake's backstory together."

"If we can order takeout, you're on." I answered way too fast, and realized that I felt good all over about the prospect of spending a few more hours with him. Even now that I'd found his first flaw. Well, you know, aside from having a serial killer for a brother and covering up his guilt and all that.

But the point here was that despite the awful circumstances, I was enjoying helping him. And, I hoped, helping those girls, too. What the hell was that about? I'd agreed to help out under duress and against my better judgment. I wasn't supposed to be enjoying it.

I reminded myself that I still missed my dog, and decided then and there that she was off her diet for tonight. Treats would abound to ease my guilty conscience.

We picked up Chinese food. The American version of Chinese food, anyway, which isn't at all accurate or all of China would be morbidly obese. I got way too much peanut chicken, my favorite. I'd never had the nerve to look up the calorie count of an average serving of peanut chicken, because why mar its heavenly perfection when I knew I'd just eat it anyway?

We spread out files across a long wooden table in a slightly larger than closet-sized room at the Binghamton PD. We had Lexus Carmichael's file open next to Venora LaMere's. We sat in hardback chairs, side by side, eating with chopsticks (I use mine like mini-spears) and flipping pages, muttering observations to each other when we came to them. The dead girl and the girl whose name she'd cut into her skin had a lot in common. Abusive relatives, absentee parents, a lot of trouble in school and a lot of trouble with the law. Both had been in the foster care system, even though living with a relative. The system still paid the relative a stipend to care for the child until said child turned eighteen. At which point, by the looks of things, a lot of relatives lost their interest in having a kid around.

Neither one of them seemed to have had many viable options when that had occurred. How either of them had any connection to a rich and spoiled girl like Stephanie Mattheson was beyond me. The only possible link was the judge. He was a family court judge, and they'd been in and out of courtrooms like his—maybe including his—for most of their lives. Investigations of their mothers for abuse and neglect, digging into absenteeism reported by their schools and finally being removed from their mothers' custody and placed into the system.

"We need to see if any of their times in court were presided over by Judge Howie," I said, reaching for another piece of peanut chicken and spearing only empty space with my chopstick. Damn. All gone. I hadn't intended to eat that much.

I looked around for my Diet Coke, which I never set down in the same place twice. Mason handed me my plastic-lidded, straw-bearing cup without looking up from his file. Someone tapped twice on the door, then came inside. Rosie.

"Damn, Mason. You haven't gotta train my replacement just yet. I'll only be off my feet for a coupl'a weeks."

"Your job is safe from me, Detective Jones," I told him.

He smiled at me, not the least bit threatened, and tossed the file in his hands onto the table. "Here's the file you wanted. Jacob Kravitz. Statutory rape and taking a minor across state lines. I took a look at it already, since you seemed to have plenty to do."

Mason looked up. "Good, that'll save me the time. You find anything interesting?"

"I did."

Mason held up a hand, turned to me. "You wanna put money on whether the ex-con is the bad guy, de Luca?"

"Oh, cute, call me by my last name like we're colleagues, right?" I looked at Rosie. "We're banging, you know."

"I…know."

"Come on, what do you say, Rache? Fifty bucks." Mason pulled his wallet out of his pocket, fished out two twenties and a ten and slapped them onto the table.

Not one to shy away from a challenge, I took my purse off the back of my chair, got out my wallet, slid out a credit card and slapped it on top of his bills.

He frowned at it, then at me.

"What? I never carry cash."

"Tell, Rosie. What did you find out?"

"Mr. Kravitz did two years for pissing off Judge Howie. For six months of that time, he shared a cell with Ivan Orloff."

I was taking another sip of my soda, and I choked on it.

Mason said, "The same Ivan Orloff I shot last November?"

"Yeah, so he wouldn't shoot me," I said, when I could talk again. "But more importantly, the same Ivan Orloff who tried to kidnap my personal assistant, Amy, and mistakenly called her Venora."

Rosie nodded. "The same." Then he sighed. "We got a positive ID on the girl we pulled out of the river. Venora LaMere. What I don't get is, she looked nothing like your Amy."

I blinked and looked at the photo of Venora in front of me. Dyed black Goth hair, nose ring. She could've been Amy's mini-me. "She did when this was taken, though."

"So Amy was a case of mistaken identity, and good ol' Jake is in this up to his neck. He's also the connection to Stephanie." Mason got up and headed for the door, leaving his cash and my plastic on the table, forgotten.

I grabbed both and hurried behind him toward the chief's office, keeping pace with Rosie. "So what do we do?"

"We find Jake," Mason said.

9

Mason made me wait in the car, which pissed me off so much I almost added it to his list of faults. Fault number one on the list was "labels all ex-cons the same and is irritatingly too often right." Number two would be "ruins all my fun by trying to keep me alive."

He didn't go busting in first, either. That was handled by a half-dozen guys in storm-trooper gear, you know, vests and helmets and shit. They ran up the stairs to Jake's apartment, and Mason went up behind them. The door got smashed in. I heard it from where I was, in Mason's car across the street. There was a lot of shouting, but no shots, thank God. I realized I was shaking and rubbed the goose bumps off my arms, then opened the car door and got out. Jeez, he did this for a living. His job was ridiculously dangerous. I mean, I knew that. For crying out loud, of course I knew it. We'd been nearly killed twice since we'd been hanging out together. But until that moment I'd kind of thought that was as unusual for him as it was for me.

Now it was hitting me that it wasn't. That it was his "just another day at the office." *Fuck.*

I got out of the car and moved a few steps closer to the building. Then Mason came out the door, shaking his head and talking to his radio mike, and the riot cops came out behind him. I was so relieved to see him upright and whole that I might have wobbled a little. Yeah, and it probably showed on my face. He came right over to me, took over rubbing my arms. "You're bone-white, woman. What's wrong?"

"Nothing. Where's Jake?"

"Gone. Place is about empty. Chief's sending a team to go over it, but it looks like he skipped." His frown deepened. "You sure you're okay?"

"No. I'm kind of done. I've had enough of this for one day. You know?"

"Yeah. Yeah, I know." He took my arm, led me around the car. "I'll take you home, okay?"

"I can get myself home. You need to stay."

"I said I'll take you home." He opened my door, and I got in, sank into the seat, closed my eyes.

Mason leaned real close to me and said, "It's nice you were worried about me."

My eyes popped open. "Funny, I didn't find it very nice at all."

We didn't even make it out of the city before the chief called to tell Mason to meet him at the hospital, pronto. So with an apologetic look, Mason changed course and took me with him. Note to self, don't ride with him. Bring your own car. Dumb-ass.

We didn't see Chief Sub in the lobby, so we headed up to the ICU in the elevator. The doors opened. We stepped out, turned right and stopped dead.

"How dare you?" Marianne Mattheson practically spat at the gorgeous brunette outside her husband's hospital room. Her face was wet with tears, her accusing pointy finger trembling. The brunette with the big glossy curls and overdone eyeliner did not back down. "My husband is fighting for his life right now. How *dare* you question me like this?"

Mason moved quickly to stand beside Mrs. Mattheson, and I did, too, so we flanked her sort of protectively. "What's going on here? Who are you?" Mason asked.

The brunette flashed an ID. "Special Agent Vanessa Cantone. So back off and let me do my job."

He didn't get a chance to reply, because I reacted first, taking a single step that put me in front of the weeping Mrs. Judge and the dead-sexy bitch. "Your *job* is harassing people in intensive care units? Do you work for the devil or the Republicans?"

"Is there a difference?" she quipped.

Shit. I didn't want to like her. She was four inches taller than me and stacked like a goddamn swimsuit model. I didn't even dare look at Mason, because I did not want to see him staring at her huge bazongas.

He came up beside me. "Take Mrs. Mattheson for some coffee," he suggested. "I've got this."

"The hell you've got this. I'm not going anywhere."
Whoa, who the hell said that? Not me. That was for sure.

"Detective Mason Brown," he said, ignoring my
comment. "The chief told me you'd be here by day's
end, but I expected to meet you at the department." He
didn't offer a handshake. Neither did she.

"I don't like wasting time." She sent me a cool look.
"And you are?"

"Rachel de Luca, special consultant to the Binghamton PD." I wanted to add *And a famous author who's
been on the* Today *show, so back the fuck off.* But instead I said, "Apparently you missed the memo, Vanessa. Mrs. Mattheson is not a suspect. Her daughter
is missing."

"So are nine other girls, including the dead girl, Venora LaMere."

"Nine?" My smooth, take-no-shit attitude had turned
to dust, and my voice sounded like sandpaper. *"Nine?"*

"Dead girl?" Mrs. Mattheson blurted. "What dead
girl? Mason, what's going on?"

Thank God the elevator doors opened just then and
Chief Sub came surging out. I never thought I'd be glad
to see that balding bastard, but I was. I had the judge's
wife by one arm, trying to lead her back into her husband's room, not out for coffee. I wanted to stay close
to Mason.

Okay, okay, stupid and petty not to want to leave him
alone with the gorgeous Fed, but it was what it was, and
I'd think about it later.

"Thank goodness you're here, Hal," Marianne said,
addressing the chief by a name I'd never heard him

called. "Tell me what's going on. Is this related to my Stephanie?"

The chief swore and swept the other three of us with a wilting look that should've melted our skin off. For once I didn't blame him.

"You three, go freaking work your shit out in the hospital cafeteria while I talk to Marianne."

"No," Mrs. Mattheson said. "No. You'll stay right here until I know everything." She sent a look through into her husband's room.

I did, too. He was in the bed, wired for sound. Monitors everywhere, IVs running, oxygen mask on his face. He looked a little gray, but better than when I'd last seen him.

His wife said, "Let's *all* move to the cafeteria. We can't have this discussion here."

So that was what we did.

I was still completely baffled by Special Agent Beyoncé's puzzling statement about there being nine missing girls when we all sat down together at a round table in the hospital cafeteria, out of earshot of other diners. I wanted to know about the nine missing girls more than I wanted to find a wart or a wrinkle or a fat roll anywhere on her person. I'd have settled for signs of surgical enhancement. But I couldn't ask my questions until the chief told Mrs. Mattheson what she needed to know. What she hadn't yet been told.

"Marianne," he said softly, taking her by the hand. "We did find a girl this morning."

"A dead girl?"

He nodded. "Yes. And we're investigating the possibility that her case might be related to Stephanie's."

She didn't react. Just stared at him like he was speaking a foreign language. Eventually she said, "What makes you think that?"

The chief looked down. An amateur would know he was holding back. Fortunately Mrs. Mattheson was too distracted by grief and worry to notice the signs. "You know I can't tell you things like that. Besides, it's technical. Trust me, Marianne, you know I'm doing everything I can."

She nodded slowly, as if that went without saying. "But…Hal, Stephanie's still alive, right? She's okay, isn't she?"

"Yes, we have every reason to think so."

Yeah, I thought. "Every reason" being that we haven't found her body yet. I wondered if poor Venora had been shot in front of Stephanie and the other one. Lexus. I wondered how terrifying that must have been for them. A blind twenty-year-old without a clue how to get by in the world and an eighteen-year-old who probably knew how a little too well.

Marianne nodded and turned to look at Special Agent Bitch-face. "And you say there are nine other girls—"

The Fed couldn't look her in the eye. "I really can't discuss that with you, ma'am."

I rolled my eyes. "Right, but you could blurt it out in the middle of the ICU. I can see how that would be okay."

Agent Cantone didn't seem to have any trouble looking *me* in the eye. I looked right back. "How do you know there are nine?" I asked her.

"As soon as we were told about Venora LaMere and Lexus Carmichael both being in the foster program and both having recently turned eighteen, we checked up on every other girl who's aged out in Broome County for the past two years."

"We were going to do that. Just waiting for a warrant," I said. Did that sound a little defensive?

"We have resources at the federal level that you don't have. We've found nine who can't be accounted for, including Venora LaMere and Lexus Carmichael."

That, I thought, was going to devastate Mr. Rodney Carr.

"You have files on them? Photos?" Chief Sub asked.

She held up her phone. "Right here."

The chief nodded, yanked out a pen and scribbled an email address on a napkin. "Send them here, will you? I'll have someone print up copies for my people."

"Happy to." She took the napkin and started tapping keys on her phone. "Now, as I was telling Mrs. Mattheson, I need access to her husband's home computer."

"And as I was telling you, Miss Cantone," Mrs. Mattheson said, "I know the law. My husband is a judge. And until I see a warrant—"

"Your husband *is* a judge. A family court judge. Eight girls who went through the family court system in his county are missing, and one is dead. Do you want to save your daughter's life, Mrs. Mattheson, or protect your husband's reputation?"

"That's out of line, Cantone," Mason said, while

Chief Sub shot a glare at the agent and put his hand over Marianne's on the table.

"The only thing waiting for a warrant is going to do is give the kidnappers more time to hurt Stephanie or one of the other girls," the Fed said, not even flinching under that wilting glare. "I'll have access to that computer one way or the other."

"Dammit, Cantone, that's enough!" The chief was on his feet.

Hell, *I'd* have flinched at that point.

Cantone just stood up and leaned closer. "Fine. I'll go get a warrant. All it'll cost us is an extra hour or two. Let's just hope it doesn't also cost us another girl." The chick had guts. Which really pissed me off, because I wanted to hate them and I couldn't.

"I have to get back to my husband," Marianne said.

"I'd like to talk to him," Mason told her. "Is that possible, Marianne?"

She shook her head slowly. "He's still unconscious. The doctors don't know when…or if…" She lowered her head, tears welling in her eyes. "Mitch tried and tried to get him to communicate, but…he just can't."

Mitch? The horn-dog disloyal boyfriend was being let in to see the ailing judge? What the hell was up with that?

"I'll stay here with you until he comes around, Marianne." Chief Sub looked at Mason. "When that warrant does come through, you'll accompany Agent Cantone to the house. Make sure nothing is disturbed but the computer and that the entire place is treated with respect."

I leaned closer to Mrs. Mattheson. "I'll go, too," I

promised. "I had cops searching my home once. I know how it feels. Don't you worry, I'll keep them honest."

She looked into my eyes. Hers were tired, dull. I could've sworn the number of wrinkles in her face had doubled since I'd last seen her. She'd aged a decade overnight. "You say in your books that everything happens for a reason, Ms. de Luca. What reason could there possibly be for all of this? What have I done to deserve—"

"It's not like that," I told her, searching my brain for some clichéd self-help sound bite to feed her that might make her feel better. "There's no judge and jury handing out life experiences as reward or punishment. But things do happen for a reason. I can tell you one thing, though. Until Stephanie went missing, we didn't even know about those other girls. They fell through the cracks of the system. No one's even been looking for them until now. Stephanie did that."

Mason was staring at me. I felt it, and when I looked back I saw that expression he sometimes got in his eyes. That one that said he was seeing something pretty fucking awesome in me. I wanted to tell him to knock it off already, but I couldn't do that without shaking Marianne's belief in me. And it was her belief that would get her through this. That particular line of bull wasn't bull at all.

"God bless you, Rachel de Luca." She reached for my hand, so I let her take it, squeeze it. Then she and Chief Sub headed out of the cafeteria and down the hall.

"What the hell was that?" Cantone blinked at me like a doe in the headlights.

"*That* was how I make my living." I hitched my hand-bag over my shoulder. "You ready, Mace?"

"Yeah." He snapped out of it. I was secretly relishing the way he'd looked at me just then, right in front of Agent Boobsalot. It was good to get it out there right up front that she shouldn't even think about putting any moves on my detective.

Jesus, who the hell was that? Was that the Rachel who doesn't want to get too romantic and serious here? Was that jealousy, *Rache?*

Shut the fuck up, Inner Bitch.

The trapdoor in the center of the ceiling opened. Stephanie heard it, and then the sound of the Ass-hole's voice. "Step back away from the rope ladder and I'll bring down some food." As he spoke, something dropped with a whoosh. She imagined it was the rope ladder he'd mentioned.

"Stevie?" Sissy said softly.

"Do what he says." No way was she going to try anything and risk another of them being killed. No way. Poor Venora.

She reached out for Sissy's arm, and they backed up a few steps. She wasn't worried about bumping into anything. She'd memorized the entire place, a giant round room with no windows, underground, she suspected, with the furniture the only thing in it besides themselves and the tiny bathroom, with a working toilet and a shower. No sink. But plenty of soap, shampoo and toilet paper. Plenty of tiny plastic combs and makeup, too. She'd gone through all of it, but unless she could think of a way to make a soft-tipped eyeliner into a weapon, there wasn't anything they could use.

"Lexi, where are you?"

Lexi came to her other side and took her by the hand. "Oughta jump him. Kill his ass and climb the fuck outta here." She whispered it very softly.

"The other one's up top, waiting, Lex." They'd noticed, a couple of times, the presence of another man, one who never got too close or spoke out loud, and they'd named him the Douche Bag. "He'd just pull up the ladder before we could get out anyway."

"How the fuck you know anyone's up there? I don't see nobody." She was leaning forward, and Stevie imagined her looking up at the opening as she did.

"I can hear him breathing, moving every now and then. Trust me."

"Yeah. I trust you. Got ears like a goddam bat."

The Asshole reached the bottom, then said, "Okay, send it down."

Lexus said, "You two some kinda geniuses, huh? Lowerin' our food down here in a basket like that. Yeah, we dealing with some rocket scientists here, we are."

"Don't antagonize them, Lexi."

Stevie heard movements, rattling plastic, and Sissy narrated. "He's taking a shopping bag out of the basket."

"That's right," the man said. "It's a bag full of pretty clothes for you girls. You're gonna put 'em on for me. You're gonna do it now, quickly, no arguments, and then I'll let you have the food. And if you give me any arguments, I'm gonna shoot another one of you." He shoved the bag into Stevie's chest. "You first."

"Okay, okay." She opened the bag and reached inside. She felt silky fabrics and sheer ones and tiny hangers. Tissue paper and price tags were still attached. "What is this? Is this lingerie?"

"Pick one and put it on. Now."

Sissy yelped, and Stevie knew the bastard had grabbed her.

"I'm putting the gun to her head, Stephanie. Are you gonna do what you're told or should I just—"

"I'm going! Don't hurt her." Stevie yanked the first item she could get hold of from the shopping bag and hurried to the little bathroom. She fiddled with the thing, a teddy by the feel of it, until she got clear on which end was up, laid it carefully across the toilet seat and then started taking her clothes off.

A distant echoing sound, a cell phone ringing, came from the shower. And then a faraway and hollow voice. "Yeah?"

She frowned and moved nearer the shower, pulling back the cheap plastic curtain, waving her arm around inside even though she knew no one was there. She would have felt them if they'd been there. And yet the voice was both definitely in there and very far away. Like it was coming from inside a tunnel or...

"I know we need another girl. What do you mean, he can't talk?"

She realized the voice was being carried through the pipes. It had a muffled, hollow sound to it that made it seem weird and alien. The water must be piped in from above, from the surface, somewhere near where the speaker was standing.

"All right, we'll find someone else." A pause, then, "Yes, right away."

There was something familiar about his voice, something telling her she should know it, but it was so distorted that she thought it might be an illusion. There was a knock on the bathroom door that startled her so badly she almost screamed. "Hurry up in there."

"Almost ready," she said very softly, so the guy above wouldn't hear and realize how voices carried. Maybe it didn't work both ways, but she couldn't be sure.

She waited another beat, but the man above had gone silent. So she let the shower curtain fall closed and turned to scoop up the skimpy garment, pulling it over her head. Its lacy parts felt scratchy on her skin, and she felt exposed and self-conscious. For the first time since the accident, she was glad she couldn't see.

She opened the bathroom door and stepped out.

"Nice. Very nice. Now smile for me." And then she heard the click of a camera shutter.

Rodney Carr woke up to the sound of his cell phone ringing like crazy and a pounding headache he couldn't explain.

He rolled over in the bed, pushing a hand through his hair, moaning in pain and finally forcing his eyes open to look for his phone.

And then he realized he wasn't in his own bed. He didn't know where the hell he was. Frowning, he sat up slowly. A sheet of questionable cleanliness slid down his body, and he realized he was naked underneath it.

"Wait, what is this?" Though he asked it aloud, there

was no one there to answer. He looked around the room, trying to remember how he'd gotten here. But there was nothing. He'd walked home from work, just like always. Stopped for two cups of Tim Horton's coffee and a pair of bear claws to take home and share with Glenn. He'd sipped his own on the way, because he couldn't resist. He'd stopped to buy a newspaper, then slopped coffee all over it when some careless, rushing idiot had run into him. The guy who'd bumped into him offered him another one, which he said he'd just purchased and hadn't even sipped yet. He took it, even though it wasn't Tim Horton's. It was true that there were still decent people in the world. A lot of them. He tried to remind himself of that as often as he could. It was easy for a guy in his job to forget that. He'd been thinking about that as he'd walked the rest of the way, sipping the coffee, which wasn't bad, but wasn't great, either.

But he didn't remember arriving at home.

The room was a hotel room. Motel, maybe. Mass-produced furniture in the style of early cheap. A bad print of geometric shapes in primary colors hung on the wall. The TV was so old it had a giant backside. His clothes were on the floor beside the bed, and when he got up and reached for them, he saw the envelope lying underneath his pants.

His phone stopped ringing. He bent low and picked up his clothes, putting them on, checking all his pockets for clues, feeling dizzy and realizing slowly that his head hurt like the dickens. All the while, he was staring at that envelope like it was going to come to life and attack him. Of course it didn't.

He finished dressing and pulled his phone out of his pocket. Glenn had called. Twenty-seven times. It was 7:12 a.m. He'd lost an entire night. Fourteen hours. Finally he reached for the envelope, vaguely aware that he'd been putting off doing so for a while. And he didn't know why. Maybe there was some part of him that knew, after all. That remembered.

He opened it and looked inside. Photos. Big ones. He tipped the envelope and let the photographs slide out onto the bed. They were of him, in various erotic poses with a beautiful nude woman. His eyes were closed in most of them, open slightly in others. They were very convincing. Even he could almost believe he'd been an active participant. If he didn't know better.

There was a note included. It began:

We know you're married. Unless you want your wife to see these photos, you'll do exactly as I say. Follow our instructions to the letter. We'll be in touch soon.

Rodney's phone started to ring again. Glenn. He picked it up this time. "Hey, honey. I'm sorry. I'm so sorry."

<u>10</u>

By 4:00 p.m., we were at the judge's place with giant-size cups of coffee we'd picked up on the way.

"Should'a got doughnuts," Mason muttered.

"News flash, Detective Brown. We can't keep eating doughnuts and junk food every time we're together. Not if we're gonna be *this* together."

"I imagine you're right. But you gotta warn a guy. I need to ease into these things."

"We'll get something after. Something healthy." He nodded but didn't look thrilled about it. I didn't pay much attention, because the Matthesons' place was so gorgeous. A fully restored Victorian, complete with pink, green and lavender touches in the elaborate trim. It had twice as much square footage as my place, and my place was big. "Damn, this is some house."

"It is."

"So where's Special Agent Foxy Galore?"

"Kitty Galore, isn't it? No, wait, it's—"

"Never mind."

"We got the warrant for the judge's office, as well," he said, "so she's heading up the team doing that while we handle this." He pulled an old receipt from his shirt pocket and read from the back of it, while punching the code Mrs. Mattheson had given him into the security panel.

I stood on the elaborate front step watching him. "Somehow I don't think that division of labor was Agent Cantone's idea."

"Chief Sub's," he said, straightening and sticking a key into the lock.

"You mean Hal?"

He laughed as he pushed the door open and waved me inside. "It's short for Harold."

"I *knew* it." I walked into the judge's lavish home and felt instantly disgusting for what I was about to do. "Damn, this does not feel right."

"Yeah, it's always bothered me, too, rifling around in people's homes. Mrs. Mattheson is at the hospital. Said she'd rather not be here for this."

"I don't blame her. So how does this work? We just start…pawing through their stuff?" I had my coffee in my hand, and I made damn sure not to spill any. The place was gorgeous.

"Warrant only covers his home office. Second floor, farthest door to the right." He led the way through an elegant foyer with velvet embossed wallpaper. It looked as if it had come from the same period as the house. Everything in the place did. The light fixtures, the furniture. All antiques. Mason headed up the curved staircase.

I couldn't help but slide my hand over the gleaming wood bannister.

"Cantone says the names and faces of the missing girls have gone out to every police agency in the country."

"Maybe someone will know something," I said. "Something that could break this wide-open." Then I rolled my eyes because I'd said "break this wide-open." "Mason, why the hell are we here? We know it was Jake. And we know he and Judge Howie hate each other's guts."

"Because whether Jake is the kidnapper or not, he's targeting girls who've aged out of the foster care system. He's gotta be getting that information from somewhere."

"Not from the judge," I said. "No way."

"Here's the office." He opened the tall wooden door by its antique porcelain doorknob, and we went in. It smelled like cigars, the only place in the house that did, and leather. Bookshelves lined the wall. And there were photos hanging in between them. Stephanie, Stephanie, Stephanie, Mrs. Mattheson, and a shot of the judge himself in front of an oversize white SUV, holding a whopper of a fish.

Mason went behind the desk, consulted his scribbled-on receipt again, and entered the judge's computer password so he could start looking at files. I walked around opening drawers and scanning bookshelves. "Makes me feel like a thief, going through someone else's stuff. How do you do this for a living?"

"Well, you know, the tradeoff of getting killers off the streets helps."

"I suppose." I moved around the desk, looked over his shoulder. "You finding anything?"

"No, but even an idiot would know enough to empty his trash. And the judge is no idiot."

"Even if he did, those files are never really gone, right?" He looked up at me, as if impressed. "Hey, I've been known to watch *CSI*."

"We'll take the computer in. Have the digital forensics guy go over it."

"We have a digital forensics guy?"

"We?" He sent me what was supposed to be a cocky grin but looked to me like a sexy one. "So you're part of the team now, huh? Careful, Rache, you might be starting to like this."

"It's disgusting."

"Yeah. You like it already." Mason went to the downloads folder, opened it and started skimming through the previews. "Oh, man, this is rough."

I leaned closer, and saw several *Binghamton Press & Sun-Bulletin* articles about Stephanie's accident. Then I wondered why Mason paused so long on a photo of a demolished red Volvo being pulled out of a ravine.

"Wait a minute, that's not right," he said.

"What's not right?" Leaning in close, I read over his shoulder. And I deliberately breathed on his neck. I was enjoying working with him. I wondered what he'd say if I told him that.

Probably "Who are you and what have you done with Rachel de Luca?"

"The date's wrong," he said. "It's too long ago to be Stephanie's accident."

"Well…what other accident would he be collecting articles about?"

Mason was nodding slowly. "I remember this. It was a couple of years back. Some asshole hit the guy in the Volvo, sent him right over the edge into that ravine and then left the scene. No 911 call, no nothing. There was white paint on the Volvo's fender, skid marks on the pavement that didn't match his tires."

"What happened to the guy in the Volvo?" I asked near his ear.

"Died. Probably instantly."

"You ever catch the guy who hit him?"

"No. The location of the dent matched up with a late-model full-size SUV. The same paint was used by three different manufacturers. There were hundreds registered locally. We spent weeks looking for one that'd had work done, found a few as I recall but ruled them out. It was a dead end."

I straightened up, turning and looking around the room. "Why do people leave the scene of an accident like that, Mason?"

"Usually because they were drunk or on drugs, so they know they'll do time if they're caught."

"That's what I thought. So then I guess the next question is, why does the judge have those articles? And, um…when did he get rid of his big gas-guzzling white SUV?"

"What?" Mason looked up at me, frowning. I just pointed at the photo on the nearby wall. The one of Judge Howie in full fishing gear from the hat to the vest to the waders, smiling and holding up his trophy fish, smiling for the camera. Right in front of a full-size white SUV.

"I wanna talk to Mitchell Kirk again," I told Mason when he was finally driving me home—home being *his* place, because that's where my dog and my car had taken up residence again this morning. The kids were still out of school, and if I had to leave Myrtle, I knew she'd rather be with Josh than Amy.

Yeah, that was the entire reason. Not.

"There we have another difference of opinion," Mason told me. "In his case, I think you just don't like him."

"His girlfriend's missing and he hits on me? Seems like a giant red flag to me, *Detective*."

"I know it seems that way to you."

"It doesn't to you?"

"Would have once." He shook his head. "Experience has changed my mind. If every guy who hit on another woman while his own was in trouble turned out to be the culprit, my job would be a lot easier."

A big sigh rushed out of me before I'd intended to let it. He shot me a quick look as he pulled the car into the long dirt driveway of his work-in-progress farmhouse. "What?"

"I…" I pressed my lips together, then shrugged. Might as well be forthright. I usually didn't beat around the bush, and this was no time to start. "You know, I don't want to know that about men. I could've gone through the rest of my life just fine not ever knowing how common it is for men to cheat on their women while they're hurt or missing or dead or dying. I'd rather be naively confident in the goodness of human nature."

He nodded. "I know exactly what you mean." He got out of the car, and so did I.

The screen door opened, and Myrtle burst out, running toward the car with her ears flapping but then slowing to a clumsy stop halfway as she remembered she was blind.

Josh was right behind her. "You're home! Awesome! You gotta come out back so I can show you the fort I'm building in the woods. Myrt loves it out there."

I looked at Mason, then at Josh. "Can I take a rain check, pal?"

"What's that mean?"

"It means I'll look at it next time. I promise. But I'm tired, and I need a bath." I looked down at my dog, who had come to my side for some loving, then returned to the eleven-year-old to sit loyally at his feet. "And I've got a book that needs finishing, and I haven't seen my house in forever. I really need to go home."

Josh looked devastated. "You're not staying?"

"Josh, I don't live here."

"Well, yeah, but I thought…"

Oh, hell, he was working up to tears here. I slammed the brakes on my determination to get home.

"Okay, tell you what, I'll stay until dinner's ready. And I'll look at your fort first. But then I really have to go home. Okay?"

He lit up. "Okay! C'mon. It's this way!" And he charged around the house with Myrtle jogging happily at his side. I frowned as I watched her bouncing away from us.

"I swear she's lost weight since we've been here."

Mason slid an arm around my shoulders, and we started following the kid. "She's been keeping up with Josh. It's the best bulldog workout ever."

"I bet." As we passed the front porch, I saw Jeremy in the doorway. He gave us a wave and went back inside.

"Mason, we have to be careful with the boys," I said. "I don't want them to start thinking…you know, that I'm trying out for substitute mommy."

"You don't want them to get too attached to you."

"Yeah. Okay, that, too."

"In case we don't last."

He was looking at me. I was looking back at him. Somehow we'd gotten sucked into one of those deep, emotional moments that made me long for some less charged topic, like religion or politics. He was asking me something. And I didn't have any choice but to give him an answer. It wouldn't have been fair not to.

"Hell, Mason, we'll *last.* I mean, things are good, right?"

"Yeah. *I* think they're good. You think they're good?"

"I think they're fine."

"Fine is good," he said.

"It is. I'm not going anywhere in the foreseeable future. You know, unless you turn into a jerk overnight. You don't plan to do that, do you?"

"Not to my knowledge."

"I just don't want the boys to start thinking of me as

their new mom. I'm not. I can barely mother a bulldog, much less a couple of kids."

"Myrtle would disagree."

"Myrtle has low standards. If I feed her, let her climb on my furniture and sleep in my bed, I'm damn near Martha Stewart."

He smiled. "It's not so different with the boys. Add in unlimited access to Xbox Live and attending most of their games, and they're content."

I nodded. "I really have to go home."

"I know you do. It's all good, Rache."

I sighed in relief. He wasn't pushing, he wasn't disappointed, he wasn't guilt-tripping me over the kids. Of course he wasn't. When had he ever? I was guilt-tripping myself, if anything. And since when did I do that?

Myrtle barked, and we picked up the pace, walking over the still soft meadow, all lush with young grasses and early wildflowers, and into the little woodlot off to the side of it. Joshua had apparently raided his uncle's toolbox. I spotted a hammer, a hatchet, a saw, a box of nails and a tape measure tossed around on the ground. There were saplings, cruelly cut down in their youth and nailed across their parent trees in a crisscross patchwork design on three sides, forming a sort of lopsided square with one side open. The kid had used what looked like a full roll of electrical tape to attach pictures to the "walls," photos he'd printed up on plain paper. There were shots of me and Mason, shots of Josh and Myrtle, shots of Jeremy, and one that broke my heart in spite of myself. A family photo of Mason's dead serial-killer brother and batshit-crazy sister-in-law, in better times, with their two sons, everyone smiling like a normal, happy, well-adjusted family. It made me wonder what business I had worrying about my own petty little problems. Dead people talking to me and whatnot.

It was a quiet night. I didn't have to walk Myrt, because she'd had more exercise hanging out with Josh for the past few days than a week's worth of walks would've supplied. She was exhausted. I whipped up a gourmet dinner in the microwave—Marie Callender's. The good shit. I had a leftover chicken breast in the fridge, too, so I chopped that up and served it to Myrtle with a sprinkle of her special healthy-weight-formula organic grain-free kibble. And then I plopped my ass in front of the TV and ate.

"It's cool to actually be able to watch the news, isn't it, Myrt? Can't do that at Mason's. If the TV's on, they're either gaming or watching baseball."

Myrt looked up from her dish, but I knew she hadn't heard a word I'd said. Food distracted her completely.

I wasn't paying much attention to the news, either. Or to my potpie. I was missing Mason.

"And that's what comes of spending so much time together all of a sudden, dumb-ass. You have to build up to these things gradually. Over time."

I heaved a sigh, and looked across the room at the desk in the corner, where my desktop with the honking twenty-seven-inch monitor waited for me to make it earn its keep. I had an office upstairs and a laptop that went anywhere I pleased, but I liked working in the living room sometimes. I knew, however, that nothing was going to happen with the writing tonight. Nothing. I'm a morning writer. I start trying to write in the evening, things could get out of whack. You just don't mess with the system when it's working well.

Not that it was, at the moment, but normally, it was a well-oiled machine, my process.

I heaved a sigh and started browsing the on-demand channels for a movie I hadn't yet seen, paid eight bucks for one that looked fascinating and then fell asleep out of sheer boredom about forty minutes in.

The flashes I'd seen when I'd touched the dead girl came pounding back to me in my dreams. Like bolts of lightning, the kind that light up the entire sky all at once. Like the blinding flash of a camera you weren't ready for.

Flash! Venora's hand, cutting letters into her impossibly flat midriff.

Flash! The beadwork blood droplets following behind her awkward cutting tool.

Flash! Cinder-block walls. Barred door.

Wait a minute, that's new.

Don't think, don't think, just lean back and let it play out.

Flash! Three young women struggling with an armed man in a ski mask. Don't look there, don't look there, don't look there.

Flash! Gunshot breaks my freaking eardrums and makes me jump out of my skin.

It'll be gone soon. Look, dammit, look!

Flash! Bunks on both sides. Like a prison cell.

Look harder! This is important.

Flash! Close-up of the bunks, the black block letters stenciled on the edge, peering out from beneath the mattress.

Flash! Closer now. Closer.

PROPERTY OF BLACKWATER STATE PENITENTIARY

I sat up on the sofa, opened my eyes and whispered, "I got it." Then I reached for the phone and dialed Mason's number.

He would've been irritated by the dead-of-night phone call if he hadn't glanced at the caller ID first and seen Rachel's name. He'd had a miserable night of second-guessing himself where she was concerned. Where this case was concerned. Where the chief's job was concerned. Where the boys and his competence in raising them was concerned.

Hell, he wasn't even sure his conscience was going to let him keep being a cop at all, much less chief of police. He'd covered up the crimes of a serial killer, let a copycat killer take the blame for all of Eric's murders. Telling himself it didn't matter because both men were dead, and because he'd given closure to the families by recovering the bodies, wasn't working so well to ease the guilt anymore.

Somehow, when Rachel was around, he felt okay about things. Not great, but okay. When she wasn't… Shit, if he confessed anything close to those feelings— to needing her—she would run screaming. Maybe.

The phone rang again. He picked it up and pushed his serious thoughts away. "Can't sleep without me, huh?"

"Slept. Dreamed. Got something for you."

He sat up straight, because she had that tone that told him she wasn't in a teasing mood or a sexy mood or a silly mood. She was dead-on balls-serious. "You got something? In a dream?" And then he said, "What's going on, Rachel?"

"If I knew I'd tell you. Closest I can figure is that the whole thing with Eric and the transplant and the visions did something to...rewire my brain. When I touched that girl's hand—"

"The dead girl's hand. You got a flash, you said. Was this the same kind of thing?"

"Yeah." She sniffed. "I think I saw Venora's murder. Dammit, why the hell me, you know?"

"Easy. Take a breath. Tell me what I need to know, okay?"

"Okay. Yeah. The girls were in what looked like a jail cell. I saw them all fighting with some jerk in a ski mask. His gun went off. I heard it. Felt it burn straight through my chest."

He nodded, fascinated by her. In so many ways. "And...?"

"And I saw the edge of the bed, stamped in black ink. 'Property of Blackwater State Penitentiary.'"

He rose to his feet in the bedroom, wide-eyed in the darkness. Speechless.

"Mace?"

"Yeah. I'm here, I just—"

"Is it a real place?"

"Blackwater prison was closed down in the seventies. I didn't even know it was still standing."

"Maybe it's not. It was a dream, after all. Where is it?"

"About fifty miles outside my jurisdiction."

"But we're going anyway. Aren't we?"

"We're going."

She was quiet for a second. Didn't hang up, though, so he knew she had more to say. "What, Rache?"

She breathed into the phone, which made him horny. Then she said, "Do we have to tell the sexy Fed?"

"You think she's sexy?" he asked, grinning.

"Don't you?"

"Not half as sexy as you are, Rachel."

"I wasn't fishing for that. I don't care about that."

"Yeah, you do."

"Yeah, I do. Vanity, thy name is de Luca."

"I think we have to tell her," he said when he could wipe the grin off his face. Okay, he was confused about things with her. But damn, he was glad they had whatever it was they had together. "Mainly because time is crucial if we want to save those girls. If we get up there and find them, we're gonna want backup ready and waiting. We don't want it to be an hour away. And we want it all on the up-and-up, so any evidence we find is admissible."

"I hate when you're logical."

"You hate when I'm right."

"That, too. So how are you gonna tell her you came up with this place?"

"Anonymous tip?"

"She'll know there's more."

"Doesn't mean I have to give it to her."

Rachel sighed heavily. He waited for her to get to whatever was bothering her, knowing she would. She always did. Eventually, she said, "Just don't let the chief tell her I'm a fucking psychic. I'm not."

"I know."

"I'm not," she said again. "I'm not, am I?"

She sounded a little bit like a scared kid. "Hey, you're Rachel de Luca," he said. "You're writing the script of your life as you go along. It says so in chapter one of your first book."

"It does, doesn't it?"

"It does," he told her. "You're whatever you want to be, Rache. You're intuitive. And you dream stuff. That's all. *You* get to decide what it means, and *you* get to decide what you want to call it."

"NFP," she said.

"Huh?"

"That's what I'm calling it. NFP, for Not Fucking Psychic."

She was quiet for a beat or two. Then she said, "If word gets out that I'm some kind of police psychic, my career will be over. I'm already walking the razor's edge between respectable self-help and new age spirituality. Something like this could push me over into the Fluff Bunny Zone. No one comes back from there."

"Really?"

"Probably. Hell, I don't know. I just know I like my work being taken seriously."

"Even though you so often refer to it as bullshit."

There was a long pause, then she admitted, "Less and less, you know."

"Good."

_11_

Back at the BPD, Rosie, among others, was working on the old hit-and-run case Judge Howie had kept clippings about. We didn't know where it would lead, or what, if anything, it had to do with the missing girls, but we were damn well going to find out.

We, on the other hand, were taking an early morning field trip to one Blackwater State Penitentiary, two hours north in a wooded area outside Utica. Special Agent Cantone had followed in her own car. Blackwater had been closed down in the seventies, replaced by the much bigger and more modern Marcy Correctional Facility. I got all that from Mason as he and I and Cantone traversed the overgrown path that had once been its driveway.

Tall fences that seemed to be made out of vines and foliage leaned drunkenly around the brick main building. If you looked closer, though, you could see razor wire loops along the tops.

The building itself was like something out of _Ameri-_

ca's Most Haunted. Its windows had fan-pattern bricks over arched tops, and bars over their blackness. Like dead eyes, those windows. Tangled masses of ivy had all but swallowed the south and east sides of the place, greedy fingers of it reaching across the front to pull itself farther along.

However, even I knew what was obvious to my companions' trained eyes. Someone had been here. The weeds and jungle-like growth were flattened down in proof that someone had walked in and out of here several times, and recently. It was even more obvious when we got to what had presumably been the main entrance. The vines had been torn away from the giant and rusted doors, and the debris on the ground in front of them had been swept aside by the trespassers' feet.

"They weren't even careful," I said.

"Could be anything. Could be kids," said Agent Cantone. She'd dressed appropriately, in jeans, a long-sleeved button-down over a clingy T-shirt and suede boots I'd have killed for. Her hair was in a ponytail. Her makeup minimal. And she still looked freaking amazing.

"Where did you say you got this anonymous tip, Detective?" she asked for the third time.

"I didn't."

"Look, if this pans out, I'm going to need to know."

"No, you're not." He opened the door, touching it with care. At the moment the possibility of rescuing several captive girls outweighed the need to check the door handle for prints first. Even so, he used his shirtsleeve and touched it as minimally as possible.

It creaked and groaned. He held it open with his back so we could go inside. Cantone held a flashlight in an overhand grip like only cops hold flashlights, her gun in her free hand as she went inside, walking slowly. I went in behind her, holding my flashlight like a normal human. I didn't have a gun, and I didn't want one. Mason stepped away from the door, letting it groan shut slowly.

This was like something out of a freaking horror movie. I hated the chills racing up my spine. The hallway was damp and musty, dark with free-range mold I hoped wasn't the deadly type. The floors were littered with debris, both natural and man-made. Broken glass, scattered pieces of brick and chunks of mortar, along with dirt and countless little shells from what looked like tiny nuts. Apparently the local wildlife had been feasting in here over the winter. Many winters.

We came to an intersection. Mason aimed the flashlight beam in each of the three directions, then nodded and picked one. The one with no spiderwebs crisscrossing the way, and with a barely discernible path through the rubbish on the floor.

And that was how we went, just following a trail that was sometimes clumsily obvious and other times almost invisible, to a stairway, and then down it into the hubs of darkness, and finally to a section marked *D,* where cells lined each side of the hallway.

One of the cell doors was open. It had a chain and a padlock dangling from it that were not only rust-free, but also looked new. And when we got closer, we saw that the inside of the cell had been swept, maybe even washed. But there was still a big bloodstain just inside the door.

"Ten to one that blood matches Venora LaMere's," Mason whispered.

"Jesus." Agent Cantone aimed her light around the inside of the cell. I didn't. Mine was holding steady on the side of one of the bunks, where Property of Blackwater State Penitentiary was stenciled in black.

"They were here," I whispered. Because whispering seemed like the thing to do in there.

"Looks like," Cantone agreed. She aimed her beam upward, at a single-bulb pull-string light fixture dangling from the ceiling, with wires that led out through the bars to a car battery sitting in a corner of the hallway. "The question is, where the hell are they now?" She turned to Mason and asked again, "Where did you get this tip?"

"Anonymous informant."

"If your informant knew, we need to know *how* he knew. These girls' lives are at stake, Brown."

"I know that. And if my source could shed any more light on this, I'd tell you. But that's just not the case."

I started to take a step into the cell, ignoring the two of them, but the Fed put a hand on my shoulder, stopping me.

"We need to get a forensics team in here before we go any farther. It's a crime scene."

I nodded. "Sure, yeah, I knew that." That forward step had been involuntary. No way did I want to go into that cell where a girl had died and feel the terror and pain and utter despondence I'd felt in my dream last night. Cantone holstered her gun and pulled out a phone instead. I saw her move its glowing screen up and left and right. "No bars."

"We're sublevel," Mason told her. "You should be able to get a signal at the top of the stairs." And I knew what he was doing, damn him. Getting her out of the way, giving me room to do…whatever the hell it was I was somehow able to do. Maybe. Sometimes.

She wasn't stupid. I didn't think he was fooling anyone, but she didn't argue, either. She aimed her flashlight back the way we'd come and started walking that way.

When we could no longer see the beam of her light, Mason turned to me. "Go on, see if you can get anything."

"I'm not going to *get* anything, Mace." But I was way more afraid than I wanted to say that I would.

"You had a flash when you touched the dead girl's hand. Get in there and *touch* something, and see if you have another."

I looked inside the cell. "I don't want to…contaminate evidence." That last part was an afterthought.

"Rachel…"

"I know, I know. Lives at stake. Civic duty. Blah blah. I'm going." I clutched the flashlight for dear life and moved inside the cell. The way the beam trembled on whatever it touched gave away my scaredy-cat shivers. I'm not even sure what I was scared *of,* but there you go. I took three steps inside, bent a little and put my hand on the mattress.

Nothing happened. I sighed in relief.

Then I turned to that stained spot on the floor. And everything in me was telling me not to go there, not to touch that. But I knew I didn't have a choice in the matter, and even if I did, I'd have touched it anyway. If I could help save the missing girls, I damn well would.

I retraced my steps backward, disturbing not even a dust mite, then crouched near the stain and lowered my hand toward it. I hesitated just for a second, then pushed past the fear and pressed my palm to the dried blood on the cold floor.

The flash was instant, and I was seeing it as if from above, somehow.

I saw Stephanie Mattheson lying still on the cell floor, near the bunk on the right. Close by, another girl…Lexus Carmichael. I'd studied her face enough to know it by heart. She, too, lay with her eyes closed. And a third girl I didn't recognize, lying perfectly still. Near the cell door, Venora lay in a pool of her own blood.

Were they all dead?

Two men in ski masks came in, speaking softly. Something about…

…*gotta move them. Someone might've heard the fucking shot.*

Something about…*the new place. It's not ready yet, but it'll do till we replace Venora and make the delivery.*

The two men began picking up the girls one by one, carrying them outside, coming back for another. Stephanie Mattheson flinched when they bumped her into the wall, and the girl whose face I didn't recognize moaned when they lifted her.

"They're alive," I whispered.

I blinked my eyes open and found myself standing up straight, staring at my upturned palm. It occurred to me then that I'd recited aloud every word I'd heard the men say. It also dawned on me that Cantone was standing behind Mason, looking at me over his shoulder like I'd just pulled off my fake rubber face to reveal an alien life form.

"What the fuck was *that?*" she asked.

I didn't answer, just stepped away from the cell without touching anything else.

"I asked you what that was," Cantone repeated.

Mason put an arm around my shoulders, and we started back down the hall toward the stairway. "Are you okay, Rachel?"

I nodded, not trusting myself to open my damn mouth again, lest some kidnapper's voice come out instead of my own, because that was what it felt like had just happened. Except I knew better.

We started up the stairs, Cantone right behind us. "Jesus, Mason, are you telling me *this* is your anonymous informant? A damned *psychic?*"

"I'm not a fucking psychic!" I spun around and shouted it at her, and she actually stumbled down a step.

"Then what the hell are you?" she asked, her voice a whole lot softer. Hell, no more hostility from this one. She was a little bit afraid of me now.

"I don't know anymore."

I went up the stairs, and when I got outside again I couldn't seem to get enough of the fresh air. It had felt like I'd been suffocating in there. Like I'd developed claustrophobia or something.

"Does the chief know about this?" Cantone demanded.

"Yes, and he wants it kept absolutely quiet," Mason said.

"I have to get out of here," I told him. I couldn't look at Cantone. I didn't want to see the ridicule, the skepticism, the speculation in her eyes. Much less the fear. Not that I gave two shits what she thought of me. More like I didn't know what *I* thought of me at this point, and I needed to get clear on that before I started letting anyone else's opinion in.

I headed straight back up the weed-entangled driveway toward where we'd left the cars, wishing I could leave behind the panicky feeling rising in my throat. It had to have come from them. The girls. Or one of the girls. Whichever one I'd been…plugged into back there.

But I knew which one, didn't I? The one whose cold, dead touch had given me the first flash, and whose blood stained that concrete I'd touched to get the second. I'd seen the room as if from above. Was that what she had seen, at the end?

Cantone and Mason came along behind me. And I moved even faster. Wanting to run away from them, from this place, and from this fucked-up enhanced vision that had come to life inside me. I wanted to run from it, because I couldn't really deny it anymore, could I? I was having visions, flashes, dreams. And it wasn't connected to Mason's brother, whose corneas had restored my eyesight. I wasn't experiencing things the other recipients of Eric's donated organs had experienced. Not unless one of the girls had received something that...

I turned abruptly and looked Vanessa in the eye. "What about those other girls? The ones who also aged out and are currently unaccounted for. What do we know about them?"

She was staring at me like I'd lapsed into Latin. There was less fear in her eyes now and more curiosity. But none of the other stuff I'd expected to see there. Like ridicule or blatant disbelief.

Then again, she was FBI. Maybe she was just good at covering up.

"I only received all the files this morning. They're in the backseat of my car right now. But their photos and fingerprints are being run through the national database right now."

"Those files have medical records in them?"

She lifted her brows. "I don't know. Probably."

I nodded, looked at Mason. "We need to go through those files."

We emerged from the wooded path and onto the road where we'd left our vehicles parked. Mason's pride and joy next to Cantone's sensible Prius. I looked back at the agent again.

"I don't like asking for favors," I said.

"I sense that about you."

Was that a slam or a compliment? Or just an observation?

"The truth is that I don't know what's happening to me. I didn't ask for this. I didn't want to be involved.

And if this…this vision thing or whatever the hell it is, ever gets out, it could do some pretty significant damage to my career as a writer."

She nodded thoughtfully. "I'll keep it to myself."

Just like that. I blinked, kind of shocked. "You will?"

"Until and unless I think doing so puts those girls or this case at further risk, sure. What the hell do I have to gain by spreading gossip about you, de Luca?" She looked at her feet, shook her head. "Shit, who'd believe it, anyway?" She actually laughed a little bit. So did Mason, but it wasn't heartfelt. Then her face turned serious again. "In return, I want you two to give me your word, here and now, that you won't keep anything related to this case from me again. I want full disclosure. Okay?"

Mason didn't agree. He looked at me instead.

"Yeah. I'm good with that," I said.

Only then did Mason say, "Me, too."

Cantone unlocked her car, reached in and pulled a big file box out of the backseat. "Here, take these and head back to Binghamton. You can read on the way. I'll wait here for the crime scene boys to arrive. Good enough?"

"Good enough," I said.

I scanned files for damn near the entire two-hour drive back, but I found nothing about any of the missing girls having had any organ transplants or even major health issues. Of course, Stephanie Mattheson's health history wasn't in the file. Maybe she was the connection.

But I knew better. It was the dead girl. That was

what it had felt like. That was whose head I'd been in. Somehow.

"I don't think you're gonna find what you're looking for, Rache." Mason had been watching me intermittently as he drove, and being even more quiet than usual.

"And what is it you think I'm looking for?"

"A link. A physical one. Between you and those girls."

I sighed, staring at but not seeing the open file in front of me. I'd been skimming all of them, but this one had a hold on me and wouldn't let go. The photo clipped to the inside of the folder showed a pretty girl with a big unapologetic afro and eyes that held sadness beyond their years. Her name was Halle Chase. She'd been in foster care since she'd turned ten years old. According to the birthdate given in the file, she was over nineteen now, and had been on her own for a year and a half. In all that time, no one had known or cared where she was or what she was doing. No one had checked in to see how she was getting by, or whether she was alive or dead.

"I think this thing is something you've always had, Rache."

"You haven't known me for always," I said, because it was an easy answer that didn't really say anything at all.

"Think about it. Think about how you always knew what people looked like when you were talking to them. How often did that inner vision turn out to be right?"

I shrugged, pretending I hadn't given that any

thought at all. The truth was, I'd given it a lot of thought. I'd even done the math. So far as I could verify, my inner TV set had given me an accurate image about ninety-two percent of the time. Way too much to be just a twenty-year series of lucky guesses.

"You had that ability long before you got the cornea transplant. You call it an extra-sharp use of your other senses, honed by years of blindness forcing you to rely more on them. You say you hear things behind and beneath someone's voice, that you sense their emotions almost like a scent. You did all of that before the transplant."

"Yeah? So?"

"So it wasn't hearing or smell that told you when Amy was in trouble last Thanksgiving. You knew it before her mother even called to tell you she'd never arrived. Remember?"

I lifted my head, looked at him in profile. He looked back at me, met my eyes head-on for a second. "Are you saying *you* think I'm psychic?" I asked softly.

He shrugged. "I'm saying it's the same thing as my cop instinct. I get hunches. Gut feelings about things. I'm right a lot of the time. There's not a cop out there that hasn't experienced that."

"But they wouldn't be caught dead claiming to have E-S-fucking-P."

"I don't give a damn what they call it. You have it, too. A version of it. Its bigger, badder brother. You've got instinct on crack. It's no different, except in intensity. That's what I'm saying. And I'm saying it's exactly what you've always said it was. Another sense getting supercharged to make up for the one you were lacking."

"Right. Just not one of the other four that actually exist."

"Just not one of the other four we know about," he corrected. He was quiet for a long moment, then he said, "You've got something, Rache. I've known it from the beginning. And I think you've been trying real hard not to know it for even longer."

"Yeah, yeah. You gonna buy me a cup of coffee or what?" I had my finger on Halle's face and a dark, dark feeling in the pit of my stomach.

"Only if we can have a doughnut, too."

"Only if we can buy an extra one for Myrtle. She's been neglected all week long."

"Your wish is my command."

He got off the 81 and drove into my little town, passed my road and then swung right into the Dunkin' Donuts drive-through lane.

His cell phone chirped while the girl was handing him two cups of coffee and a paper bag through the window.

He handed everything over to me and picked up the phone, looked down at the screen and swore. "They got a hit on one of the girls. A Jane Doe found in the New Mexico desert six months ago."

I looked at the open file folder with the three-by-five glossy photo paper clipped to it. "Halle Chase," I said softly. I didn't even need to ask.

He looked at me sharply, then at the file folder. "Damn, woman, this is getting almost eerie."

"You think it's eerie for you, try being me for a day." I looked sadly at the doughnut bag, my appetite gone.

12

The body of Venora LaMere was in the morgue in the basement of Binghamton General. The autopsy had been done by Dr. Jack Nagawa, who'd come down from Syracuse to tackle the job. Broome County didn't have its own FP, but we were fortunate to be close enough to the Salt City to borrow one of theirs from time to time. In this case, we'd borrowed their best. I knew Dr. Nagawa's name because I'd seen him on Court TV. The guy was kind of a big deal.

He'd just completed the procedure, and Chief Sub had asked him to stick around a bit longer to compare notes with the autopsy done on Halle Chase six months ago in Taos, New Mexico. That file had been emailed and was waiting for us when Mason and I arrived at the morgue. We had to take the elevator down to the sub-level of the hospital, and we emerged into a cold, gray hallway lined with extra-wide wooden doors. Mason led me through a set of them into an even colder room. Still gray, lined with drawers just like you see on TV detective shows. A couple of stainless-steel gurneys, sans sheet-draped bodies, thank God, stood around, and there was a huge double sink nearby. A set of scales. A tray with stuff on top that was draped with sterile paper. I didn't want to know what instruments that paper covered, but I imagined scalpels and bone saws.

Dr. Nagawa was as good-looking as a Japanese rock star—compact, buff, with dark hair that looked like some beautiful groupie had just finished running her hands through it. I knew this because Amy was something of a Japanese rock-star groupie of late, and was constantly making me watch YouTube videos and telling me how hot they were.

He met my eyes and smiled like he knew what I was thinking. "Hello, Ms. de Luca. It's very nice to meet you. I'm familiar with your work." He extended a hand.

"I'm familiar with yours, too." I shook his hand, hoping he'd washed really well, and then *flash!* I saw it buried to the wrist inside a body. I let go fast and tried to blink away the image, while the chief introduced Rock Star Nagawa to Mason.

Vanessa wasn't there. I presumed she wasn't back yet from the prison, though she had to at least be on her way by now.

The chief had a laptop under his arm and said, "There's an office down the hall we can use. They sent someone down to open it up for us."

"Then what the hell are we doing in here?" I asked. But my eyes were drawn to the third drawer from the left, bottom level. I knew that was where Venora was. Poor goddamn kid.

I didn't know how I knew that. No extra-sharp sense of hearing, smelling, touch or taste had told me. But I didn't have a hair's width of doubt about it.

So was this the new norm for me? Because I didn't freaking like it.

I hurried out the door into the drab-as-dirt hallway again, feeling like maybe the walls might start closing in pretty soon. The others filed out behind me, following Chief Sub down the hall. I got a couple of concerned glances but not much else. Not till Mason came out, anyway, and walked straight to me. He plopped his giant hands firmly on my shoulders.

Close call, though. The guy was good for me.

"You okay?" he asked.

"Am now." I took a deep breath, nodded hard and smiled at him. "Stop looking so damn worried. I'm fine."

And touched. Right to my sarcastic, shallow, "don't take this shit too seriously" heart. Damn him.

He gave my eyes a lingering exploration, then, with a nod, took my hand and walked me into the office at the end of the hall. I saw the chief and Nagawa notice and pretend not to. Then, from behind us, the voice I loved to hate.

"Well, doesn't *that* explain a few things."

"Fuck you, Cantone," I told her without even looking over my shoulder.

"You wish," she snapped back at me. Then she squeezed past us and around to Dr. Nagawa. "Good to see you again, Jack."

"It's a shame we only meet when someone's been

murdered," he replied, looking up only briefly. He was leaning over a long Formica meeting table, the chief's laptop open in front of him. Never breaking eye contact with the screen, Nagawa pulled a chair out and sank into it.

Agent Cantone hurried around the table to look over his shoulder. "What is this?"

"It's the autopsy of a New Mexican Jane Doe who turned out to be one of the missing girls." Chief Subrinsky pulled out a chair and nodded at Mason and I to do the same, so we did. Cantone stayed standing. "Dr. Nagawa?" the chief said.

The intense doctor nodded and spoke. "Both women had marks on their ankles and wrists that suggest they'd been bound. In the case of the girl from New Mexico—"

"Halle. Her name was Halle." Rude to interrupt, but dammit, called for.

Dr. Nagawa nodded. "Probably quite frequently and over a long period of time. The marks go deep and had begun to callus."

I looked at Mason, who looked at the chief, who looked at Cantone, who asked, "You think they were held prisoner?"

"I think they were kept in restraints, in Halle's case on a regular basis. I can't speculate on anything beyond that. This one—" he looked at me, gave an almost imperceptible nod "—Halle, died from a shot to the back of the head. She'd had recent intercourse, and while a condom was used, there was enough genetic material for a DNA sample."

"That'll help," the chief said. "If we ever get a suspect to compare it with." He nodded at Mason. "How long has Halle been missing?"

Mason looked at me, because I'd read the files and he'd done the driving. We'd made several calls on the way and had a rough time line. "The last time anyone saw her was August, year before last. She'd been working eight-to-five at a convenience store and staying in a friend's vacant apartment. The employer was named in the file, so we were able to contact him, and he pulled her work record. Said she'd worked late on August fourteenth, until 8:00 p.m., then didn't show up on the morning of the fifteenth. She was supposed to start at eight, as usual."

Dr. Nagawa nodded. "The Taos ME notes symptoms of Vitamin D deficiency. A loss of pigmentation, an inflamed liver…"

"What does that mean?" Mason asked.

I answered softly. "Lack of sunlight."

Dr. Nagawa nodded at me, eyes locking on mine, a little smile of approval crinkling the corners, making me think he was older than my first estimate of about seventeen. He had that kind of face. Most women wouldn't know whether they wanted to make out with him or adopt him. Except for Amy, of course. She'd know exactly what she wanted to do with him.

But he was also talking. "She was pregnant," he added.

We all felt the shock ripple through us. "That's probably why she was killed," Mason said softly.

"She'd been spending most, possibly all, of her time

indoors," Dr. Nagawa continued, listing what he knew in a dispassionate, clinical tone.

"I spend most of the winter indoors, Doctor," Cantone said. "Why don't I have those symptoms?"

"Everyone gets exposed to the sun's radiation. Through windows, in the car, just opening the front door. And more so in that part of the country."

Cantone looked at me, and I looked back at her. No windows? No car rides? No exposure to sunlight? In Taos?

"She was held prisoner. Long-term." Mason said what we were all thinking.

"Yeah, but in freaking New Mexico?" I asked. "How can that have anything to do with this? With Venora and Stevie and Lexus?"

"She came from here, same as all of them," Cantone said. "She'd aged out of foster care just like Lexus and Venora, and she could've been connected to the judge, same as Stephanie. But what's the connection with this—" she consulted her notes "—Amy Montrose?"

"Mistaken identity," Mason said. "Pure and simple."

She nodded and turned to the chief. "Any sign of Stephanie's ex-boyfriend, Jake Kravitz?"

"No, but we have an all-out manhunt under way. We'll find him."

"I still don't think he was involved," I said.

"Him being cellmates with the brother of Amy's kidnapper and the ex-boyfriend of one of the victims is just coincidence, then?" Cantone asked me.

She wasn't being sarcastic.

I shook my head. "No such thing as coincidence.

It has to mean something. And I hate to say it, but the judge is as big a common denominator as Jake is. Maybe bigger."

The chief nodded slowly, pushed his chair back away from the table and stood up. "Then it's time we push him harder. He's not telling us everything."

"You can't push him very hard while he's unconscious, Chief," Mason said.

Chief Sub nodded. "He's awake and stable. They've moved him out of the ICU. Marianne called, said he was asking for me. I'm heading upstairs to see him now."

He reached past Nagawa to close the laptop and then picked it up. "Thank you, Doctor."

"I'll have a report with my findings on the second victim sent to you tomorrow, Chief Subrinsky," he said, rising and shaking the chief's hand again.

We all filed out, crowded into the elevator and rode it up. When it hit the ground floor it stopped and Dr. Nagawa, who was standing right against my side, pressed something into my hand, then got out, saying a polite goodbye to everyone and giving me a particularly lingering smile.

Oh, hell.

The doors slid closed. Mason glanced down at me, and I knew that he'd noticed that smile and was looking to see if I had. Or maybe to see what my reaction was. "What?" I asked him, wondering when the hell I could gracefully stop playing Nancy Drew and go the fuck home. I glanced down at the paper in my hand. The guy had given me his phone number.

"Nothing." He said it in a tone that meant "something." Then he added, "Last stop before home, I prom-ise," reading my mind better than I could read tea leaves. (That was sarcasm. I cannot read tea leaves. I mean, not unless someone lines them up in the shapes of letters.)

The doors opened again, and we spilled into the hos-pital corridor and followed the chief to Judge Howie's door.

Chief Sub went into the room, and as the door opened wide I glimpsed the judge in his bed, cranked upright, Marianne sitting beside him. A nurse was hanging an IV bag. The blinds in the window behind her were pulled up, admitting the maximum possible amount of sunlight into the room, and I thought for a minute about how much Halle Chase would've liked to see sunlight before she died.

Judge Mattheson caught Mason's eye and waved a hand. "You might as well come in. This will be for the record."

So Mason and I went in behind the chief, and Can-tone came in behind us. The nurse pushed a few buttons on the IV pump and hurried out of the room. Man, talk about overkill. She had the puffy hat, surgical mask, gloves, even the goggles. Whole nine yards. That was weird, wasn't it?

"Why was she dressed like she just came out of a leper colony?" I asked.

"You should go, Marianne," Judge Mattheson told his wife.

"I'm staying." She took his hand in hers and held tight. "Whatever it is, I'm here for you, Howard."

He met her eyes, and something really beautiful passed between them, completely diverting me from the dark shiver that had just crept up my spine for no apparent reason.

"I'm so, so sorry, Marianne. I'm so, so sorry." He pulled her hand to him and bent his head over it, kissing the back of it.

Gooey emotions bubbled up in my chest. He lingered there, mouth on her hand, eyes closed. And it was really sweet, until it went on just long enough to slip over into uncomfortable.

About two beats after that it turned from uncomfortable into *something's fucking wrong* when he slumped over her forearm.

"Howard?" Marianne whispered.

The chief grabbed Judge Howie's shoulders and pushed him back onto his pillows. "Howard! Nurse! Get a nurse!"

People were crowding into the room now, shoving us unceremoniously out of the way. The first nurse to the bedside yelled to the one behind her, "Call a code and clear this room!"

I got out of the way, stumbled down the hall a few steps, then turned around and practically stabbed Mason in the chest with my nose.

The chief hurried out with an arm around Marianne Mattheson, Cantone right behind them. They came our way, but the judge's wife turned to look back toward the room, one hand hovering near her mouth. The chief tugged her on until we all came to the waiting room, where she stopped and couldn't be coaxed farther. And then we just stood there, and maybe I wasn't the only one eyeing the comfy-looking sofas and well-stocked vending machines with lust in my heart. But we didn't go in. We stayed around Marianne like it would help her somehow, and watched people rushing in and out of that hospital room. Each time the door swung open, we were afforded a glimpse inside. We saw the paddles being applied. We saw the exertion of battle in the faces of the staff. And we saw when that look turned to crushing defeat, and all the activity ground to a sudden and devastating halt.

Marianne collapsed, and Mason and the chief scrambled to gather her up and carry her into the waiting room to a sofa. I was still staring at the door opening and closing, but more slowly now. Giving me strobe-effect pieces of something I couldn't put my finger on just yet. I didn't realize I was walking toward the door until Cantone fell into step. "What? What is it?"

I looked at her face, wondered if she was fucking with me or serious. She sounded serious. "There was something off about…"

The door opened one more time, and a nurse inside the judge's room demanded, "Who the hell hung this?" She was staring at an IV bag.

"That nurse," I said. "It was that nurse!" I burst back into Judge Howie's room, and Cantone ran the other way, toward Mason and the chief and that murderous nurse. As I skidded to a stop, the nurse with the IV bag in her hand lowered it and said, "You can't be in here."

"I want to see that IV bag," I said. "Come on, I'm

with the police. And he was a judge. We're not fucking around with you here. I want to see that bag."

She lifted it up, held it out. "Hang it up like it was," I told the nurse. "And try not to touch it any more than you already have. And…and we might have to finger-print you for comparison, so don't go anywhere. Okay?" I pulled that straight out of my butt, but it sounded right.

"Okay." She hung the bag, then scurried out of the room, probably to call her union rep. I figured she knew this was a lawsuit waiting to happen and would have liked to spirit that little IV bag away before anyone no-ticed it. And I didn't blame her. Nurses get sued, too.

I looked up at the bag. It had another patient's name on it, and a different room number. The label read In-sulin.

Shaking my head, I looked at the judge's body in the bed. "What were you gonna tell us, Judge Howie? What the fuck were you into?" I even tried touching his hand, waiting for a vision. But Judge Howie didn't give me a thing.

There was no sign of the nurse—if she even was a nurse—who'd hung the IV bag. She was long gone by the time we realized what had happened and went look-ing. And from there the afternoon had been endless, as Mason and Vanessa interviewed witnesses and I stood around trying to pick up on their underlying issues.

And I did. I knew, for example, that a hunky orderly was sleeping with a female surgeon who didn't want anyone to know. *He* did, though. He was busting with pride, and it was written all over his face. I knew that the nurse in charge of the floor at the time of the judge's murder was scared to death of being blamed and losing her license. She had that look people have when they get caught doing something unforgivable and have been found out. I thought she was blaming herself more than anyone else would, and hoped she didn't lose her job or her license over it. I mean, it happened in a roomful of cops, an FBI agent and me. How the hell could she blame herself?

I got lots of shit like that. Nothing useful.

The insulin had been taken from another patient's room. There was a tiny bit of video surveillance footage of the imposter nurse walking out of the room and down the hall with the IV bag in hand, going directly into the judge's room and leaving again. She had a way of fitting right in, moving with that quick, confident efficiency nurses always had, and keeping her face averted from the cameras all the time.

I'd been going over it in my head nonstop, wondering what good this extra sense of mine was if people could commit murder right under my nose without me even fucking noticing.

I *had* noticed, though. I'd felt a dark little niggling in the back of my neck when she'd walked past me, even wondered why she was hiding behind all that gear. Why the hell hadn't I trusted that feeling? I could've kicked myself.

I didn't need to keep going over it in my head in search of details about the murderer. There was video footage. But it didn't do a hell of a lot of good. The woman had been dressed in clothes normally used in the O.R. I hadn't even noticed the shoe covers. Aside from female and five-four, we had no clue who she was. She probably didn't work for the hospital. She had some medical knowledge. Enough to know the right dose of insulin to use to kill and how to operate an IV pump. Although they were uncomplicated enough, I supposed, for an amateur intent on murder to figure out ahead of time. She'd taken a crowded elevator when she'd left the judge to die. The police were still going over security camera footage on every floor where it had stopped, but there was no footage of her getting off. They suspected she'd removed her getup a piece or two at a time, as other people got on and off, and eventually exited with a group, probably looking entirely different than she had earlier. She might have even ridden up and down a few times to throw off the search. It was going to take time to identify and rule out every person picked up on video. And she'd probably kept her face averted from the cameras, anyway.

In the meantime, I was home, and it was a warm night. A beautiful night. Almost like an early taste of what the coming summer was going to be like. Mason had dropped me off, and we'd gone our separate ways.

But it had hurt more than it usually did this time. I don't know why. Being around all this death shit, maybe. I took Myrtle out on her leash, but only to keep her from slipping and falling into the lake. We walked down across the lush lawn and the little dirt road, and then down the sloping grass to the big dock I'd had built near the water's edge. It was time to get the patio set out of the garage and set it up out here. Time to drag out the barbecue grill I'd bought. This was going to be my first sighted summer as an adult, and I intended to enjoy it. I might even get a boat.

I didn't go out onto the dock but down to the water's edge beside it. Myrt started sniffing immediately, front paws in the water, her entire butt wiggling in joy. I saw an unsuspecting frog a foot or two ahead of her and waited. Soon she sniffed her way nearer, and just as she bumped the creature with her nose, it sprang away and splashed her in the face. She wriggled and barked for sheer joy, then started sniffing for another.

I didn't know what she'd ever do if she caught one. Not eat it. There wasn't a mean bone in Myrtle's body. Though she *was* perpetually ravenous, so I supposed there was a slight chance. More likely, though, she'd try to hold the thing still with a forepaw so she could sniff it thoroughly and it would wind up squashed.

I wasn't going to let that happen. If she caught a frog, I'd make sure not to let her squash it.

I sat down in the grass, and let her wander and sniff to the end of her lead. It was one of those extending ones, so she had plenty of room to explore. I sat there looking out over the water, watching the sun sink slowly on the other side. It was gonna be one helluva sunset. Damn, it was a shame Mason wasn't here to see this.

My phone rang. I pulled it out, saw his face on the screen and got all mushy inside. This was rapidly approaching pathetic.

I touched the screen. "How'd you know I was thinking about you?" Oh, God, did I really just say something that sappy? Gag!

"Maybe I'm the one who's psychic."

I didn't flinch or cuss at the word. I supposed that was progress. "I'm out by the dock with Myrt. The sunset's going to be killer."

"You want some company?"

"You'll never make it in time."

"Yeah, I will. I'm at the end of your road. With the boys. And an entire vat of takeout from Uncle Louie's Backyard Barbecue."

"What were you doing in Cortland?"

"*Lords of Battle Seven* was sold out everywhere else."

"*Lords of Battle Seven?*" I repeated.

"For Xbox."

"Ah, of course."

"I promised the boys we'd get it on release day. I just forgot to preorder."

"Hence the forty-minute drive. After the day we just had." I shook my head, because it hit me how good he was. He really was just plain good right to his bones. That was something I didn't think most people were. I didn't even really think I was. At least not compared to him. I'd have ordered the game on Amazon and told the boys the world would not end if they got it a few days after release day. I'd have told myself it was a good life lesson and refused to feel any guilt about it.

Yeah. He was good.

"So we grabbed the best takeout known to man and we were heading home when Josh asked if we could bring you some. He misses you."

"He misses my dog, and it's only been two days."

But I was smiling like an idiot and wondering when I'd developed such a mushy spot in my heart for an eleven-year-old.

"I don't want to stomp all over your serenity, Rache. I know it's been a rough week."

"It's too damn quiet around here, to be honest." My stomach growled. "And you know, there're the ribs."

"And a surprise for dessert."

I smiled and looked up the winding dirt road. "I can just see your headlights."

"I can't see yours at all from here."

"Smart-ass."

The sunset was spectacular. I was standing there on the little patch of lawn on the reservoir side of my dusty dirt road, my arms loaded down with deadfall I'd gathered for firewood. Mason was on the dock, setting up my lawn furniture. He'd dug it out of the garage for me after we'd devoured the ribs in my dining room. Four woven folding lawn chairs now surrounded our small but burgeoning campfire, and the wicker set was almost ready for use on the dock.

I dropped the firewood and turned to look his way. And there he was, on the dock, a silhouette against the red-orange blaze of the sun just kissing the distant hilltops on the far side of the lake.

"Wow."

He looked up from his deep study of the white wicker patio set that included a love seat, two side chairs and a glass-topped coffee table, and straight at me. His brows went up. "Wow, what?"

I smiled. No way was I gonna reply with a breathy "you," as much as that was what I was feeling. Instead I nodded, aiming over his left shoulder, and he turned around to look out across the water. The lake's surface reflected the fiery sunset like a mirror. "Oh," he said. "Yeah. Wow."

"I think it's the best sunset I've seen so far," I told him. Barely taking my eyes off the spectacular display, I knelt and started laying some of my gathered wood on the fire, using slightly larger pieces than were already taking hold.

"You've been keeping track, I'll bet." He gave the coffee table a last adjustment, then came off the deck and toward the fire, nodding in approval as the flames snapped and licked at the newly added logs. Then he looked across the road to where the kids were. Jeremy was messing with their fishing rods in the back of the Jeep, and Josh was rolling around in the grass with Myrtle, who had apparently reverted to puppyhood.

"Give me your phone, Mason."

He pulled it out and handed it over, and I snapped a few shots of Josh and Myrt.

"At first I was taking pictures of every sunset I saw. And every sunrise. Fall, oh, man, fall! And then winter…" I shrugged. "My computer has more than seven thousand pics on it, a thousand of them just of Myrtle. But I'm…easing up a little bit." I handed him back his phone.

"Why's that?" he asked, pocketing it before heading across the grass to where a few young willow trees dipped their long fingertips into the shallow water. He pulled out a jackknife and started sawing off some branches from a nearby apple tree.

I added some even larger wood to the fire. "I think I've finally accepted that I can't really capture the beauty of being able to see, and that I don't need to. I'm going to keep on seeing it day after day, sunset after sunset, stupid dog trick after stupid dog trick, for the rest of my life." I shrugged then. "And if I lose my eyesight again, pictures aren't going to be much help."

"That's very practical."

"Yeah, well, how many sunset photographs does one person need, right?"

He came walking back, sharpening the ends of his sticks, and stripping off their twigs and greenery. He sank into one of the lawn chairs and kept on working. "This is your first spring. Maybe you should keep taking pics at least until it's fall again." He set his knife down, pulled his cell phone out of his pocket again and said, "Here," just as he tossed it my way.

I caught it like a pro and crinkled my brows at him.

"What?" he said. "Take a pic of that sunset. You might have plenty, but I don't."

By now the fast-sinking sun was almost down to half. Grinning, I snapped a shot, then another.

A second later he joined me, slid an arm around my waist and spun me around, while stealing back his phone with his free hand. Guy could'a been a pickpocket. He held the phone up and tugged me closer to his side. "Smile, Rache."

"Been smiling since you came over and grabbed me, big guy."

He snapped a selfie of us. Then he tucked the phone away, leaned down and kissed my neck. "You ready for that surprise dessert?"

I looked at the sticks he'd been working on and the lightbulb finally snapped over my head. "S'mores?"

"Oh, yeah."

And I felt something just then. Something very slightly…off. "Why did you come over here tonight bearing ribs and chocolate?"

"I told you, it was spur-of-the-moment."

Then why did his energy sort of flicker when he said that? "Spontaneous, huh? And the fishing poles just happened to be in the Jeep?"

"They're in the Jeep from April to October."

"I see. And you just happened to take the Jeep instead of the Beast tonight?"

He shrugged. "I haven't got around to taking her off the road for the summer yet. Figured I'd give her a glory run."

"Winter rats don't rate glory runs. Feels more like this was planned because you've got something to tell me that you think I'm not gonna like."

He held my eyes for one more second, then rolled his. "Why do I even bother trying?"

"Damned if I know. What is it?"

"Cantone," he said. "She's after the chief's job." Then he whistled to get the boys' attention and waved them over. "Bring the grocery bag."

So I was left without much time to rant about the underhanded federal agent swooping in to steal Mason's dream job.

Okay, not *his* dream job. My dream job for him. Because as much as I didn't want to get overly attached to the guy, I'd be pretty damned devastated if anything happened to him. And in his current job, that was a constant threat. Day in, day out.

And yeah, I was breaking one of my own multipublished cardinal rules of life here by thinking *I'd feel better if only he would...* Doesn't matter what you use to fill in that blank, it's always the same result. In my case, the blank was filled with "get a nice, safe desk job."

One of my other cardinal rules for living was to do what you loved, not what you felt you should. Yet I was expecting him to do what he should, what would be better for the boys and better for me, though I hadn't mentioned that part. I was pushing him—subtly, but still pushing him—to do what we wanted him to do, rather than what his own soul wanted. And it wasn't because I didn't agree 100 percent with my public stance on the matter. No, in this case what I wrote wasn't bullshit at all, and I knew it. My happiness was my job, no one else's, and the notion of "I'd be happy if only he would" was a false one anyway.

And still I was feeling like I'd be happier if he would take the nice safe chief's job. Because I was scared he'd get himself killed, and I didn't think I could handle that.

I looked at him sitting there with the fire making his face look harsher and tougher than it did in daylight. Josh had claimed a stick and stuffed multiple marshmallows onto the end of it. He was toasting them now, leaning forward from his chair. Myrtle was, predictably, right by his side, waiting for handouts. Her nose was twitching like crazy with the smells of the campfire and the water and the rapidly charring marshmallows. Jeremy had wandered out to the end of the dock with his fishing pole, cast it into the water and then sat in one of the white wicker chairs. He was too cool to hang with the adults eating chocolate. Mason was looking at me, had been watching me survey the entire idyllic scene. I read his eyes. They were smiling, and saying, *Not so bad, huh?*

I gave him a slight nod. *Not so bad. Not bad at all.*

13

The Asshole had lowered a radio down with the latest meal. Once he'd gotten his pictures he hadn't ventured down into the hole with the girls again. But the radio was good. The radio was just what Stephanie had been waiting for.

She turned it on nice and loud, then gathered the girls around the coffee table, over a board game, and tilted her head downward, as if she were staring at the game board.

"Sit just like I'm sitting."

"What?" Lexus asked. "What the hell you staring at, girl? You can't even see."

"Do what she says," Sissy said. And Stevie heard and felt her sit on the other end of the couch. Lexi heaved a sigh, and dragged a chair closer to the table and the game board.

"I don't really think they're listening to us or even watching us," Stephanie said softly. "But just in case, pretend we're playing the game and keep your heads down so they can't read our lips."

Lexus popped the popper in the middle of the game board, then moved a plastic token. "Happy?"

"I heard something the other day when I was in the bathroom changing."

That got the other girls' attention. "What do you mean, you heard something?" Lexus asked.

"Just what I said. There was another guy. He was up top. The water must be piped down from up there. I could hear everything he said."

"Holy shit. Who was he talkin' to? What he say?"

"Lexi, shut up and let her talk," Sissy whispered loudly.

"Ssshh." Stevie reached out for the popper, and pressed it down, then felt for a plastic token and had Sissy help her move it around the board. "I don't know who he was talking to. But I do know he's planning to get another girl. Just one more, to replace Venora."

"What good does it do us to know that?" Lexus asked. "Jeez, girl, it's not like we can do anything about it, and anyway, we always figured there was going to be four of us."

"Once he has all four, we're going somewhere else," Stevie said. "When they move us again, that'll be our chance. Maybe our last chance."

"But…but I thought you said it was too dangerous, Stevie?" Sissy's voice came from an angle that told Stevie she was looking directly at her.

"Head down, Sissy," she said.

The other girl sniffled but obeyed. Stevie could tell when Sissy spoke again. "Last time you tried to escape, your friend got shot."

"I know, Sissy. I know that, and I regret it right to my bones, but—"

"What choice do we have?" Lexus demanded. "You tell me that, Sissy. What choice do we have? Are we gonna spend our lives in this hole or some other one? In chains, maybe? Who knows where we end up? Dead, most likely. Sooner or later, dead and dumped like poor Venora. It's not like they can let us go. Ever. We'd tell, right? We'd tell what happened here. Even if we swear up and down we won't, they can't risk it. They gonna keep us till they done with us, and then we dead." Lexus paused for a breath, then, more softly, asked, "Right, Stevie?"

"Probably. I have to admit, I've been thinking the same thing."

"Oh, God." There were tears in Sissy's voice.

"They gonna kill me anyway," Lexi said. "I'll be damned if I'm gonna make it easy for them. I'm gonna go out fighting. And I'm gonna make them sorry sons of bitches before I do."

Stevie nodded. "I'm right with you, Lexus. A hundred percent." Then she waited, but she only heard soft, shallow breaths coming from the newer girl. "Sissy?" she prompted.

"I'm scared."

"I know. I know you're scared, Sissy." Stevie reached out to run a hand over the girl's hair. It was curly and short and she wished she could see it. "But I've also been thinking that once we leave here, we can't be sure they won't split us up."

"No!"

"Shhh."

"They try that shit, I…" But Lexus didn't finish the thought.

Probably, Stevie thought, because there wouldn't be much she could do about it if it happened. "We have a better chance together than we ever will apart," she said.

Sissy was crying softly, but finally she seemed to pull herself together. "Okay. I'll do whatever you think we should do," she said.

"Somebody else might get killed," Lexus said. "That's gotta be said right up front. We gotta know what we risking."

"You're right." Stevie nodded hard. "But what's the alternative? Just give up? Let them take us wherever they want? Do whatever they want to us? We're being held prisoner, Lexi."

"I know." Lexus gave a heavy sigh. "Move your game piece, Sissy."

Sissy popped the popper and moved a piece accordingly. "What's the plan?"

"I don't know yet," Stevie said. "But I think we start by being cooperative. We make them think we're resigned to our fate. That we've given up. We act beaten, you understand? Submissive. No mouthing back. No resistance. Like the weakest dogs in the pack."

"So they don't expect no trouble," Lexus said slowly. "Yeah. Yeah, that make sense. Maybe they get lazy, don't bother drugging us the next time we gotta move."

"Exactly. They don't drug us, we wait for a chance to run for it, and then we do," Stevie said.

"I think we might be better off waiting for a chance to cut their throats," Lexi said.

Stevie reached out, felt for the popper and popped it. "What'd I get?"

"Six," Sissy told her. "You get to go twice."

Stevie found her game piece, and Sissy helped her count six spaces with it, tapping each one. "If we get the chance to kill them, then yeah, I think we have to kill them. I don't think we have a choice."

She stopped after she said that, just sitting there and feeling the disconnect in her mind. When, in her wildest dreams, had she ever imagined she would say something like that? Much less that when she did, she would mean every word of it?

But she did, she realized. She meant it. And she didn't feel like it was going to be all that hard, either. She didn't think she'd even hesitate.

Then she popped again. The game of *Trouble* was easy enough without eyesight. Getting out of trouble, maybe not quite so much.

They slept over. The boys in two of my five guest rooms, and Mason with me, in the master suite that was kind of my notion of a royal palace. Before my transplant, everything in it had been cream-colored. I'd redecorated it in a style I liked to call Early Jeannie's Bottle, because I just loved the rich bright jewel tones. I'd done it in February, when the dull blahs of an upstate New York winter grew too dull even for my innocent recently reborn eyes. Grays and whites, grays and whites, grays and whites. I was going to need a winter home, I decided. Someplace colorful.

Anyway, my bedspread and drapes were matching red velvet with gold brocade accent pillows and tiebacks, and short fringy trim. I'd painted the walls a creamy white, and the carpet and woodwork were emerald-green. Then I'd chosen blue glass pieces for the dresser, and artwork with rich Hindu themes, lots of ruby and gold, emerald and sapphire. The theme carried through to the attached bathroom, and I loved it.

Mason said it looked like a Valentine card on crack. I wanted to add a canopy and draping wispy bed curtains. Yet another reason we could never be together. You know, under the same roof.

Holy shit, when had I even entertained the thought of cohabitation before?

Mason had planned to go to bed in another guest room, wait for the boys to fall asleep and then sneak into my room, like we did on my frequent visits to his place. But Jeremy called him on it when he said goodnight, and I was lucky enough to be standing nearby when he did.

"You can quit playing games with us, Uncle Mace. We both know you're gonna go sleep with Rachel."

"Yeah, Uncle Mace," Josh added. He was in bed, under the covers, hugging my bulldog. "You always do that after you think we've gone to sleep. But it's okay. We understand."

Mason had been stunned by such an observation coming from an eleven-year-old and asked, "You do?"

"Yeah. Whenever I'm around, Myrtle sleeps with me

instead of her." He hugged my traitorous little bulldog closer. "Rache must get lonely all by herself."

"Yeah," Jeremy said. "She must get *lonely.*"

I poked my head in through the doorway. "Watch it, Jere. *She's* standing right here."

Jeremy shrugged but had the good manners to blush a little. Mason sighed, gave Josh a final tuck and a kiss on the forehead, then squeezed Jeremy's shoulder, because apparently that one was too old to appreciate being kissed on the forehead. Jeremy rolled his eyes and headed next door to his own assigned room.

When he'd closed the door behind him, Mason slung an arm around me and we headed down the hall to my room.

"So it looks like we haven't been fooling anyone," I said. "Guess they inherited your detective genes."

"My brother was adopted, remember?"

"Then they got them by osmosis."

He nodded. "You know, I really thought they'd believe me. I mean, they've seen the inside of your bedroom. The colors alone ought to keep me from sleeping in there."

"I'll change it again in six months."

"To something I'll hate even more?"

"Possibly. I was thinking maybe a jungle theme. Will that drive you away?"

"Only if I don't get to be Tarzan." He swept me close for a passionate, walking kiss, and stumbled me backward right through my bedroom doorway and across the bed, kicking said door closed behind us.

And I thought to myself, this really isn't so bad *at all.*

And it wasn't. Not until the dream came. It was about Vanessa Cantone, of all people. And that didn't make any sense at all, if this new connection of mine was to the dead. Because Vanessa wasn't dead at all.

At first.

She was in some kind of big industrial-looking room that might've been round, with three girls and two men. One of the girls was Stephanie Mattheson. I knew her right away. Hell, I'd been looking at her face for days now on the Missing posters and police files. The other two, I had only seen in the photos with their files. Cecelia "Sissy" Dunham was a beautiful black girl, and Lexus Carmichael was as white as anyone I'd ever seen. She had short, sassy platinum-blond hair and eyebrows so pale she damn near looked albino. There were two men, too, both wearing ski masks. One of them was pointing a gun at Cantone.

No, no. No no no.

He pulled the hammer back. Cantone looked him dead in the eye. She didn't flinch. She didn't beg.

I don't want to see this. Wake up, wake up, dammit!

But I didn't wake up. The gunshot exploded. So did Agent Cantone's head. She was dead before she hit the floor.

I sat up in bed with my heart choking me, gasping for breath and feeling like I wasn't getting any.

"Rache?" Mason was there. I knew he was there, but I couldn't rip my brain away from that vision of Cantone hitting the floor with her head blown apart.

"Rachel, come on, look at me." He patted my face a little.

It worked. I blinked the dream away and locked on to his eyes.

"You okay?"

"Yeah."

"What happened?"

"I dreamed…I saw…"

Flash! The same scene blazed into my head, only this time Mason played the role of Vanessa, and it was him on the floor in a pool of blood and brain matter.

"Jesus," I said softly. And I wasn't cussing, I was praying.

"Rache, come on. Talk to me. What did you see?"

"I…" I looked at him, sitting up in bed beside me, shirtless and alive and perfect, and tears blurred my vision. I slid my arms around his waist and laid my head on his hard chest. He hugged me close, rocked me slowly. "I don't remember," I whispered.

I hated lying to him. But what was I gonna tell him? That Cantone was in danger? So he could get in the way of that and get *his* brains blown out instead? Because it was pretty clear that was what was going to happen. And there was no fucking way I was going to help it happen. Not to him. There had to be a better answer than that. I'd just damn well better hurry up and find it.

Mason was sure that Rachel remembered whatever the dream had been. He would have turned in his shield if he hadn't been able to tell that much. But if she wouldn't tell him, there wasn't much he could do to find out.

She was shaken up by it, that much was obvious. And

for the moment, he thought the best thing he could do was give her a little time to work through it. She would tell him when she was ready.

His cell phone rang. He looked at the time—3:37 a.m. Shit, calls at this hour were never good news. He answered the phone. "Brown."

"Detective?"

"Yeah, who is this?"

"I—I need to talk to you."

"And I repeat, who is this?"

"Rodney Carr, sir. From Social Services? We spoke in my office…about Venora and the—"

"Yeah, okay. I know who you are. What's going on, Mr. Carr?"

"I need to see you. Alone. I have… Something happened."

Mason sighed, pushed a hand through his hair. Rachel was looking up at him now, curious and blinking tears from her eyes. Tears. Damn, she didn't cry easily. That must've been some dream.

"I know you were checking on the other girls who'd aged out, Mr. Carr. I'm sorry we didn't contact you to tell you that we got that information already."

"That's not why I'm calling. I think…I think I have information that can help. I need you to come here. But be careful. I think I'm being watched."

That got Mason's attention. He sat up straighter, and turned on the bedside lamp. "Where are you right now?"

Rachel sat up straighter, too, watching him with eyes so perceptive he almost thought she could hear both sides of the conversation.

"I'm at my apartment. I'm using my partner's cell."

"Okay. I'm writing the number down. I'm gonna call you back when I get close. Gimme your address."

Rodney rattled it off, and Mason winced a little at the neighborhood as he scribbled it down. "Don't go anywhere, and don't talk to anybody until you hear from me. Okay?"

"Yeah. I'm not going anywhere."

"All right. I'll be…ah, jeez, a half hour. You want me to send someone who's closer? Do you feel like you're in danger?"

"No, they won't hurt me. They need me. Half hour."

"Yeah. Less if I can."

"Thanks, Detective Brown."

"See you soon." Mason disconnected and rolled out of bed, pulling on his jeans and pocketing the phone practically in one motion. He grabbed his shirt as Rachel got out of bed on the other side.

"What's going on with Rodney?" she asked.

"He thinks he's being watched. Thinks he knows something about what was going on with the case and wants to talk in person."

"I *knew* he was a good guy." She grabbed a pair of jeans from a drawer.

"Rache, what're you doing?"

"Getting dressed. We have to hur—"

"Not we, babe. Me."

She blinked, and he thought she was probably wondering if he had really just called her "babe." It had slid out naturally, and he was a little embarrassed.

"You've got to stay here, Rache. There are the kids, and the dog—"

"Hey, the kids are yours," she said teasingly. He thought. "How about you stay and I'll go?"

"Because he called *me*. Because I'm the cop and you're the self-help writer. Because of a thousand other things, Rache, and just because—" He grabbed her and kissed her hard. "Because that. Okay? I'll be back as soon as I can."

He turned around and left, grabbing his wallet and keys off the nightstand, buttoning his shirt on the way down the stairs.

Fuck. Fuck, fuck, *fuck!*

I followed him to the front door and stood there watching him go, mad enough to spit. Since when did I take no for an answer that easily? Dammit, what if he needed my help? What if…what if he was the one who was right about Rodney Carr and this was all a setup? He'd been right about Jake, after all. Apparently.

Jeez, what if something happened to him?

The phone rang, the house phone, not my cell. I thought it might have been him, so I raced across the living room to pick it up. "Yeah?"

"It's Vanessa Cantone," said my arch-nemesis. Oh, wait, not anymore. Now she was a potential victim in need of protecting in some way that didn't ensure Mason was going to wind up taking her place in the slo-mo nightmare produced by my brain. "Is Mason there?"

"Why would you think he was here?" I asked.

"Because I tried his place and he didn't answer, and he's not picking up his cell."

"So maybe he doesn't take 3:00 a.m. phone calls, Vanessa. You ever think of that? It's a practice I'm striving to emulate."

"He's a cop, and he took a 3:00 a.m. phone call a few minutes ago, didn't he?"

I stood there gaping like an air-starved trout.

"I have his phone tapped. I know where he's going."

"Well, that makes one of us." I frowned hard. "You tapped his phone?" Man, was he going to be *pissed*.

"I just need to know how long it's going to take him to get there," she went on, never stopping to let my comment get through the gates. "Did he leave from your place or his, Rachel?"

"Mine."

"Thank you."

"Vanessa, wait. Don't hang up."

She didn't. She waited two beats, then asked, "What?"

"I—I think you might be in danger."

She was quiet for a second.

"I saw—"

"No, don't. Look, thank you, Rachel. Thank you. I just… Don't tell me, all right? I don't want to know. I don't want it changing the way I do my job. Just…just don't, okay?"

"Are you fucking kidding me?"

"No, I am not fucking kidding you."

It had never occurred to me that she might not want

to know. Jeez, why not make this as difficult as possible, Universe? "Okay."

"Okay. I gotta go now. Mason might need backup."

"Okay." I pulled the phone away from my ear, about to hang up, when I heard, very clearly, a little girl's voice calling, "Mommy?"

Frowning, I jerked the phone back to my ear and heard Cantone's voice, sweeter than ever before. "I'm right here, honey." *Click.*

Holy crap, the woman had a child! A little girl. Oh, hell, how was I supposed to hate her *now?*

Mason checked the entire block around Rodney Carr's apartment but didn't see anyone lurking, no one watching. The local bars were closed, and the sidewalks empty except for the occasional newspaper skittering in the breeze. He circled twice more just to be sure. The guy was probably just being paranoid. Still, better safe than sorry. He parked a block away and then texted him, rather than risking an overheard call.

I'm here. I don't see anyone watching.

Ok. Come to the back door, I'll let u in.

He walked the block back to Rodney's address, hugging his jacket around him a little more tightly against the chill. It was cool tonight, clear. On the drive over, the stars had been thick and bright overhead, but here, near downtown Binghamton, they were barely visible against the competing lights of the city.

The building was a converted Georgian house that had probably been a landmark once. Now it was four apartments, two on the ground level, two on the second, with a chain-link fence around the small backyard. He went through the gate, around to the back door, and he didn't have to knock. Rodney Carr was waiting on the other side.

He opened the door, looked warily past Mason, then ushered him inside and closed the door behind him. They were in a small kitchen with the usual accoutrements. A Formica table had a manila envelope on it, and that, Mason suspected, was why he was here.

"Are you sure no one saw you come in?" Rodney asked. He was pouring coffee into two mugs.

"I'm sure."

"He must think I'd be too scared to talk." He shook his head slowly, adding cream and sugar to his own cup, then setting both mugs on the table. "Sit down, Detective." He handed Mason a cup without asking.

Mason sat. He sipped. Then sipped again. It was damn good coffee. The maker, he now noticed, was bright red and expensive-looking. None of the other appliances in the kitchen seemed to be of the same quality, so it was either a gift or Rodney had a passion for coffee.

Rodney sniffed, cleared his throat. "Okay, I guess I just have to say it. Two days ago I woke up naked in a no-tell motel with no idea how I got there," he said, pushing the envelope to Mason's side of the table. "This was on the bed with me."

Mason opened the envelope, slid the photos out. He saw naked limbs, recognized the social worker in one shot, and that was enough. The poor guy was red to his roots. He slid the photos back into the envelope, deciding to take a more thorough look in private.

"What do they want?" he asked, disappointed that Rodney hadn't called him with something more useful than a personal problem. He'd thought this was about the missing girls. In fact, the guy had led him to believe it was. Was that a ruse just to get some help with an attempted shakedown?

"They want the name and last known address of a girl who has recently aged out of the foster care system and has no known relatives, or at least none who give a damn about her."

Mason jumped to his feet. "You're shitting me."

He nodded at the envelope. "There's a note."

Mason took the note out, read it. "'We know you're married,'" he said aloud. Then he looked at the guy again. "Married?"

"It's legal in New York now, you know. What they didn't realize is that my *wife* is a man and would no more fall for this obvious frame job than I would."

Mason smiled. "They sure picked the wrong guy." Then he frowned as more pieces started to snap into place. "Why didn't you call me sooner?"

"I was waiting to see what they wanted. I know it was stupid, but I thought they might never call, and then I wouldn't have to deal with all this. But they did. And when they told me what they wanted, I realized they must be responsible for all those missing girls." He shook his head. "Someone's been giving them names of girls they can…they can prey on. And for whatever reason, that someone stopped."

Judge Mattheson, Mason thought. And he'd stopped because he'd stroked out. He'd been about to confess when they killed him. "When do you have to give them the information?"

"Noon tomorrow," Rodney said. "They said if I told anyone they'd do worse than show those photos."

Mason said, "They mean it." Then he looked at the guy. "And yet you called me anyway."

"Of course I called you anyway. If these people are the reason nine of my girls have gone missing…" He met Mason's eyes. "It's worth the risk. I mean there's only one of me."

Mason nodded. Rachel had been right about this guy. He'd been dead wrong.

"So…what should I do?"

"Help me take them down. If you're willing."

"I am. How?"

"By doing exactly what they asked you to do. Give them the name and last known address of a girl. Only the girl is gonna be an undercover cop, and when they take her, they're gonna lead us straight to the others." He shrugged. "I hope."

I couldn't go back to sleep, so I ground up some fresh beans and made coffee. The whole downstairs smelled like heaven as my Bona Vita chugged and steamed. The boys were still sleeping. They'd sleep through a hurricane. Myrtle, on the other hand, had probably heard everything. The phone call, and us getting up and moving around the house. She'd heard Mason leave, and there was no question she could smell the coffee. I didn't think her other senses were necessarily sharper due to her blindness. I think dogs' hearing and smell are always supercharged, blind or not. Hell, of the five senses, sight is probably the least important one to a canine.

And when the hell were we going to stop listing our senses as five? Animals clearly had more than that. And so did I.

When I saw headlights in the driveway I smiled, and went to the kitchen to pour two mugs full of the fresh, luscious brew. Mason was a man who appreciated a great cuppa as much as I did, and it wasn't like a couple of caffeine junkies like us would be kept awake long by a single mug. I was carrying the cups back into the front of the house when I heard the knock on the door. Weird. Mason would've just come in. We were way past knocking. On that aspect of our relationship we were in complete agreement. See? It wasn't *all* confusion and fear of commitment.

I set the mugs down on the coffee table, tugged my very short but very luxurious silk robe a little more snugly around me and wished I had more on underneath it. Then I went to the door and peeked out through the glass panes. Shit. It was Agent McPretty. I opened the door. "Cantone."

"De Luca." She came in, then lifted her perfect brows and sniffed. "God, that smells good. Can I have a cup?"

I nodded at the coffee table where two mugs sat steaming and saw her eyes go round as she headed for the sofa. "Damn. You *are* good, aren't you?"

"I'm a fucking genius." I took a quick look outside, in case Mason was in sight, but no luck. Then I closed the door but didn't lock it. "I thought you were going to back Mason up. What are you doing here?"

"I finally got him on the phone. He'd already left and was on his way back. He asked me to meet him here." She picked up her mug and looked around the living room. "Man, this place is gorgeous. I guess you must do okay."

"I do all right. Sit down, make yourself at home. Cop conventions in my living room are my favorite. Especially at—" I glanced at the clock "—4:45 a.m. Yeah, it's the best time." I headed for the kitchen to pour another mug for Mason.

Instead of sitting, Cantone followed me into the kitchen. "Damn, de Luca, you really know how to live."

"So I've been told." I grabbed another mug. "So he was on his way back when you talked to him?"

"Yeah." She spied the sugar and cream I'd left out on the counter and helped herself to a bit more of each.

I filled Mason's mug and fixed it the way he liked it. "Did he say anything about what happened?"

"No."

"I guess he'll tell us when he gets here, then."

"Guess so."

It was a little awkward. She knew that I knew something about her. I knew that she wished I didn't and didn't want to know herself. The phrase *elephant in the room* was an understatement.

I sighed and carried Mason's mug back toward the living room, where the slightly rumpled blanket tossed haphazardly over the back of the sofa probably revealed that I'd been sitting there all wrapped up and cozy, awaiting my man in a scene of domestic bliss.

I set his mug down on the coffee table and pulled the blanket around my shoulders. Then I sank onto the cushions of the biggest armchair in the room. That was better. Now I was feeling more like a queen on her throne than a half-dressed, half-asleep, wild-haired writer with her nipples showing through her silk bathrobe.

"So how old is your little girl?" I asked.

Cantone had been perching in the rocker, but now she froze and sloshed coffee all over her hand. "Where the hell did you get that?" Then she frowned. "Did you…?" She pointed at her head and moved her forefinger in a circle.

"Um, no, I heard her voice on the phone. And that's the gesture for bat-shit crazy, not NFP, by the way."

"NFP?"

"Not Fucking Psychic."

She smiled a little. I thought she appreciated my brand of sarcasm. "So, your little girl. She sounded…what, seven?"

She finished sitting down. "Six. Good guess, though."

"What's her name?"

"Lilly."

"And you bring her with you when you're on cases."

"No. That was a Skype call in progress." She sipped her coffee. "She had a nightmare. She often does when I have to leave town on a case."

And just like that, I got it. "That's why you're after the chief's job."

"How do you know about that?" She rolled her eyes at her own question. "Why do I keep asking you that. Yes, that's why I want the chief's job. I heard through the grapevine he was getting ready to retire and might be scouting potential replacements. That's why I volunteered to come out here when this case came up."

I nodded, getting nothing but honesty from her. I didn't volunteer anything. She didn't need to know that Mason wanted the job. Okay, that wasn't accurate. She didn't need to know that I wanted Mason to want the job.

"It would be nice to have a desk job in a nice place like this. It's quiet."

"It's fucking pastoral."

She grinned. "Good word."

"Words are my specialty."

She pressed her lips together, thinking about something. Deciding on something, I thought, and then she nodded, decision made. "I need to ask you for a favor, Rachel. Woman to woman. Just between us."

I must not have been as gifted as she thought I was, because I had not been expecting that. What could I possibly do for her? "Shoot," I said.

"Don't tell them."

I blinked, and my brain tried to decide what she was referring to. "You're gonna have to be more specific. Are you talking about the job now, or—"

"My daughter. Don't tell Mason or the chief or anyone about my daughter."

"Why the hell not?" I asked.

"I'm a woman in a man's world. Trust me, it wouldn't be good for my chances at the job."

And there it was. The easiest way in the freaking universe to put her out of the running for Mason's future position. And would I use it? Come on, now. I'm a bitch, but I'm not a backstabber.

The front door opened, and Mason walked in, met my eyes and told me without a word that he was glad to be back. And that his mysterious late-night meeting with Rodney Carr had been a good one.

I held up his mug. He said, "You're a mind reader." Then he grinned. "Sorry. It slipped out." Then he came to take his cup and glanced at Cantone. "Did she tell you she's been monitoring my cell phone?"

"Yeah. And I know all about those 900 numbers you've been calling, pal."

He crooked a brow at me, I winked and he relaxed.

"I'm sorry about that," Cantone said. "Look, I'm FBI. You were keeping some pretty significant things from me when I made that decision. I'm sharp enough to know that much. I just didn't know what they were." She paused, then added, "Now that I do, I'll cancel the monitoring. I understand why you two were playing things so close to the vest. I get the need for discretion. And I want you both to know that this…NFP thing—" she smiled when she said it "—is off the record."

"I appreciate that," I told her.

"Well, you know, I wouldn't do anything to fuck up another woman's career if I could help it."

Oh, man. Subtle, she wasn't. I sighed. "Neither would I."

She looked so relieved it should've been obvious, but she quickly leaned back and sipped her coffee, trying to act like nothing important had just happened.

Mason looked from me to her and back again, clearly aware something had transpired between us, so I changed the subject before he could ask what. "So? What did Rodney Carr have to say?"

He smiled. "He said he's gonna help us nail the kidnappers, save the girls and put this case to bed. So Jake Kravitz and whoever else he's working with are toast." He smiled a little bit bigger. "In other words, we've got 'em."

"We do?"

Mason nodded, and then he filled us in. Rodney Carr had been set up with a half-naked hooker, photographed and then blackmailed for the name of another girl who'd aged out of foster care. A girl no one would miss.

"Which means whoever was supplying them with names before, stopped," Vanessa Cantone said. "They need a new insider."

"It has to have been the judge," Mason said. "He's been supplying the names of the girls. He must have said no more, or maybe he threatened to turn Jake in, so Jake took Stephanie to shut him up and force him to comply."

"And even though he had to know that was what happened to his daughter, the bastard wouldn't tell us the truth." I shook my head in disgust. I could hardly believe it. "I knew he was hiding something, but I had no idea he was that vile."

Mason said, "Maybe he honestly wanted to make

sure Jake really had taken her, that she hadn't just run off on her own again."

"Bullshit."

"It's not bullshit. I think Jake had something on him. Blackmailed him into providing those names."

I nodded. "The judge had photos of an unsolved hit-and-run that resulted in a death. The suspect vehicle was narrowed down to a full-size white SUV."

Mason picked up there. "And the judge owned a full-size white SUV at the time."

"Holy shit," Vanessa said.

"But when the judge saw Stephanie's name cut into Venora's body, he knew for sure the people blackmailing him must have taken her," Mason said. "You saw him, Rachel. You felt his reaction to that. He had a stroke, for God's sake."

I lowered my head, wanting to hate Judge Mattheson, to condemn him. But I couldn't really do that. "Okay, maybe he didn't know what was happening to the girls whose names he was providing. Maybe when he saw Venora, it all hit him at once. That the girls were being harmed. And that now his own daughter was with them."

"And he *was* going to come clean. Probably right before he stroked out. And then again, once he came around, right before that fake nurse killed him," Cantone said. "Doesn't excuse his behavior. He made bad choices. Real bad."

"So what do we do next?" I asked.

"We set up a sting," Mason said slowly. "We give Rodney a fake name and last known address to pass on to these assholes. We get a female officer to pose as the aged-out foster girl. And we let Jake and his goons come and kidnap her."

"Me," Cantone said. "We let them come and kidnap me."

I managed not to shoot to my feet and shout no at the top of my lungs. Barely. Instead, I calmly set my coffee down, and said, "There's no way you're gonna pass for eighteen, Vanessa. No offense."

She lowered her head and lifted her brows. "Offense taken."

"We don't need her to pass for long. It'll be dark. We'll use a lot of makeup."

"Jesus, you two are good for my ego." She got to her feet. "It's my case. My call. I'm the one." She looked me right in the eye. "It's my job. My choice. Okay?"

I nodded. "Okay."

"Okay." She looked at Mason. "Set it up." Then to me. "Thanks for the coffee. See you both tomorrow." And she headed out the front door.

As I watched her go, my dream came rushing back. Vanessa Cantone, standing with three young women, including Stephanie Mattheson and Lexus Carmichael, and getting her brains blown out.

I had something. A gift. A curse. Maybe I was born with it. Maybe I got it from the transplant and the circuits that seemed to have opened in my brain. Maybe I got it from twenty years of blindness. Or maybe it was some combination of all of the above, or something completely different that I hadn't even thought of yet.

Regardless of how I had it, or where it had come from or what I called it, I had it.

I had to believe I had it for a reason.

The dreams I'd had right after the transplant had helped stop a serial killer and return the bodies of his victims to their families. The gut feelings that had helped Mason and me save Amy from these same goons. The visions that had come to me later, over Christmas, had helped us stop a very sick woman from continuing her own murder spree. Now it was happening again. And this time the reason was to put Jake Kravitz away, to set free the girls he was holding captive somewhere, and to save the life of six-year-old Lilly Cantone's mom.

I could not let Vanessa Cantone walk head-on into her own execution. And I wouldn't.

14

I worked with Rodney Carr to print up a phony file that would look identical to the others Jake might or might not have seen before. After quite a bit of discussion with Mason, Cantone and the chief, we'd agreed this was the best way to do it.

Jake. Yeah, I guess I'd been wrong about him. I hated that, and wondered if some people were just harder to read than others. Because I really had thought he'd seemed like a decent guy, and his concern for Stephanie had felt genuine to me.

I guess if I were 100 percent all the time I wouldn't be human. Jake had a look about him, that tall, lanky, carelessly longhaired look that my brother, Tommy, had. So had my best friend, Mott. Maybe my personal experiences could cause static in my receiver. So to speak.

I handed a photograph to Rodney Carr. He looked at it, nodded thoughtfully. It was a deliberately grainy black-and-white, heavily altered shot of Federal Agent Cantone. I had a plan, though, and I'd come prepared with a twenty-something headshot of myself that didn't look too dated. It was in my bag, sitting beside me on the chair in Rodney's office. And I was absurdly glad that Mason was waiting out in the car, to avoid being spotted near Rodney and blowing the whole thing.

"Are you nervous?" I asked the social worker.

"I'm petrified," he said.

I understood that. I was petrified, too.

"But I shouldn't be," he went on. "I just drop the file and walk away. That's all." He looked toward the stapler on his desk, ready to attach the photo to the folder and seal Cantone's fate.

I reached out and picked it up before he could decide to do it himself. "Let me take one last look before we make this permanent," I said, and held out my hand.

He handed me the file. I opened it on my lap, where he couldn't see it. That gave me the cover to slide Cantone's photo into my purse and my own into the file. I stapled it where it belonged, right above the fake name Carlotta Bennett, closed the folder, then leaned forward and took the waiting envelope off the desk. I slid the file into the envelope. Licked and sealed it.

There. Done.

Finally I handed it back to him. "You're gonna be fine. Just like you said, you just drop this envelope and walk away. Then your job is over and you can relax."

He nodded. I knew Mason would be going over all this again with the guy before the drop, but I couldn't seem to help myself.

"There'll be police watching you. You'll be wearing a vest. And then you and Glenn are heading out of town immediately after, just in case anything goes wrong. All right?"

"Yes. I've got it. And we haven't told anyone where we're going."

"Mason's going to give you a secure phone before you take off. Either he or the chief will call you if there's anything you need to know to stay safe," I said.

He nodded firmly. "If I'd known all these precautions were going to be necessary I might not have been so willing to volunteer," he said.

"Yes, you would have."

He looked at me in surprise. "Why do you say that?"

I shrugged one shoulder. "I'm a good judge of character. And I think you care about these girls almost as much as if they were your own kids."

His smile was crooked. I liked that, too. "Thank you for saying that."

"It's true, isn't it?"

"Yes. I do care. I really do. I've always wished there was more I could do for them than what the job and the rules and the budget allow."

"Well, your wish was granted. You're doing more now. You're saving their lives, Mr. Carr. Rodney."

We shared a moment. His smile got a little watery, and he looked away. "And yet it's nothing, what I'm doing is nothing, compared to what Agent Cantone is going to do. I can't believe they're sending her in like this. She could be killed."

"Well, you know that's what they sign up for when they take the job, right?" I said, repeating what Cantone had said to me almost verbatim. And then I thought of a little more. "As a matter of fact, I think it's kind of what we *all* sign up for when we come here to Planet Earth. Helping each other out. Taking care of each other. Looking out for the innocent, helping the helpless. That's kind of the point, when you think about it."

He blinked and tipped his head slowly to the side. "That was beautiful."

I gave my head a shake. "Sorry. I've been neglecting my writing and it's apparently decided to leak out my piehole without permission. Sermon over."

"You should make a note. Remember that bit for the next book."

"I will." I got to my feet and reached across the desk to shake his hand.

"Please tell Agent Cantone to be careful."

"I'll make absolutely sure she is."

Mason was waiting in the car. My car, for a change. He hadn't wanted to risk being seen in the office with Rodney, and parking the Beast out front would've been just as bad. If Jake were watching personally, my own presence here might have raised a red flag, as well. But he'd never seen my car, and I'd worn a glamorous scarf and matching sunglasses like Thelma or Louise (or Myrtle) might have worn, and Jake had only seen me once. I thought we were safe.

I jumped into the driver's seat and said, "Okay, he's good to go. He'll deliver the envelope to the kidnapper at noon. Do you think they'll go after 'Carlotta' tonight?"

"I think so, yes. Whatever they're doing, they clearly need four girls to do it, or they'd have been long gone by now. Things heated up for them when Venora's body was found. I think if they thought they could cut their losses and move on, they would have."

The planted information specified that the fictional Carlotta Bennett frequented a certain street corner most nights. There was no other information they could hope to use to locate her. I figured they'd take the bait.

"That's it, then," I said.

"Nothing else to do but wait," Mason said.

I looked at him and kind of got stuck on his face. I was growing pretty fond of that face. I hoped today wasn't going to be the last time I would see it.

I hoped he wasn't going to be too furious with me tonight, when the proverbial shit hit the proverbial fan. Then again, what difference did it make? If I survived, he'd forgive me. And if I didn't, then it wouldn't really matter.

He dropped me at home after that but promised to pick me up when I said I wanted a nice dinner with the kids before everything went down tonight.

When he returned, he had the Beast. The boys, freshly picked up from baseball practice, were in the backseat.

I stuck Myrt in her happy place, right between Jeremy and Joshua with room to spare. "Hey, guys. Good day?"

"It was all right," Josh said. "I got an eighty-five on my spelling test."

"That's great, Josh. What words did you miss?" I was curious.

"*Existence* was one of them."

I nodded. "Spelled it with an *a,* didn't you?"

"How'd you know?"

"'Cause that's how I always spell it. Thank goodness for spell-checker and editors."

Josh grinned and returned to hugging my dog.

"How about you, Jere?" I asked.

"Every day closer to graduation is a good day," he said.

"I remember that feeling. What are you doing after graduation? I don't think I've ever heard you say."

"I've been asking him the same thing," Mason said. "It's not too late to apply to a two-year school. He keeps saying he's still thinking about it."

Jeremy looked at the back of Mason's head. "I have been. And I've decided. I want to be a cop."

Mason looked up at the rearview mirror, adjusting it so he could see his nephew's face. "You didn't tell me that."

"Yeah, well, I wasn't sure. But now I am."

I knew this wasn't setting well. Mason had sort of cringed into himself. Not visibly, but still… "What about college?" he said at length. "You're gonna want at least a two-year degree before you—"

"All I need is my high school diploma and a good score on the civil service exam. I checked."

Mason blinked, then set his jaw and said, "You're gonna want at least an associate degree," for the second time.

"But it's not required."

"No, it's not required. So let's say you apply." Mason

sounded very calm, very reasonable, but I could tell it was fake. The notion of Jeremy risking his life shook him, I knew it did. Served him right. Maybe he'd figure out how I felt about him doing the same thing every day.

That wasn't fair.

Mason went on. "Say six other guys apply, too. And say there are only two positions open and four of the other six guys have degrees. You think you're gonna get the job?"

"Yeah, I do," Jeremy replied. "I think with my uncle being a supercop, I'd get the job easy." He crossed his arms over his chest, apparently sure the argument had been won.

"You need to get a two-year degree, Jere. You *need* to."

Jeremy heaved one of those giant sighs that only teenagers are capable of producing. Probably had something to do with lung capacity. I don't know. But he let the matter drop. Not for long, though. I'd learned a thing or two about teenagers in my day. This discussion was far from over.

Mason drove us to the nearest Pizza Hut for dinner. Carbs and cheese. Not Myrt's most healthy snack of late. I ordered her a Personal Pan Meat Lover's with extra meat, then picked the bits of flesh off and fed them to her. Better than giving her the whole thing, right?

The place was retro. It still had the big table-sized Pac-Man game in the middle of the dining room. The boys wolfed their food and went to play it. Well, Josh played it. Jeremy leaned on a pillar with his eyes on his cell phone and his thumbs tapping away.

It occurred to me that kids could easily take over the

world. They could hack in and use our own technology against us. Or just decide to stop helping us figure it out to begin with. Either way, we adults would be relegated to a life of servitude and there would be weekly keggers in the White House rose garden. The only reason this hasn't already happened is that the kids haven't figured it out yet. When they buy a clue, it's gonna suck to be a grown-up.

With the boys occupied, I went straight to what was most on my mind. "How did Rodney do with the drop?"

"He did great. Took the bus three blocks, left the file on the seat just like they told him, then got off and got the hell out of there."

The chief had decided putting an officer on the bus might be too obvious and blow the entire thing. So they'd just let it go.

"Why do you think Judge Howie gave those girls up like that? Could it really all have been just to save his own ass?"

Mason sucked fast-food coffee, the worst kind of coffee there is, in my opinion. I'd ordered a vanilla shake solely to avoid the coffee. "I think he was forced to," Mason said. "I had the lab email me what they had on that hit-and-run. The paint the other vehicle left on the victim's car was used on three types of trucks and SUVs, and the one in Judge Mattheson's photo was one of them. I talked to Marianne. She—"

"You didn't tell her why, did you?"

"No, of course not."

I sighed in relief. That poor woman had been through enough.

"But she did tell me he drank quite heavily at one time, and that he'd suddenly given it up and started AA right around the same time as that accident. She says he never drank again. And DMV records show he also sold the SUV the very same week of the hit-and-run."

I closed my eyes. "Did he have it repaired first?"

"I haven't had time to dig that deeply, but I wouldn't be surprised."

"So you think Jake knew and blackmailed the judge into giving him those girls' names?"

He nodded. "I still think he must have tried to put a stop to it," Mason said. "And that's why they took Stephanie."

I lowered my head. Then lifted it again fast. "God, Mace, what's gonna happen to Stephanie? They killed her father, for God's sake. Holding her isn't gonna do them any good now."

He looked grim. "They'll either kill her…or they'll do whatever they're doing with all those other girls."

"What do you think that is?"

He met my eyes like he thought I already knew. "Halle Chase was last seen almost two years ago. She'd been kept in restraints, away from sunlight, and showed signs of recent and frequent intercourse. Rough stuff."

I closed my eyes slowly. "You don't think they're…" I lowered my voice to a whisper. "They're being kept as…sex slaves?"

He nodded. "And who knows how big this thing is? Halle was found in New Mexico. We still have six other girls missing."

"In our district," I said. "It might go farther. You never know."

"Cantone's already got people at the field office in Albany looking into that possibility."

I nodded, glanced over at the boys. He followed my gaze as I said, "I've gotta tell you something. But you're sworn to secrecy. I gave my word I wouldn't tell anyone, but I trust you completely."

"You do?"

"Yeah. I do. What, you didn't know that?"

He shrugged. "I hoped that. I thought it. It's nice to know it. So what's the big secret?"

"Cantone has a kid."

He shot me a look. "She what?"

"She has a little girl. Six years old. At first I thought she was with her over at the Holiday Inn, but—"

"She's at the DoubleTree."

"Right. I knew that." I did now, anyway. And that was what I'd been angling to find out. "She doesn't wear a ring. You think she's a single mom?"

"I don't know. I didn't know she was a mom at all."

"Anyway, I was wrong. I heard the little girl's voice on the phone, but it was 'cause she was talking to her on Skype from home. So somebody must be back in Albany, taking care of the kid while she's out chasing bad guys, right?"

"I guess so." He was looking at me a little too closely. I had to be careful. His way of reading people was almost as good as mine.

That's not quite true, though, is it? His powers of perception were as good as mine *used to be*. My skills, however, had apparently been bitten by a radioactive spider.

Either way, he was sensing something, noticing, maybe, that I was holding something back. I decided on distraction because he would see through denial. "I was thinking it's no wonder she wants the chief's job."

He shrugged.

"And I was thinking that you *don't* want it. And you wouldn't be happy in it. And that if you were anybody else, I'd have been telling you to follow your heart. To do what you really *want* to do and not what you're being told you should. But instead, I'm the one telling you what I think you should do, and I feel bad about that."

"So…?"

I shrugged. "Do what's gonna make you happy."

He seemed to be waiting for me to say something more, but I didn't know what, so I let it go at that. After a minute he nodded and returned to watching the boys.

"Will she be safe?" I asked.

"Who? Vanessa?"

"Yeah. How's this gonna go down, Mason? I'm nervous as hell, not knowing."

He frowned like he was surprised I wanted this level of detail, but then he said, "She'll be safe. We're outfitting her to look a little younger."

I nodded. "Jeans, a T-shirt, cross trainers or army boots instead of anything remotely presentable."

He blinked at me. "Where are you getting that?"

"Nieces, remember?"

"Oh. Well, not exactly. She's gotta look young, but hooker young."

"Hooker young," I repeated, trying to visualize what that meant so I could costume myself appropriately when I took Cantone's place. "So you're just gonna... What? Drop her off on the corner and let her stand there all alone?"

"She won't be all alone. We'll be parked nearby. And we'll follow when they pick her up."

"So she'll be...wearing a wire?" I had no idea if that was actually the correct term for it, or whether all the cop shows had it wrong.

"No, they might find a wire, and that could get her dead. But she is gonna plant a GPS on the vehicle as backup."

I nodded. "How does she do that? Plant a GPS?"

"It's magnetized. All she's gotta do is slap it onto the vehicle someplace it won't be seen right away."

"Right. As they grab her."

"Or right before. They don't know that she knows she's about to be abducted. She's gonna lean over any cars that stop and proposition 'em like any hard-working street girl would do."

"What if the guy's a real john and not the kidnapper?"

"She pretends to change her mind or gets a phone call or something, and backs out of the deal. If he lets her walk away, he's a regular perv looking to get his rocks off. If he *grabs* her, he's our boy."

"Or girl," I said. "That nurse... She was a woman."

He looked at me sharply. "That couldn't really be verified from the footage. It was grainy, out of focus. Could've been a guy in drag."

"If it had been a guy in drag, I think I'd have picked up on that. It's unusual enough that it would've tripped my triggers."

"But it didn't."

"No. So when he grabs her? Then what? You just let him?"

"Well, yeah. We're close. We follow. But yeah, we have to let him take her to wherever they're going so we can—" He stopped there, tipped his head a little bit. "You're awfully interested in all this."

"Well, of course I am." I lowered my eyes, using my milk shake as an excuse. After a long pull, I said, "I'm an official police consultant. It's my case."

That made him smile, just as I'd intended. He wanted me to get excited about sleuthing. Or consulting. Or whatever it was I was doing. It was his passion, after all, solving crimes, protecting the innocent, tracking down the guilty. Rescuing damsels.

But it wasn't mine.

And I wasn't warming to it as I had led him to believe just now. In fact, the more I worked around crime and death and darkness, the better I liked making my living writing happy-happy, joy-joy books from the peaceful, safe haven of my own home.

Several hours later I was knocking at Vanessa Cantone's hotel room door with two cups of Dunkin' in a tray with a bag in between them. The DD approach was kind of becoming my all-purpose solution to any problem. I was supposed to be with the kids. But I'd pawned Josh, Jeremy and Myrtle off on my sister, Sandra. Misty had been delighted by the excuse to hang with Jeremy again so soon, and Sandra didn't mind too much. She liked Jere. Had even told me she wished *he* had a twin, because the boys Christy had been bringing home lately were trouble with a capital *T*.

When Cantone opened her door and peeked out at me, she lifted her brows, looked past me—for Mason, I knew—and then at me again. "What are you up to, de Luca?"

"Peace offering?"

"I didn't know we were at war."

"Even better. And since you liked the coffee so much, I brought you a pound." I held up the bag. "And a couple of doughnuts for good measure."

She pursed her lips, and I knew that she knew better, but she opened the door anyway. I walked in, looked around. No sign of anyone but her. That was gonna make this a whole lot easier. I set the coffee on the table in the corner of her hotel room. She'd made up her bed. There was an empty Walmart bag on it, with price tags and stickers on top of it and the clothes that went with them laid out nearby. A pair of skinny jeans, capri length. A super low-cut green cami, a push-up bra and a torn-up T-shirt that was either designed that way or bought secondhand from an extra in a zombie flick. I was betting on the latter. There was also a framed photo on the nightstand. A woman who wasn't Vanessa, pretty and blonde and very pregnant, and standing beside her, the little girl I'd heard on the phone. I knew it without asking. Lilly.

"She looks just like I thought," I said. "Is that your sister?"

"That's my partner."

I sent her a surprised look before I could cover it, and she muttered, "Some psychic."

"You got that right." I looked at the photo again and refrained from asking, "You're having another baby?" because I didn't want to hear "No, she swallowed a hot air balloon."

Then I started to laugh and shook my head. "Damn," I told her. "I was afraid you were gonna try to get into Mason's pants. 'Some psychic' is right."

"I read somewhere that negative, petty emotions block a person's natural gifts," she said, grinning now, relaxing a little.

"That sounds like something I would say," I told her, wiping my eyes.

"You did. I've been reading you on my phone. Trying to figure you out."

"Welcome to the club." I picked up my cup, held it up to her. She picked up hers, tapped it against the rim of mine.

"Did you come to try to warn me not to go tonight?"

"Would it do any good?"

"No."

"Then I'm not gonna try. But I figured I could still tell you anything I've seen that might help."

"Seen? You mean…?" She tapped her forehead with a short, clean nail. "Seen?"

I nodded. "There are three girls. Stephanie and Lexus Carmichael and one I'm pretty sure is Sissy Dunham.

I looked at the photos of all the missing girls, and she looks most like the one I...*saw*." I had snapped pics of the file photos of Lexus and Sissy with my phone, and I showed them to her even though I knew she'd seen them before. Hell, I needed some kind of legitimate excuse to be here. "And there are two men. One just lurks out of sight, but I know he's there. I feel him. That's probably Jake Kravitz. And then there's the one the girls call the Asshole, who seems to be doing most of the hands-on work from behind a ski mask. He's white. Average build. You know, not lean and toned, but not fat, either. Five-ten or so. Always has a gun on him, and he's real careful not to give the girls access to it. He doesn't get too close to them."

She was with me, intense and interested. She sipped her coffee and sat down on the bed opposite me. "This is good intel, if it's accurate."

"And harmless if it's not."

She reached for a little notepad by the phone, but I didn't want her hands occupied, so I was ready for that. I tugged a folded piece of paper from my pocket, showed her, but didn't give it to her. "I wrote it all down for you."

She set her pen back down. "You get anything about where they are?"

"It's underground. But not a cellar or basement. There's no house over it. It's kind of...round. I know that sounds unlikely, but..." I shrugged. "It's in my note there." Then I drank my coffee. Subliminally triggering her to drink hers. Half-gone. It would be enough.

"That's all I've got."

"If any of this pans out, I'll pass out from shock, de Luca."

She was going to pass out, all right. But not from shock. "Well, you know, some of it probably will and some won't. It's hit-and-miss with this stuff."

She sighed, looked at her watch. "I gotta finish getting ready for this thing. I need to leave in..."

"About an hour. You want to ride over there together?"

She looked surprised that I had asked. "Sure. I've gotta hit the shower, though." She slugged down most of the remaining coffee in a single gulp.

"Go ahead. I'll wait in the lobby." I got up to go.

"You can wait here if you want." She opened the bathroom door and looked back at me, like she was more curious than before about what the hell I was doing here. Then she seemed to change her mind, went into the bathroom and closed the door.

"Some FBI agent," I muttered.

As soon as I heard the water turn on, I went through the clothes she'd been wearing earlier in the day. I found her rental car key in her pocket and threw it into my purse. I didn't think she'd make it even as far as her hotel room door with the amount of Ativan I'd put in her coffee, but better safe than sorry. Besides, if Mason saw my car pulling up when I was supposed to be home with the boys, he'd be on to me.

The pills had been Amy's, prescribed right after her abduction last Thanksgiving to help with the post-traumatic stress. She'd brought them with her to house-sit for me in February, and then she'd left them in my medicine cabinet. I guess she hadn't needed them again. I'd forgotten all about them until rummaging for something I could use to knock out Cantone, sure I'd find nothing and have to settle for Benadryl or just sabotaging her car. That little brown bottle had appeared like an answer to a prayer.

"Wish and it is granted," I said softly. I'd done a little internet research to figure out how much to use. Risking my life to save hers wouldn't be worth a lot if I killed her in the process. Besides, I only needed her out for an hour or so.

I rummaged through her purse, found the little electronic box she was supposed to attach to the bad guys' vehicle and took her cell phone, too. Just for good measure, I unplugged the landlines and took the cords. She would never know what had happened until it was too late.

Then I changed into the clothes that were laid out on the bed. The jeans were skintight but otherwise comfy. The bra gave me cleavage I never knew I had, and the torn-up T-shirt hung strategically off one shoulder and had what looked like claw marks across the breast area to reveal said cleavage. Subtle. Not.

I used the Walmart bag to carry my own clothes and grabbed one of the doughnuts for the road. I heard the shower turn off, a little movement in the bathroom, and then it got really quiet in there, so I opened the door to take a quick peek.

Cantone was wrapped in a towel, sitting on the floor,

sound asleep. I took pity and shoved a pillow between her head and the wall, and draped a blanket over her.

On my way out of the room, I hung the Do Not Disturb sign on her door.

About thirty minutes later I arrived. I'd driven Agent Cantone's rental car. My brown hair was pulled around to one side, and my face was hidden beneath the low brim of a funky painter's cap with a sequined peace sign on the front. I stayed out of the light, and pretended to study my fingernails as I waited for kidnappers to come and abduct me.

And I was shaking like a stray dog in a thunderstorm. How the hell had I reached the conclusion that this was the only solution? I didn't fucking know. I knew that Vanessa Cantone's little girl needed her mommy. Both of her mommies. Not to mention they had a baby on the way. And I'd seen Vanessa die. I'd seen it. I was never wrong.

Well, almost never. And not about things like that.

I'd made the right call. I'd seen what I'd seen for a reason, and here it was, handed to me on a silver platter. A reason. So that I could save the life of Vanessa Cantone. Mother and, who the hell knew, maybe soon-to-be Binghamton chief of police. And I wasn't risking *my* life, because I hadn't seen *me* getting killed in this thing.

Then again, I hadn't seen me *not* getting killed, either. The way I figured it, you couldn't ask for things, demand things, have them handed to you and then refuse to take them. Could you? I'd asked for there to be a reason for this. I'd asked to understand *why me?* And here were my answers, being handed to me.

Mason was inside the van with Rosie and Chief Sub, watching the GPS monitor, when Vanessa's car pulled over a block away.

"Here she is," Rosie said. "And here she comes."

Vanessa's car door opened and she got out, locked it and then started walking up the sidewalk. She didn't wobble in the heels at all the way he'd expected her to.

After five steps he got a real good notion why.

"That's not Cantone," he said.

The other two men looked at him. He watched her move, the sway of her hips, the length of her stride, the swing of her arms, the bounce of her hair. He knew them all. Intimately. "That's Rachel."

"What?" The chief was looking at him like he was crazy. "Rosie, call Cantone."

Mason started to get up, but Chief Sub clapped him on the shoulder. "Just wait. Rosie?"

"It's ringing." He held out the phone he'd used to dial Cantone's number and hit the speaker button.

Mason watched the woman he knew better than any other stop walking and fumble inside the little purse on the long chain. She brought the phone to her ear. "Yeah?"

Mason snatched the phone from Rosie and yelled into it, "Rachel, what the hell are you doing?"

"I'll explain later. Someone's coming." She clicked off and headed up the road toward the corner where Car-lotta was supposed to have set up shop. A pair of headlights caught her, and a van slowed down and veered toward her.

Mason saw Rachel tapping on Vanessa's smartphone. Then she apparently finished and shoved it down the front of her shirt just as the van came to a stop.

She walked right up to the rolled-down window, smiling, but wisely staying in the shadows. She was a hottie, but she wasn't gonna pass for barely eighteen on close inspection. Her hand was inside the purse, and when she pulled it out, he was sure she had the GPS.

"I can't let this happen," he said. "I gotta stop this. She doesn't know what the hell she's doing." He was reaching for the door as he spoke, but then the chief said, "Too late," and he looked.

The van's side door slid open. A guy jumped out and grabbed her, hurled her inside. The GPS went sailing out of her hand and hit the sidewalk, pieces flying everywhere as the van lurched into motion. The door was slammed shut, and then they sped around a corner.

"No. Dammit, no!" Mason shouted.

Rosie dove into the front seat. He was too big to be graceful, but he was damn fast. "Get out your keys, bro, I'll drop you at your car. It'll move way faster than this thing."

Mason got out his keys while the chief shouted into the radio. "I want triangulation on cell phones belonging to Rachel de Luca and Special Agent Vanessa Cantone. If either of them has location tracking turned on I want remote access, and I want Cantone's supervisor on my phone twenty minutes ago. Got it?"

Rosie hit the brakes, and Mason had the side door

open and was jumping out before the police van even came to a stop. The chief closed the door from inside, and Rosie stomped on the gas.

Mason slid behind the wheel of the Beast, twisted the key and put the car into gear, very glad that he had installed a supercharger.

I'd blown it. Oh, hell and damnation, I'd blown it. The GPS thingie had gone flying, and I'd heard it smash into a zillion pieces on the sidewalk when the jerk had yanked me into the van. I buried my face in my hands, pretending to be terrified and crying, cringing down into a corner on the floor. Keeping my face hidden was the top part of my plan. Okay, it was, as of right now, the *only* part of my plan. If one of these guys was Jake Kravitz, then he would recognize me. End of story. I needed them to lead the good guys to those captive girls before that happened.

I knew I'd been in sight of the cops when I'd been taken, and I knew Mason and the guys were following us. Or trying to. I didn't know how successful they'd be now that the GPS was busted to bits.

"Shoot, this one's barely any trouble at all," said the guy who'd grabbed me.

The driver didn't speak, but I figured I'd better do something before they caught on that this was going down way too easily. So I lunged for the side door.

"Whoa, whoa, spoke too soon!" the guy with me said, grabbing me by the hair and hurling me back. My head cracked against the side of the van and I yelped. That part wasn't fake.

Then he was kneeling across the backs of my thighs, jerking my arms behind my back and tying my wrists real tight. So tight it hurt. Then he flipped me over. My hair fell across my face, and I left it that way.

He grabbed my purse off the floor where I'd dropped it and unzipped it while I watched him from behind my hair. He took out everything I'd put in there. All the props. Dummy wallet with nothing but cash, the shit-ton of makeup, my phone.

Shit, my phone. I'd meant to leave it in the car, but I'd been so damn nervous that I'd forgotten it. And if they started going through it, they'd know I wasn't Carlotta Bennett, barely eighteen and a part-time hooker.

But I still had Vanessa's phone stuffed down the front of my blouse. I'd tucked it up underneath my right boob, and now I thanked my stars I was well-endowed enough to pull that off.

My kidnapper didn't even bother looking at my phone. He opened a window and tossed it out. I yelped again, and it wasn't fake that time, either. My fucking phone!

Then he felt me up and down, both sides, both legs, even grabbed my crotch through the jeans. Up my front, giving me a breast exam for free on the way. He didn't feel the phone crammed between my boob and the bra's brutal underwire. And he didn't check underneath, just down the front, then down my back. Big smack to my ass.

"Now you just lay there and be quiet, you understand me?"

I nodded, thinking, *The Asshole, I presume?*

Then he sat down. I stayed where I was on the floor, but I scooched up a little, resting my back against the far side of the van, my head hanging down but my eyes angled up, trying to see where we were going. I caught a couple of street signs and committed them to memory, wondering as I did why they didn't care that I was looking out the window. Then suddenly we turned so sharply I almost fell over. The van pulled into a garage with an empty car and a door on each end, and skidded to a sharp stop that slammed my head against the seat in front of me. The driver shut off the engine and the lights. The garage door closed behind us in slow motion while I watched, praying to see the headlights of the cops who were supposed to be following us.

The Asshole tied my feet together and wrapped a blindfold around my face from behind. Apparently what I'd seen up to now wouldn't help me or they would've done it before now. "You start yelling, I'll duct tape your mouth. Got it?"

I nodded, glad he was hiding my obviously not-eighteen-year-old face for me. I almost screamed so he'd add that promised tape to my mouth, because then everything but my nose would've been hidden. But I didn't quite have the courage to do it.

Then he gripped my upper arm and started dragging me. I damn near fell out of the van when he pulled me through the door, badly banging one knee on the way down. He jerked me upright and forward, and I stumbled and cursed at myself inwardly. After twenty years blind, you'd think I could manage being yanked around in a blindfold without inflicting this much damage.

This didn't feel like an act. I didn't feel like bait in a trap or an amateur sleuth catching a killer. I felt like a victim. I felt like I was being kidnapped and roughed up and terrorized.

Because I was.

Then I was shoved into the back of a car.

"There, they drove right on by, just like we planned. Let's go," said the one doing all the talking.

I heard the hum of a second garage door, this one in front, and we drove out, turned right and sped away, leaving Mason and the rest of the cavalry chasing ghosts on the wrong road.

15

Mason pounded the steering wheel in frustration and peered through the windshield until his eyes watered, but it was no use. He'd lost them.

He'd lost *her*.

His cell phone rang, and he picked it up without looking first. "Yeah?"

"Brown?"

He frowned at the phone, pausing at an intersection before pulling a U-turn and going slowly back the way they'd come. "Cantone?"

"Yesh."

"Where the hell are you, and why do you sound drunk?"

"Your girlfriend spiked my coffee. I figured it out just before I passed out, managed to hack up what wasn't in my bloodstream yet. She took my keys 'n' phone."

He frowned. "Where are you calling from?"

"Front desk. Why did she—"

"She found out you had a kid."

She sighed. "She had a vision. 'Bout me. Somethin'

bad. Tried to warn me." She paused. Then she said, "She took my clothes. She's gonna try to take my place."

"She already did. They got her."

"Ah, hell. You following?"

"Lost 'em. She dropped the GPS, and they tossed her phone a block from where they grabbed her."

"She has my phone, Mason. If you haven't found it, if they didn't toss it with hers, then—"

"Then maybe they didn't find it. We know and we're on it. You okay?"

"Yeah. Been in worse shape than this 'n' called it fun. Go find her. I'll get some coffee 'n' be there ASAP."

"Will do." He disconnected, scanning the buildings as he passed. They had to have pulled in somewhere. They couldn't have gotten that far ahead of him that quickly. They'd been out of sight, around a bend…that bend, right there. And just this side of it there was a garage attached to an empty storefront. He killed the headlights and pulled over. Then he got out, flashlight in one hand, gun in the other, and ran over to check.

Flashlight still off, he looked through the glass quickly, then ducked below it again. He'd glimpsed the big boxy shape of what he thought might be the van. And darkness. No movement.

He got up and looked inside again, this time using the flashlight against the glass to get a better look. The van was there, and beside it was an empty space big enough to have held a second vehicle, and another garage door on the front wall.

He grabbed his phone and hit the chief's number as he raced back to his car.

"Mason?"

"Look for Mike's Garage," he said, looking at the building and giving them the address. "They ditched the van, switched vehicles."

He reached his car and dove behind the wheel, cranked the engine and slammed it into gear before he'd closed the door. He shot around the block and up the alley to the other side of the garage and stopped again, taking his light and his gun to examine the pavement from the overhead door to the road.

Sure as shit, someone had burned rubber as they'd turned right out of the garage. He got back into the car and drove. When he saw headlights his pulse jumped like a runner at the pistol shot. Hand on his gun, he was ready to ram the bastard right off the road if that was what it took.

Almost immediately he recognized the familiar shape of the police van.

He slammed the Beast into Park and got out, walked up to the driver's side. "They must have turned off. The van's in a garage a mile back. We need to call it in. Any hits on Cantone's phone?"

"Not yet, but if it's on, we'll find her," Chief Sub said. "We'll get a team on that van…the garage. We'll find something."

Mason nodded. "Keep me posted."

"Mason, they could have taken any of six streets back that way."

"Or four my way," Mason said. "I'm gonna keep looking."

"Why?" Chief Sub asked. "You have no idea yet which way they—"

"Because that's what Rachel would do." He paused, then nodded firmly. "And you know what? She'd find me, too."

I was terrified. I hadn't expected to be. After all, this was part of my plan, right? Cops did this sort of thing all the time. I wasn't *really* a kidnap victim. I was just pretending to be. It was all an act.

Yeah, except that was bull. That was the sort of fucked-up thought process that got me into this mess to begin with. I'd dropped the tracking device while trying to slap it onto the side of the van—where it surely would've been seen anyway. I hadn't expected it to happen so fast. I'd expected to have more time, to slide the thing underneath the wheel well or something.

Dammit.

I had two things going for me. Cantone's cell was still snugly underneath my boob, inside my bra. It was uncomfortable as all hell, and I wouldn't have taken a cool million for it. As soon as I was alone for long enough, I was going to get it out and use it to call for help.

And I had Mason on my trail. Yeah, I'd fucked up the means he'd been planning to use to follow me, but I knew that man. He was good. He never quit. And he was pretty damn fond of me for some reason. I'd have to ask him why sometime. I hoped I got the chance.

I cringed in the corner of the backseat, hunched up and pretend-crying into my forearms so they wouldn't see my crow's-feet and catch on to the fact that I was far from eighteen. But I managed to push the blindfold down enough that I could see a little, and I peered out as often as I could, getting a clear look at the driver when he pulled off his mask.

It was Jake. The ex-boyfriend I'd wanted to trust. The one who'd reminded me of my brother. I think right up until I saw him with my own eyes I'd been hoping it wouldn't be him. That Mason had been wrong about him and I'd been right. Like with Rodney Carr.

And that was the first time I got really freaking scared that he would look at my face and know me. Up until that moment it had been an abstract possibility that probably wouldn't happen.

But when he took off his mask, when I saw his face and knew in just that much of a glance that it was him, I realized he could recognize me just as easily. For crying out loud, if he looked me in the face he'd know this was a sting and would never take me to the girls. And oh, yeah, he'd probably put a bullet in my head, too, and toss me into the nearest ditch.

Okay okay okay, just stay calm. Look around.

The other guy was in the passenger seat up front. Ski mask still in place. Smarter than good ol' Jake up there.

Jake. That bastard was nothing like my brother. Tommy wouldn't have hurt a fucking fly.

Jake looked up into the rearview mirror, and I lowered my head just in time. I gave him a few shuddering shoulders and loud sobs for good measure, then dared to check again. He was looking straight ahead, driving.

"This has dragged on way too long," he said. "I haven't even been paid yet."

The one on the right didn't say anything, and Jake heaved a sigh. "No more till I get paid. I mean it." Then he took a sharp turn off the main road, and I rocked up against the door so hard I hit my head again.

The car jerked to a stop, and the guy in the passenger side reached back and pressed a damp rag against my face. I forgot about hiding from them and thrashed hard, but only about three times.

I was going, going... The car stopped, the door opened, and the interior light came on, so I tucked my face into my hair... Gone.

"We've lost the signal, Mason."

Mason was behind the wheel of the Beast in the middle of fucking nowhere. Up to now he'd been driving according to the chief's instructions, relayed from the tech boys who had finally homed in on Cantone's cell phone.

He was in the right area, according to that signal... until it had vanished just now.

"What do you mean, you lost the signal?"

"They must have driven out of range. Or hit a tunnel or some interference."

He pulled the car to the side of the road, shut off the headlights and looked around him. "No tunnel. And I can't imagine interference out here. There's just... nothing." Rolling hills, some cattle, a lot of pines. A farm here and there. No towns, nothing that looked like a village in the past fifteen minutes, and roads getting steadily less roadlike. Broken pavement, then oil and stone, now dirt.

He didn't even know where the hell he was.

He pounded the steering wheel and hung up the phone. Then he got out of the car and stared at the distant horizon like it might hold an answer. There were a zillion stars, no moon. The sky tonight would've had Rachel oohing and ahhing like a little kid seeing her first fireworks display.

If anything happened to her...

Wow. He hadn't realized just how much he cared until it had hit him in the gut just now.

"Be okay, Rache. Dammit, be okay."

"Hey, c'mon. Wake up."

There was loud music, but the voice came from close to my ear. There were hands on my face, patting me, hands on my shoulders, shaking me. My eyes flew open and I sat up fast, sucking in a breath. The three girls jumped away from me, and I looked from one to the other, recognizing them. "Holy shit, you're still alive!" I clapped a hand over my mouth as soon as I said it, darting a look at the room around me, frowning.

"It's okay, they're not here. Just talk low in case they're listening." The girl kneeling beside me was Stephanie Mattheson, in the flesh. She wasn't looking directly at me, but her blue eyes, though blank and sightless, were beautiful.

"You ain't no foster child," said another girl.

"Lexus," I said, looking at the platinum blonde with the nose ring. Then I shifted to the frightened-looking caramel-skinned beauty, who seemed way less than eighteen. "And you're Sissy, right?"

"How do you know?"

I lowered my voice even further. "I'm working with the cops."

"Some cop," Lexus drawled with a roll of her eyes. "Girl, they knocked you out and tossed you in here like a dead rat they found under the sink. You the cop they sent to save us?" She talked like a rapper, and I got that it made her feel tough. It puffed her up, like a little animal trying to look bigger when facing a predator.

"I didn't say I was a cop. I said I'm working with them. My name's Rachel de Luca. I'm—"

"You're shitting me," Stephanie said. "Rachel de Luca?"

"Yeah."

"So what are you gonna do, positive-think us out of this hole in the ground?"

"Hole in the—" I frowned, spotting the odd door in the ceiling about fifteen, maybe twenty feet above us. No ladder, no stairs, no way to get to it. And it was the only opening in the entire place. Not another door or window, except for the open one through which I could see a tiny bathroom. The room was round and underground, just like in my vision. I shook my head. "It doesn't matter. I'm here to help."

"How?" Lexus asked. "How you gonna help us?"

I smiled. "With this." I reached up under my blouse, into my bra and pulled out the very warm cell phone. Immediately I dialed Mason's number. Then I waited.

And then I waited some more.

Then I looked at the screen.

"Girl, we underground," Lexus said.

"Shit." I got up, looked around the room. "Okay, we have to get up high. Close to the door."

"You think they didn't lock it?" Stephanie asked.

"Even if they did, we might get a signal if we get close enough."

"There's no way."

"There *is* a way." I put my hands on her shoulders, softened my voice. "There's always a way, Stephanie. There's *always* a way. There's a way when you can see. There's a way when you can't. And there's a way out of this. Trust me."

She shook her head hard. "If they catch us, they'll kill one of us. We tried to fight our way out of here and it got Venora killed."

"I know. We found her."

Stephanie's eyes welled up. She closed her eyes to block the tears.

"She'd scratched your names into her skin. That was a huge help in us finding you."

Sissy and Lexus looked at each other.

"She knew she was gonna die," Stephanie said softly. "She said she dreamed it right before they took her. It's my fault. It's my fault."

"Stephanie, it's not your fault," I began.

"Don't even try to tell me she attracted it somehow. Don't do it, 'cause there's no way—"

I took a deep breath, because this was an argument hurled at me by my critics. If you create your own reality, why do people die? Why do they get sick? Why do they experience poverty or pain?

I knew this wasn't the time or place for a discourse on the nature of reality, but I knew, too, that I had to get her on my side. I had to give her reason to believe, in herself and in me.

"Venora had a bad dream," I said. "She believed it was going to come true, believed it so much that she made preparations for it to come true. And then it did." I rubbed my sore head, and saw zip ties on the floor, realized the girls must have cut me loose. "Those are the facts. So either she foresaw it because it was going to happen, or it happened because she foresaw it. We're never gonna know which or what it all means, Stephanie, so there's no point arguing about it. But either way, she did a wonderful thing on her way out and maybe saved your lives in the process. Don't you think you can find some meaning in that?"

Lexus blinked. "Meaning?"

"Like that her time was up, but yours wasn't," I said. "Like that her life is over, but yours is supposed to go on. Like that maybe whatever you were born to do, you haven't done yet."

"But how do you know Venora had done whatever *she* was born to do?" Sissy asked.

"'Cause if she hadn't, she'd still be here," I said, and I found that I meant it. "Maybe this was it. Maybe being the clue that led us to you was her whole thing."

"It's bullshit. Don't listen to her," Stephanie said.

I looked at the girl, and realized that she didn't know her father was dead, or that her ex-boyfriend was one of her kidnappers. And I didn't really think it would do her any good to know either of those things right now, but I felt guilty keeping the truth from her all the same.

"We've gotta try to get out of here," I said, and I got to my feet, pacing around the place and finally stopping beside the sofa, which was about five feet long. Lexus and Sissy were sitting on it. I said, "Get up."

The girls looked at me curiously, but they got up without a word. Then I squatted and put my hands under the edge of the sofa, and started lifting it. I grunted, but Sissy jumped up to help, and then Lexus did, too. In a second or two the sofa was standing—none-too-steadily—on end. I braced it with one hand.

"Great. Push that coffee table over here, Stephanie."

"Uh, yeah, I'm kind of blind."

"Will you stop changing the subject and push the fucking coffee table over here?"

She frowned, but I watched her walk to that coffee table as easily as if she had 20/20 vision. She bent and shoved it, and stopped with a quarter inch between the table and the couch. She knew she wasn't helpless. She might not have known it before all this, though, I thought. In fact, from what I'd heard about her from her parents and her life coach, I was sure she hadn't. But she knew what she was capable of now.

"Okay, I need two of you to hold the couch up. Stephanie—"

"Stevie," she corrected me. "I go by Stevie."

"Stevie and Sissy, hold the couch upright, one of you on each side. Lexus, we're climbing up on top. Ready?"

"You are crazy, woman."

"I'm not crazy. I'm smart. I wasn't, but then I spent twenty years being blind, and that was an education." I shoved the phone down the front of my shirt, kicked off my shoes and climbed up onto the coffee table. "I've gotta jump a little. You guys got that sofa?"

"We've got it," Stevie said. "Go on."

I jumped, grabbing the arm of the sofa and pulling myself up onto it. Then I held on for dear life while Lexus did the same. I helped pull her up. Then I stood up, balancing like I was on a damned surfboard. Pulling Vanessa Cantone's cell phone out of my bra, I typed a text to Mason.

"C'mon, Lexus. Stand up."

She did, but she was wobbling big-time. "You've gotta boost me up. I've gotta get as high as I can to send this."

"You need to get as high as you can and try the door. Not that it matters, 'cause the minute you climb up on me, I'm gonna fall over."

"Lexus," Stevie called. "Stand with your legs wide apart and your knees slightly bent."

Lexus frowned, but she set her feet wider, as wide as the sofa would allow, holding her hands palms-down as she wobbled.

"Are you bending your knees?" Stevie asked.

"Yeah," Lexus said, and bent her knees.

"Put your hands on your hips. You know, like Superman."

Lexus did.

"Rachel, put your knees between her hands and hips to start with."

"Where the hell did you learn this, Stevie?" I asked. "Are you some kind of ninja?"

"Ex-cheerleader. Do it."

I gripped the younger but larger girl's shoulders and hopped up, shoving my knees into the triangles made by her arms on either side. We wobbled, then steadied.

I let go with one hand, plucked the phone from my bra and held it up, watching for a signal to show up. Nothing.

"I've got to get higher."

"Pull your knee out on one side and put your foot there instead, and then push yourself upright," Stevie called.

I did that, and it was hard, but I was standing a little higher.

"Need more?" she asked.

"Yeah," I said.

"Stand on her shoulders, then. Lexus, grab her ass to help boost her up there, and once she's up, wrap your arms behind her thighs to hold her."

"I *know* you didn't just tell me to grab another woman's ass, Stevie."

"Our lives depend on it."

Lexus was pissed, but I felt her give in and started climbing onto her shoulders. She put her arms behind me, bracing them on the backs of my thighs, not my ass, as I fought to straighten up to my full height. My knees were still partly bent when my palms made contact with the wooden trapdoor over my head. I gave it a shove, and it lifted an inch, then stopped. I heard a chain and knew it wasn't going any farther. Still, I grabbed the phone, held it so it was sticking out through the narrow opening as far as I could poke it without letting go. Bracing my other hand on the door above me, I hit the send key.

"Shit!" Lexus tipped sideways, and my sock feet slid off her shoulders. I bounced off the sofa and went crashing to the floor before I knew what had happened. I hit hard, and then the couch came down like a felled redwood. Instinctively, I rolled onto one side and curled up, arms shielding my face. Lexus hit the floor on my left, the sofa on my right. They both missed me, thank God.

"Are you okay?"

"Oh, my God, are you okay?"

Stevie and Sissy were speaking at once.

I lowered my arms, blinking and surprised that I was still alive. "Yeah, I'm good. I'm good, nothing broken. Except maybe that phone." I looked around the floor but didn't see it. "You okay, Lexus?"

"Cracked my damn head." She sat up, rubbing her head as she did. "Yeah, I'm a'right."

"Did you send the message?" Stevie asked.

"I think so. Check the phone. Where the hell did it—"

"Sheee-it," Lexus said softly, pointing upward. We all looked.... Well, all but Stevie. The phone was sticking out from underneath the door, which had fallen closed and trapped it there.

"What? What is it?" Stevie asked.

"The phone's stuck under the trapdoor," I said softly. I knew how bad it was not to know what was going on because you couldn't see and having people take their damn time about filling you in.

"They're gonna know. When they come back here, they're gonna know," Stevie said. "They're gonna shoot one of us."

"Yeah, well, if they get a good look at my face, they're gonna shoot me anyway, and the three of you are worth money to them, so you're probably safe. From that, anyway."

"Money," Sissy said. "What are they going to do with us?"

"Sell you," I said. "To some pervert who wants a real live sex slave chained up in his basement dungeon, near as we've been able to figure."

Sissy's eyes went big as saucers. Lexus shook her head, looking more pissed off than before and limping pretty badly to a spot to sit down. No use trying to get the phone again. I'd never get Sissy to dare stand on my shoulders, and she was too small for me to stand on hers. And while I hated to admit it, being blind limited Stevie from performing acrobatics on the upturned end of a sofa.

"I figured that when they had us dress up in that fucking lacy shit for pictures," Lexus said.

I got up, and we started righting the furniture, which was none the worse for wear. "Stevie, they've been forcing your father to give them the names of girls who've aged out of foster care and are on their own. Girls they thought no one would miss."

She was quiet for a moment, then asked, "Something's happened to him, hasn't it?"

I hadn't wanted to tell her that. "Yeah. He had a stroke. He…didn't make it. How did you know?"

"I heard them talking. Saying something about needing a new informant." She lowered her head slowly, and I saw her tears. "He was an asshole. But he was still my father."

"I'm sorry. For what it's worth, he was about to come clean. Tell us everything. And he only did what he did because he was being blackmailed."

She nodded. "It was that drunk-driving thing, that man he killed and never took the blame for. Wasn't it?"

"You knew about that?"

She nodded. "I heard him and Mom arguing about it. I couldn't believe he wouldn't turn himself in. When another drunk driver blinded me, it was like fucking divine retribution or something." She lowered her head to hide her tears.

I took a deep breath. I was about to destroy this poor kid's world. "Did you tell Jake about that, Stevie?"

"Jake?" she asked. "Jake? God, Rachel, are you telling me Jake is involved in this?"

"He was one of the guys who kidnapped me and brought me here," I told her. "I'm really sorry."

She sank onto the newly righted sofa, put her head down and cried. The news about her ex seemed to hurt her more than the news of her father's death.

There were teams combing the area where the cell phone signal had been lost, but there was no way to be sure the kidnappers hadn't gone much farther. Dogs were on the way. Mason was damn near sick with fear,

searching a wooded area with the chief. Chief Sub, ex-
amining the ground a few yards away, was acting more
like a zealous rookie than a man looking to retire. He
was worried, too.

He liked Rachel. He'd even admitted it to her.

Mason's phone chimed and he picked it up, looked
at the screen. "It's a text. From Rachel!"

He stood perfectly still, almost afraid to move as the
chief came running and read over his shoulder. Circular
underground room w trapdoor top center. Bunker not
basement. 3 girls r ok. Jake was driver. Hasn't seen my
face. Find us b4 he does.

The chief's phone chirped, and he took the call.
Mason wanted to text Rachel back, but he didn't dare.
The sound might give her away. If Jake had found the
phone...

Jake. And Rachel hadn't believed him. Her damn
radar was off for sure where that guy was concerned.

Chief Sub said, "The garage was owned by Ivan
Orloff."

"Jake's former cellmate? The guy I shot when he kidnapped Amy last November?" Mason muttered.

"Yeah. He left it to his sister."

"Sister?"

The chief nodded. "His widowed sister. Whose married name is Loren Markovich."

Mason's head came up. "Stevie's blindness coach?"

"One and the same." He looked at his phone again.
"They've picked up a signal from Cantone's cell phone
again. Wait a sec." He tapped buttons, then held his
phone up, showing Mason the green dot on the map

screen that marked Rachel's location, and the smaller red dot that marked the spot where he was currently standing.

"Hold on, Rachel," he said. "Hold on. I'm coming."

16

"You've come a long way in a few days, haven't you, Stevie?"

The other two girls were engaged in a game of checkers.

Stephanie didn't look at me at all. "How would you know? You didn't even know me before."

"No. But I've talked to your mom and your coach, Loren."

She hissed through her teeth.

"Yeah, I found that a little ridiculous, too. A sighted person teaching a blind person how to be blind. But it is what it is."

She perked up a little. She was curled in the corner of the sofa, a blanket wrapped around her shoulders. "So you didn't have a coach?"

"No. I mean, I had my parents, my sister, Sandra, and brother, Tommy. It was plenty."

"But they couldn't teach you anything about being blind."

"The only thing that can teach you about being blind is being blind, kid." She pressed her lips together in irritation. I should have left off the "kid" part. It offended her. "There's more to it than not being able to see, though. Have you noticed that yet?"

She blinked twice. I could tell by the subtle shift in her attitude that she had. "I hear ten times better than those two."

"Yeah. And you feel things in front of you before you walk into them, so long as you're paying attention. It's like you can sort of feel the vibrations bouncing off them as you get closer."

"Ye-e-a-ah." She drew out the word, crinkled her nose. "Yeah, I *can*. Sort of."

"There's no limit to how far your other senses can grow, you know. They keep trying to make me believe I'm psychic because I pick up on so many things."

"They? Like who?"

"Like the cops. One cop in particular. And my assistant, Amy, who was kidnapped by these jerks last Thanksgiving when they mistook her for Venora."

"Really?"

"Yeah. We got her back, though." I shook my head. "Maybe I do have something extra. I knew which way to drive when we were looking for Amy. I also knew there was more to it, that it wasn't an isolated incident. And the minute I walked that sidewalk where they took you, I knew it was related to what happened to Amy."

She blinked a few times, then lifted her head to look in my direction. That showed a lot of trust. You don't like showing people your eyes when you're blind. I didn't, anyway.

"Maybe you *do* have ESP."

"I've decided to call it NFP."

"NFP?"

"Yeah, for Not Fucking Psychic."

She laughed, and it was real, right from her belly, which made me feel good.

"Maybe I don't dislike you as much as I wanted to," she said.

"Ditto." I was on the other end of the sofa from her. "Why'd you want to dislike me?"

"Your books. My mother's been trying to force-feed them to me. All that positive bullshit."

"Yeah, I know. My mother force-fed me on the same kind of thing. That's why I wound up writing them. I figured if someone was gonna get paid for that crap, it might as well be me."

Her smile died. "Really?"

"Yeah, really. And then... I don't know, stuff started happening. Stuff that made me think maybe it wasn't all bullshit, after all. I mean, damn, I'm here, right? I'm here, with you. I used to be blind, you're currently blind. I wrote the books, you read them." I frowned. "You *did* read 'em, right?"

"Enough to want to barf."

"Gee, thanks."

"You're welcome."

I took a breath, then went back to my topic. "They took my phone, but I had another one they didn't find. Was that just luck, do you think?"

"Yeah. Bad luck. They're gonna find it as soon as they get back here. How are you going to put a positive spin on this if they shoot you?"

I shrugged. "That'll suck, I admit it. I'm really enjoying my life lately."

"Yeah, I'll bet. How long have you been able to see again?"

"Since last August. But it's not having my eyes back that's making me so…sickeningly happy. This sounds sappy, but it's true. It's the people in my life now. Mason—he's the detective who's gonna get his ass here to save us if he knows what's good for him. His boys, Jeremy and Josh. And Myrtle. Damn, I miss my Myrtle."

"Myrtle?"

"English bulldog."

She smiled. "I'd like to meet her."

"She would fucking love you," I said. "She's blind, too, but she barely seems to notice."

We were quiet for a long moment. Then I slid close to her and said, "The other girls look up to you, you know. You're like their leader in this mess."

"I know. It's weird."

"Not weird at all. You're the most capable, the most mature. You're smart, and you're tough. You didn't lose any of that when you lost your eyesight. You just…lost track of it for a while."

The other girls finished their game and came over to where we were. Lexus poured water from a gallon jug into a plastic tumbler. It was the only refreshment. Fuckers could have thrown down some chips or something.

"I don't want them to shoot you, Rachel," Stevie said.

"Well, then maybe we should think about how to prevent it. You have one advantage against them that can't be overemphasized."

"What's that?" she asked.

"They're not expecting anything from you. Maybe from Lexi and Sissy. Maybe even from me. But not you. They don't see you as a threat."

"You got that right," Lexus said softly. "I hadn't even thought about it before, but the Asshole barely pays any attention to you when he comes down here. He always got his back to you. Watchin' us two like we're gonna try something but never payin' much attention to you."

"That's right. He does." Sissy nodded enthusiastically.

"Last time we tried something, he shot Venora. Right in front of us." Stevie said it softly, and shivered a little.

"I know," I said. "I know. I also know there are other girls missing besides you three."

"There are?" Stevie asked, stunned.

"Yeah. And Venora isn't the only one who's been killed. Another girl was missing almost two years before her captor finally killed her. She was pregnant, too."

Sissy bit her lip. Stevie lowered her head. "How many others are missing?" she asked.

"Besides the two dead girls and you three, there are five more that we know of."

"We got to kill these bastards," Lexus said.

"At least you have to ask yourself what you'd rather do. Fight to get free, even though it means risking your lives, or go be someone's sex slave for a year or two until they get tired of you and kill you anyway."

"Do you know for sure they'd kill us?" Sissy said.

"I know for sure they can't just let you go when they use you up. How would they keep you from going to the cops?"

"We know you're right," Stevie said. "We had this discussion just last night. We're dead for sure if we don't fight. If we do, we've at least got a chance." She drew a deep breath, nodded and let it out again. "The only question is how the hell we can fight them. But... but now I think I have an idea."

Mason was with Chief Sub and Rosie, who was still limping and didn't give a shit. The chief had called in reinforcements, so they and a half-dozen officers fanned out, searching the woods and fields. The initial ping had narrowed the phone's location down to within a five-mile radius, and the chief was now tapped into its GPS signal, which was leading them even closer.

Mason had a headset on, leaving his hands free to hold his flashlight and gun, and enabling him to communicate with the chief, who also wore a headset, without shouting and giving away their presence. "I don't know why anyone would build an underground bunker in the woods, Chief. There's gotta be a clearing or—"

"Keep going the way you're going. We're getting closer."

Mason did, but he knew it was an impractical strategy. There had to be a way around the woodlot that would bring him to her faster than this. The limbs of the pines were so dense he could barely see two feet ahead of him. And the underbrush was thick enough that he could step right over top of her and not see her.

He was shaking. And he did not shake on the job. Not ever.

"Mason, wait—we've got something," the chief said.

"What?"

"Cantone's phone. We've activated it remotely. We should be able to hear anything within range of its… Wait, listen."

Mason could hear a car motor, followed by slamming doors. Footsteps growing louder.

"It'll be easier if we drug them first," a man said.

"The buyers will not be impressed by unconscious rag dolls, Jake."

"The buyers will have an easier time getting them home if they're—"

"What they do with them after we deliver them is their problem. Let's just get the girls out here and follow orders."

The footsteps grew even louder, then one of them said, "What the hell is *this?*"

Then silence. The transmission had abruptly ended. Mason swore. "What the fuck just happened?"

"I think they found Cantone's cell. Keep going, Mason, you've got a couple hundred yards and then… Wait, wait, it's coming back online. And it's moving."

"Shit."

"Turn slightly west. You can intercept them when you get to the road if you hurry."

* * *

"They're coming," Stevie said. "Get ready." She came running out of the bathroom, where she'd been listening for the kidnappers near the pipes she'd said carried their voices.

Sissy lay on the floor, facedown, sprawled like she'd fallen there, and Lexus and I knelt near her, shaking her and making a fuss like something was wrong, while Stevie stood a few steps away, looking helpless, which she most definitely was not.

The trapdoor opened and a rope ladder dropped down. Then the Asshole came down, his expression furious. "What the fuck is going on with the cell phone I found up there?"

Lexus shouted at him, "We had a cell phone, you think we'd still be down here?"

"Something's wrong with Sissy," I said, still looking down, my hair curtaining my face. "She had some kind of a fit and fell over, and now she's not—" I leaned closer to her. "She's not breathing!"

"I'm not falling for that." The Asshole held up a gun, waved it at me. "You first, newbie. Get over here."

"She's gonna die!"

"Then we'll get another. Get over here. Climb up the ladder. I'm done screwing around with you girls."

He worked the action of the gun. It scared me, but I didn't give. "I'm not leaving her. She needs help." I rolled her over and tipped her head back, bending close, like I was going to start mouth-to-mouth.

Then I sat up again and positioned my hands over her chest, as if I were about to start compressions.

"Jesus, get off her," the Asshole said, striding toward me. "You two, back up. I mean it."

So I stood and took Lexus by the arm, and we backed right up against the wall so he'd feel nice and safe. And that was when Stevie clocked the back of his head with the leg we'd unscrewed from the coffee table.

He went straight down, and we all hurriedly started searching him. I took his gun and shoved it down the back of my jeans. But I couldn't find the damned cell phone. He didn't have it on him.

"Now what?" Sissy whispered.

"We get out of here." I looked at the dangling rope ladder, the open trapdoor and the dark expanse of star-dotted sky above it.

"What if the other guy is out there waiting?" Sissy asked.

"Then we shoot him," Lexus snapped. "We got the gun. The question is, what if this prick comes to and starts yelling?"

I rolled the Asshole over and pulled his hands behind his back. Then I pulled my bra out of my pocket, where I'd stashed it earlier in preparation for just this moment, and used it to tie his hands behind him.

Three sharp raps had us all freezing in fear. The second guy was peering down, dead silent and well-hidden behind his ski mask. He couldn't see us. He could only see straight down and we were off to one side.

"There's the other one," Sissy said softly.

"Yeah," I said softly. "It's Jake."

"It's Jake?" Stevie asked.

"You can't let on that you know. Okay?"

She nodded, but I saw the tears welling in her eyes. Better she be prepared. I think she'd been hoping I was wrong about him. Well, so had I.

"You guys have to go first," I said, "so he'll be distracted and not notice the gun. Just go up like the Asshole told us, stand there and be docile, keep your heads down, but be alert, be ready. Don't do anything until we're all out of this hole. Okay?"

The three nodded. Stephanie whispered, "Yes, okay."

"Okay. You first, Lexus." I knew that was best. Sissy was too afraid to go first. Lexus grabbed hold of the rope ladder, and even gave a shout back down to the unconscious idiot. "I'm goin', I'm goin'. Stop pointin' that gun at me."

She climbed up the ladder. I glanced up top, saw Jake grab her by one arm and pull her out of sight. I hoped he wasn't going to drug her or tie her up right away.

"Go on, Stevie. Hurry, so he doesn't have time to think about tying her up or anything." I took her hands, guided them to the ladder, and she found the first rung with one foot and started up.

Sissy went next. I pulled my T-shirt down over the gun in back, and went last. When my head emerged from the top, I looked around, trying to quickly see where we stood.

Jake had the girls lined up, on their knees, heads down, a gun in his hand. Another person was getting out of a waiting van, ski mask in place, stripping a long piece from a roll of duct tape while moving behind the girls and using it to tie their hands.

It was a woman.

I reached behind me for the gun, wondering if I had it in me to shoot them both. Just as my hand curled around its grip, Jake turned toward me with his gun aimed and saw my face. His went lax. "You!" he said.

I jerked my gun around fast, knowing he was about to shoot and hoping I could pull the trigger before he did. At the same time Stevie came upright, throwing herself at him just as the gun bucked in my hand so hard that I dropped it.

My bullet hit his shoulder and spun him in an almost full circle, and he hit the ground. The crouching bitch behind Lexi pulled a gun, but Lexus head-butted her hard, and she went down, too. And then I grabbed Stevie by one arm and screamed, "Run!"

The next second we were all heading for the nearby woods.

Mason didn't like it. He let the others go off in pursuit of the moving cell phone ping, but he kept heading in the same direction he'd been heading, straight through the woods toward the clearing the chief had told him was on the other side. Something in his gut told him that was where he would find Rachel. And he'd seen too much since he'd met her to doubt his gut feelings. She might have a little bit more of whatever *it* was than most people did, but he was rapidly coming to the conclusion that everyone had a little bit of *it* in them.

Then he heard a gunshot, and he knew he was right. He ran flat-out, crashing through brush, breaking branches, leaping deadfall and stumps like a freaking athlete, everything in him turning to ice as the image of Rachel with a bullet in her head kept flashing into his brain.

He burst out of the woods to see Rachel and three other women running toward him, two with their hands behind them as if bound. Rachel was holding one of them by the arm. Stephanie Mattheson.

And beyond them he saw a woman, Loren Markovich, pulling off her ski mask and picking herself up off the ground, raising her gun and pointing it right at Rachel's back just as Rachel spotted him and smiled in relief.

He couldn't reach her in time, but he tried, stretching out his arms and pouring on the speed, shouting *"Down!"* as he lifted his gun to take aim. But he knew he couldn't get a shot off in time. There was no way.

And then a gunshot rang through the night and Mason relived the worst horror he'd ever felt in his life. He flashed back to that nightmare moment last year when he'd walked into his apartment just in time to see his brother put a bullet into his own head. This time he saw Rachel arching forward as the bullet ripped into her back, then falling facedown in the thick, tall grass.

And beyond her, Loren Markovich also went down.

What the hell?

Behind the fallen blindness coach, Jake Kravitz rose to his feet, holding his hands over his head and throwing the gun he held away.

The other girls crowded around Rachel.

Mason ignored Jake and raced toward them, unable to see past them to Rachel, moving them carefully aside.

Rache was pushing herself upright in the grass, looking for him, finding him. "You found us. Dammit, you really waited till the last possible fucking minute, didn't you?"

"You're hit. Stay still."

She frowned at him. "I'm not hit."

"You went down. She shot you and you went down."

"You yelled *down* at the top of your fucking lungs, Mace. When someone yells *down* at me like that, I get down."

He helped her to her feet, searching her face, still unclear on what had just happened. "You're okay?"

"I'm okay."

He felt like every muscle in his body wanted to go weak all at once. He wanted to grab her, kiss her, hold her and feel for himself that she wasn't shot or bleeding.

One of the girls, the blonde, was unwrapping the duct tape from the other.

"We're all okay," she said.

He nodded. "All right, get into the woods out of sight and wait there." He handed his phone to Rachel, told her to call the chief, then shifted his attention back to the man who was standing out there with his hands on top of his head. Mason hurried forward across the grass. When he got to Loren lying facedown, clearly shot in the back, he paused to kick the gun away, then bent to check for a pulse but didn't find one. "On your knees, Jake," he called.

Jake dropped to his knees, hands still on his head. Mason walked over and cuffed him quickly. Then he went back to Loren, rolled her over and double-checked.

Yup. Dead as a doornail. That shot hadn't been Loren's, it had been Jake's.

"There's another one down in the hole," Rachel said, her voice coming from close by. He hadn't expected that.

"Dead?"

"I don't think so. Stevie beaned him with a table leg, and I tied him up with my bra."

"Stevie?"

She nodded. "Oh, yeah. She's totally found her girl power again." Then, shaking her head, she looked at Jake, who was sitting on the ground with his legs crossed and his hands cuffed behind him. "Why did you shoot your partner, Jake?" Rachel asked.

"I was never really working for her," he said.

"Yeah, right. Tell it to the judge," Mason said.

"Just not the one you killed."

"I didn't do that. Loren did. And I didn't take Stephanie, either. It was Loren and her fucking family. One of whom, by the way, took off with that cell phone we found to lead you guys away."

"So then why…?"

"I was trying to save Stevie."

Rachel looked at Mason, one brow cocked upward. He said, "Right. You have the right to remain silent—"

"No fucking way. I want to hear this," I said.

But Mason went on, finished Mirandizing the guy, then asked him point-blank if he wanted to give up the right to remain silent.

Jake looked at Rachel, looked at Mason, nodded. "This was my fault, all of it. I ran my mouth in jail about the judge. I hated him for making me do time for the cardinal sin of loving his daughter. I was an idiot, ranting to my cellmate about how the judge had killed someone when he was driving drunk and covered it up. Fucker. I hated him for that as much as for what he did to me. It didn't seem fair, you know. He could kill a guy and walk away. But I was doing time for taking Stevie across state lines."

Mason nodded. "And your cellmate was—"

"Ivan Orloff," he said. "So then I get out of jail and I forget all about it. Then Ivan's brother, Uri, comes to me. Offers me a job. Tells me about this cherry setup with his sister. Says Ivan bought it last November, so they're short a guy. He tells me how they kidnap girls and sell 'em as sex slaves for a cool hundred grand apiece. Tells me how they're using what I told his brother about the judge to blackmail him for info on girls who age out of the foster care system. Girls who don't have families or anyone to go looking for them. Says it's the perfect crime, that no one ever even knows the girls are missing."

"And you said yes," Rachel all but spat.

"No, I didn't say yes! I said no. I was racking my brain to figure out what to do with the information. I mean, I knew I had to tell someone, but Jesus, I was gonna look guilty as hell if I did. My cellmate blackmailing the guy who sent me up the river with info I gave him?"

Mason nodded. He could see where that would look pretty bad.

"Before I could figure out what to do, you guys

showed up at my door asking about Stevie. Shit, I knew damn well you'd never believe I didn't have anything to do with it at that point. My ex-girlfriend, right? And she'd been calling, too, but I didn't answer. I didn't want to get into that mess again, not with a powerful guy like the judge looking to mess up my life." He lowered his head. "But I had to save Stevie. Somehow. And I knew they were the ones who had her. So I called Uri back, told him I'd changed my mind, that I wanted the job. I figured I could save her from the inside."

"You realize one of the girls you helped kidnap and hold hostage was killed, right?"

"I wasn't anywhere near that. I wasn't even working for them yet."

Mason looked at Rachel. "Is he telling the truth?"

"He is. I was right, and you owe me fifty bucks."

"You already took my fifty bucks."

"I was right about Rodney Carr, too."

"We didn't make a bet about Rodney Carr."

She rolled her eyes. "Details." But beneath the banter, there was something else. Mason was just about eating her up with his eyes, and she was doing the same to him. She turned to Jake. "I hope you can prove some of this."

"I hope so, too."

Mason took Jake by the arm and led him toward the headlights that were bounding into the clearing now.

Epilogue

Jake would have a trial, Mason said, but he was pretty sure that with the judge's widow and daughter speaking up for him, he'd wind up with a suspended sentence.

Loren Markovich was dead, and so was her brother, Uri Orloff. He'd had a blood clot in his brain that Stephanie had knocked loose when she'd pasted him with the table leg. Poetic justice, if you asked me.

Their other henchman, a cousin—this was entirely a family business—had been tracked down easy as shit, because the dumb-ass had been driving around with the pinging cell phone trying to lead the cops away from the rest of the gang and their captives. The bomb shelter—that was what our hole in the ground turned out to have been—had belonged to a distant relative who claimed to have no idea it was being used as a prison but did admit to having been the one who'd had it built, and so recently that it wasn't considered finished yet. Since the Cold War was long over, the cops figured it had never been intended for bombs but for the exact purpose for which it had been used.

Loren's computer had given up the names of her customers. She had kept careful records, including photos that looked as if they'd been taken secretly, of them taking possession of their girls and handing over stacks of cash. This, Mason presumed, was just in case she ever needed to blackmail any of them.

Aside from Halle Chase and Venora LaMere, the rest of the girls were found alive and rescued. Thirteen arrests had been made and more were pending.

It was over. I was alive and well, and so was Mason. And there was something between us that hadn't been there before.

I sat on the lawn near the little lakeside campfire that would probably be a summer staple around here. The boys were on the dock, fishing, and couldn't have cared less about Mason and me, and it was a good thing. He was sitting on the ground, and I was nestled in the crook of his arm like a devoted lover. Didn't have any desire to move away, either. I was sipping a lovely vodka Diet, and he was working on a beer. First drink of the evening for both of us, and while we might go for a second, that would be the limit. We had the kids to take care of, after all.

He'd been different since that rescue. I felt it but couldn't put my finger on what it was, exactly. He looked at me oddly all the time. And he seemed as interested in just hanging out as he was in sex. Weird.

"So you gonna tell me what's going on with you, Mace?"

He nodded. "That was the plan, yeah."

"Anytime soon?"

"Any minute now, actually."

"What are you waiting for, then?"

He shrugged. "The beer to kick in?"

I elbowed him. "You thought I was shot dead out there. That's what it is, isn't it?"

"Yeah, that's what it is."

"And it shook you up. I know, 'cause it would shake me up, too, if it were you."

"Would it?"

"Oh, hell, yes. Big-time. More than you know, I bet."

He looked down at me, smiled a little. "That's good to hear."

"The thing is, I'm here. I'm alive and well. Jake—who I was right and you were wrong about, you'll recall—saved me by shooting what's-her-name."

"Loren Markovich."

"Yeah, whatever. Blindness coach, my ass. I was right about that, too."

"You're always right. I concede on that, so you can stop pointing out each incidence of your rightness."

"I will never stop pointing that out."

"I know you won't."

I sighed and snuggled a little closer.

"I'm not gonna take the chief's job," he said.

"I know you're not. I'm not gonna give you a hard time about it, either. And the only reason I did to begin with was because I'm afraid you'll get yourself killed one of these days."

"Has that changed?"

"No. I'm still afraid of it."

"Then why did you change your position?"

"Because I decided that I really do believe we're all here for as long as we're supposed to be. And then we're not. And that it doesn't matter what we're doing. When it's time, it's time. So it's really better to make the most of the moment, right now and right now and right now, than it is to worry about what might be coming later."

He nodded really slowly. "So you believe your own widely published philosophy at long last."

"Parts of it, at least. That's progress, right?"

"That's progress for sure."

I tipped my head back against his shoulder and stared up at the stars. "Gosh, it's a beautiful night. I don't think I've ever seen so many stars. It's amazing, isn't it?"

"It is." He lowered his head so his cheek rested on top of my hair. And then he said, "So here's the thing," he said.

"Ahh, at last, he gets to the crux of the matter. I knew something was on your mind."

"Yeah. Something."

"So?"

He inhaled, exhaled again. "When I thought you were dead, it hit me that I'm probably in love with you."

I sat up fast and stared into his eyes, mine wide as a thousand things tumbled through my mind. Fear? Yeah. Surprise, too. And love? Hell, was that what this was? I didn't know. How could I know? It was my first time. Out of sheer panic, I said the first thing that came to me. "You're shitting me."

I don't think it was the response he was expecting.

* * * * *

Look for the next Brown and de Luca novel,
DEADLY OBSESSION,
coming soon from Harlequin MIRA

New York Times Bestselling Author

MAGGIE SHAYNE

Rachel de Luca has always had a gift for seeing people's most carefully hidden secrets. But the secret she shares with Detective Mason Brown is one she has promised to keep. As for Mason, he sees Rachel more clearly than she'd like to admit.

After a single night of adrenaline-fueled passion, they have agreed to keep their distance—until a string of murders brings them together again. Mason thinks that he can protect everyone he loves, including Rachel, by taking them to a winter hideaway, but as guests disappear from the snowbound resort, the race to find the murderer intensifies.

Rachel knows she's a target. Will acknowledging her feelings for Mason destroy her—or save them both and stop a killer?

Available wherever books are sold.

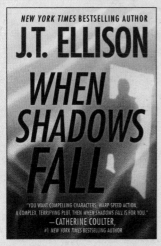

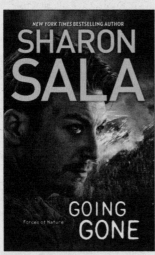

REQUEST YOUR
FREE BOOKS!

2 FREE NOVELS
FROM THE SUSPENSE COLLECTION
PLUS 2 FREE GIFTS!

YES! Please send me 2 FREE novels from the Suspense Collection and my 2 FREE gifts (gifts are worth about $10). After receiving them, if I don't wish to receive any more books, I can return the shipping statement marked "cancel." If I don't cancel, I will receive 4 brand-new novels every month and be billed just $6.24 per book in the U.S. or $6.74 per book in Canada. That's a savings of at least 22% off the cover price. It's quite a bargain! Shipping and handling is just 50¢ per book in the U.S. and 75¢ per book in Canada.* I understand that accepting the 2 free books and gifts places me under no obligation to buy anything. I can always return a shipment and cancel at any time. Even if I never buy another book, the two free books and gifts are mine to keep forever.

191/391 MDN F4XN

Name _____ (PLEASE PRINT) _____

Address _____ Apt. # _____

City _____ State/Prov. _____ Zip/Postal Code _____

Signature (if under 18, a parent or guardian must sign)

Mail to the Harlequin® Reader Service:
IN U.S.A.: P.O. Box 1867, Buffalo, NY 14240-1867
IN CANADA: P.O. Box 609, Fort Erie, Ontario L2A 5X3

Want to try two free books from another line?
Call 1-800-873-8635 or visit www.ReaderService.com.

* Terms and prices subject to change without notice. Prices do not include applicable taxes. Sales tax applicable in N.Y. Canadian residents will be charged applicable taxes. Offer not valid in Quebec. This offer is limited to one order per household. Not valid for current subscribers to the Suspense Collection or the Romance/Suspense Collection. All orders subject to credit approval. Credit or debit balances in a customer's account(s) may be offset by any other outstanding balance owed by or to the customer. Please allow 4 to 6 weeks for delivery. Offer available while quantities last.

Your Privacy—The Harlequin® Reader Service is committed to protecting your privacy. Our Privacy Policy is available online at www.ReaderService.com or upon request from the Harlequin Reader Service.

We make a portion of our mailing list available to reputable third parties that offer products we believe may interest you. If you prefer that we not exchange your name with third parties, or if you wish to clarify or modify your communication preferences, please visit us at www.ReaderService.com/consumerchoice or write to us at Harlequin Reader Service Preference Service, P.O. Box 9062, Buffalo, NY 14269. Include your complete name and address.

MAGGIE SHAYNE

32980	TWILIGHT PROPHECY	___ $7.99 U.S.	___ $9.99 CAN.
32906	PRINCE OF TWILIGHT	___ $7.99 U.S.	___ $9.99 CAN.
32875	BLUE TWILIGHT	___ $7.99 U.S.	___ $9.99 CAN.
32871	TWILIGHT HUNGER	___ $7.99 U.S.	___ $9.99 CAN.
32808	KISS ME, KILL ME	___ $7.99 U.S.	___ $9.99 CAN.
32793	KILLING ME SOFTLY	___ $7.99 U.S.	___ $9.99 CAN.
32498	ANGEL'S PAIN	___ $7.99 U.S.	___ $7.99 CAN.
32244	COLDER THAN ICE	___ $5.99 U.S.	___ $6.99 CAN.
31555	WAKE TO DARKNESS	___ $7.99 U.S.	___ $8.99 CAN.
31554	SLEEP WITH THE LIGHTS ON	___ $7.99 U.S.	___ $8.99 CAN.
31421	BLOOD OF THE SORCERESS	___ $7.99 U.S.	___ $9.99 CAN.
31333	MARK OF THE WITCH	___ $7.99 U.S.	___ $9.99 CAN.
31267	TWILIGHT FULFILLED	___ $7.99 U.S.	___ $9.99 CAN.

(limited quantities available)

TOTAL AMOUNT	$ _____
POSTAGE & HANDLING	$ _____
($1.00 for 1 book, 50¢ for each additional)	
APPLICABLE TAXES*	$ _____
TOTAL PAYABLE	$ _____

(check or money order—please do not send cash)

To order, complete this form and send it, along with a check or money order for the total above, payable to Harlequin MIRA, to: **In the U.S.:** 3010 Walden Avenue, P.O. Box 9077, Buffalo, NY 14269-9077; **In Canada:** P.O. Box 636, Fort Erie, Ontario, L2A 5X3.

Name: _____
Address: _____ City: _____
State/Prov.: _____ Zip/Postal Code: _____
Account Number (if applicable): _____

075 CSAS

*New York residents remit applicable sales taxes.
*Canadian residents remit applicable GST and provincial taxes.

HARLEQUIN® MIRA®
™ www.Harlequin.com

MMS1014BL